Entwined Publishing books by Jennifer Moffatt

Falling Hard
A Hard Sell
A Hard Fit

Falling Hard

A HARD FIT

JENNIFER MOFFATT

ENTWINED PUBLISHING

A Hard Fit
ISBN # 978-1-80250-717-1
©Copyright Jennifer Moffatt 2024
Cover Art by Kelly Martin ©Copyright November 2024
Interior text design by Entwined Publishing
Published by Entice, an Entwined Publishing imprint

Published in 2024 by Entwined Publishing, United Kingdom.

Entwined Publishing is a division of Totally Entwined Group Limited.

A HARD FIT

Dedication

For my brother Kyle (1983–2024),
whose laugh I'll never forget.
We would have loved watching *Godstrike*
together.

Chapter One

Love ~~Love~~ Lust at First Sight

Love at first sight? Not real.

Probably not, anyway. Maybe it happened to some people, but not everyone. It was certainly not something Finn expected to happen to him.

Well, maybe it could.

It wouldn't.

But it might.

If it was going to happen, now was the perfect time — new job, fresh start, a whole city full of people. It would just take one, after all.

Worth trying, anyway.

His first date in Oakport was with Albert. They matched on a dating app. It was definitely *something* at first sight, although Finn suspected that something was lust... Hard to tell the difference in the moment.

"Albert?" he asked the man at the bar, even though he knew Albert from his profile pics. He was Finn's type — tall and lean, smiley, tousled hair.

"Finn?" Albert grinned.

"Great to meet you," Finn said, shaking his hand.

"You too." Albert studied him up and down in a way that made Finn's dick twitch. "Want to go back to your place and fuck?"

Finn laughed as he sat considering the offer. "You're on the wrong app, Albert."

Albert's green eyes twinkled. "Doesn't change my question."

Finn pushed his ginger curls back, taking in the way Albert's cuffs were rolled up, displaying sculpted forearms. "Why arrange to meet here if you just want to fuck?"

Albert shrugged and tossed back the rest of his cocktail. "Making sure you matched your pictures." He eyed where Finn's T-shirt pulled tight over his biceps.

Finn rested an arm on the bar and leaned in. "So you like what you see?"

Albert nodded and inched closer on his stool, gaze now dropping to Finn's lap. "And now I want to see the rest."

Albert came back to Finn's place. And came at his place. Finn hadn't even gotten his breath back yet when Albert rolled over and looked at his phone. "That was great. I've gotta get going. I'll call you."

He never called.

So, lust—definitely lust.

It wasn't quite as easy to tell with Safa. They had sex on the first date too, then there were more dates. At least five, by Finn's count, plus he ran into her at the charity 5K. Anyway, they spent enough time together that there was something more than lust, but she broke up with him because, quote, *My cat thinks you're too loud.*

You're choosing your cat over me? was the question that came to Finn's mind, but that was where it stayed, because there were some questions he shouldn't have to ask. Plus that cat was an asshole.

Scott was hot but had no sense of humor. He didn't laugh at a single thing Finn said, not even his standard first date dirty jokes.

Wynn was rude to servers. *Next.*

With Luka, gorgeous Luka, there had been promise, at least. When Finn had seen him for the first time, he had felt warm all over. Luka was new at their office — young and sparkling, brown hair flopping into his forehead, killer blue eyes, sharp dresser. The two of them were the only openly queer men at Breakpoint and had gravitated toward each other instantly. In fact, Luka asked him to go for a drink after work at the end of his first week. Finn said yes without hesitation.

Finn took him to the Bitter Exchange, a new pub that had opened only a few blocks from the office. It was dim and already grimy somehow, but the wings were excellent and the beer was cheap. After the requisite chit-chat and delivery of their pitcher, they started diving into more personal topics.

"So, where did you go to school?" Luka asked before taking his first sip.

"U State, you?"

"Bryerson."

"I dated a couple from Bryerson once." Finn remembered it fondly.

Luka quirked his brow. "Like…at the same time?"

Finn shrugged. "Not exactly. I went out with her first a few times, and then him, but when he brought me home, she showed up."

Luka grimaced. "Awkward."

The grin stretched across Finn's face. "It was at first, but then we had a threesome."

Luka almost choked on his drink. "How did that go?"

"It became a bit of a competition between the two of them to see who could get me off first, so…really, really good."

Luka's laugh warmed Finn's heart. He laughed a lot at all of Finn's dumb jokes.

They swapped stories with not a single lull or awkward pause in the conversation the whole night until the place was closing and the owner was glaring at them from behind the bar. There was a moment, though, watching Luka lick a stray drop of beer off his lip, when Finn realized there was no zing, no lust *or* love. But there was a lot of laughter and warmth and the beginnings of friendship, and that felt exactly right.

Toward the end of the evening, Luka asked Finn for his hair-care regimen. Finn did have the softest, shiniest hair around, and he spent a decent chunk of money on products to keep it that way. He couldn't leave those curls to their own devices.

"That would be telling," Finn said, narrowing his eyes at Luka. "Can't have you stealing my Sexiest Guy at the Office crown. Shiny hair might push you over the top."

Luka stuck out his lower lip. "Pretty please? I'll be your best friend."

Finn only paused for another second before giving up his secret. Luka ordered the whole product line right then on his phone.

Finn didn't mind if his new friend had hair just as shiny as his.

* * * *

So the dating continued, for a year, then two, then more. There were lulls where he didn't bother with the app as much, ignoring the notifications, spending more time with Luka or at the gym, or on his painting or charity work. He even took up the guitar at one point. Other times it was a whirlwind. Remy. Sonja. Wu. Benjamin. But no matter how many dates he went on, it was just a string of *not for me, no way in hell,* and *are you fucking kidding me?,* plus one *oh shit, should I be calling the police right now?*

Tonight's date was with Tiana, a pretty nurse with a four-year-old daughter and a dry sense of humor in her profile that made Finn chuckle. Finn had chosen a place he'd never been to before — an imposing wine bar with black and scarlet walls and gothic accents. He and Tiana had agreed to meet at the main bar, so, a few minutes early, he settled onto a stool to wait.

When the bartender asked if he could get a drink started, Finn glanced at the time. Tiana was only a couple minutes late at this point, but why not? He ordered a glass of the Sartini Courbis and relished the first sip as it tingled over his taste buds. At least if the date sucked, it sucked over top of a truly stellar glass of wine.

He finished it off examining the wall of fancy wine bottles behind the bar, gaze drifting down the collection of gold and silver labels. At the far end, where the bar turned to meet the wall, his gaze landed on a person sitting alone. The buzz that swept over Finn left the tingle from the wine in the dust.

The person had a lean, compact frame, with toned biceps revealed by short black sleeves. The T-shirt read 'they/them' in white letters across the chest. Straight black hair fell onto their forehead but was shaved short on the sides. Tattoos wound down both arms, with two piercings glittering on the ear Finn could see, and one in their nose.

Finn's heart pounded. The person suddenly glanced up, but Finn dropped his eyes before they could meet, face flushing. Shit, how much wine had he chugged? He dared to risk another quick look, but the person's attention was drawn by a man who had arrived and was leaning up against the bar right next to them.

Finn narrowed his eyes as he studied the intruder. At first, he couldn't make out anything the man was saying, but his body language—broad gestures, swaying on his feet and listing right into the other person's space—screamed 'drunk.'

The person in black nodded politely a few times, then began to study their phone. As the one-sided conversation went on, Finn could tell by the tightness in their jaw and shoulders they were not enjoying the attention.

The drunk man's voice was growing louder, then, as he put his hand on their shoulder and tugged, his words reached Finn. "Hey! I'm tryna talk to you!"

Finn was on his way. He didn't hit the gym every single morning for nothing. He was at the end of the bar in less than a breath, inserting himself into the drunk man's space.

"Excuse me, is there a problem here?" he asked, voice deep and authoritative.

The man slid his gaze over to Finn, blurry and unfocused. *Really* drunk.

"Nah," the man said. "Jus' chatting with my frien' here."

"I'm not your friend." It was quiet but firm. "And yes, there is a problem."

"Look." Finn shuffled a step closer, glare cranked up a notch. "Your attention is not wanted here. Move on."

"Wha's your problem? I's just talking."

Finn waved an arm, indicating the direction in which the man should begin moving.

The man sneered, expression sliding from annoyed into surly. "What're you gonna do, Red? You gonna kick my ass?"

Finn chuckled, scratching his nose and flexing his biceps.

The man's eyes bulged, perhaps now noticing Finn's broad shoulders and thick chest.

"I don't want to," Finn replied evenly, "but if you don't fuck off on your own in about five seconds, I will make you."

The man grunted and stumbled away, jostling Finn and a few others as he passed. He couldn't resist yelling "fucking prick" over his shoulder once he was a safe distance through the crowd.

Finn barely heard it because he was drowning in the deep, dark-brown eyes that were locked onto his.

"Thanks," the person in black said, lips quirking into a shy smile.

Finn's heart fluttered. "No problem." His fingers twitched with the bizarre urge to push those black strands off their forehead. *What the fuck?*

A head flick tossed them back without Finn's help. "That was really nice of you."

Finn's face burned. It had to be a brighter red than his hair by now. "Happy to help."

The face watching him was impossibly beautiful and serene. "I'm Rory."

Finn tried not to trip over his tongue. "Hi, Rory. I'm —"

"Finn?" The voice came from behind him.

He whirled. "Oh." His mind scrambled to put a name to the face. "Tiana?"

"That's right."

She was cute and smiling and all Finn wanted to do was turn around and get back to Rory.

"I grabbed us a table, if that's okay?" Tiana pointed toward the back of the bar, smile faltering for a moment at the extended pause from Finn.

"Of course, yeah, I just—" He turned to say goodbye—or something—to Rory, but the manager had come over to apologize for the disturbance, and Rory was facing away from Finn, talking to her over the counter. "Sounds great." Finn smiled at Tiana and followed her to their table. He couldn't see the bar from his seat, but he didn't stop thinking about Rory the rest of the night.

* * * *

The next morning, Finn flopped onto the extra chair in Luka's office, his favorite place to be at work. Luka had a way of making the sharp edges of the world a little softer, and the world had been especially sharp lately.

"Do you believe in love at first sight?" he asked Luka without any preamble.

"Oof." Luka stopped typing and spun in his chair to face Finn. "Does that mean your date went really bad or really good?"

Finn rubbed his beard. "She grilled me for twenty minutes on why I'm still single, so I pretended I had a work emergency and left." With no sign of Rory on his way out.

Luka cringed. "Shit. Sorry, man."

"So." Finn straightened the pleat on his pants. "Do you?"

Luka stretched out a long leg as his mouth curled in an apologetic smile. "Yeah. I think so. It was love at first sight for my parents. They've been together for almost forty years."

Finn nodded, not sure which answer he had been wanting to hear. "Have you ever been in love?" Luka had had a few boyfriends along the way, but none stuck, and there hadn't been anyone lately.

Luka sighed. "I wanted to be, for a bit... Have you?"

Finn shook his head so hard his hair bounced. "Nah, man. Not yet."

"Hey, guys." Tawney's tight brown curls and bright smile popped into Luka's office as she rapped on the doorframe. "Did you see the email? Ilona wants us in the conference room in twenty. The new head of Analytics is here."

"Already?" Luka asked. "Didn't they just fill that spot like yesterday?"

Tawney shrugged. "Guess they were eager to start. See you there!"

Luka clicked over to his email and began reading. "'We are thrilled to welcome Rory Barrett (they/them) to Breakpoint Advertising. Rory joins us as head of analytics with a wealth of experience —'"

Finn's heart stopped. "Rory?"

"That's right... Why?"

Finn's heart slammed back into action, hammering his ribcage. *There's no way...* That would be impossible. "*Rory*? You're sure?"

"Yes, Rory! What's up?"

Finn shook his head. "Nothing, it's just... I met someone named Rory last night before my date arrived and..."

"And what?"

"Nothing. It's probably not them."

Luka eyed him. "Are we hoping it's them?"

Finn shrugged dismissively. "Whatever."

"Hmm." Luka cocked an eyebrow, way too smug. "Sure."

Finn's heart only beat harder as the appointed time approached, and he crept into the conference room behind Luka, terrified and hopeful at the same time. He examined the room, then his stomach crashed into his shoes.

It *was* Rory. *That* Rory. Beautiful, calm, impossibly deep eyes Rory.

The black T-shirt had been replaced with a short-sleeved button-down, black with a subtle gray pattern, but otherwise they looked pretty much the same.

Rory's eyes lit up with recognition when they saw Finn. Finn was smiling before he could play it cool, but Rory smiled back.

Don't stare, Finn told himself, looking down to avoid tripping over his chair. *Jesus, man. Get it together.*

He might have stared a little, though, leg jittering under the table, as the introductions began.

Ilona went around the table until she got to Luka, who was sitting on Finn's left. "This is Luka Moreno, one of our project managers…"

Luka flashed Rory his patented killer smile as they nodded and murmured greetings.

"And," Ilona continued, "this is Finn Owens, lead designer."

"It's nice to meet you, Finn," Rory said warmly, eyes bright.

Finn's brain spun madly, discarding the stupid joke he would normally have made about IT nerds, then the dumb comment on Rory's tattoos, searching for something witty…charming…welcoming to say instead. "Hello, Rory," was what he came up with.

He could feel Luka looking at him sideways. Finn ignored him, dizzy, as the introductions continued around the table.

And this time, he hadn't even had any wine.

Chapter Two

Just Lunch

The next morning, Finn and Luka were wandering down the hall on their way to the staff kitchen for a coffee refill when Luka asked, "So when's your next hot date?"

Finn flipped through his mental calendar. "Dinner Saturday night, with another ginger. He seems... needy? I figure he'll either suck my dick in the car before we go in, or get drunk over appetizers and tell me his entire life story."

Luka chuckled. "I mean, both options sound not bad, as far as dates go."

Finn rounded the doorway into the kitchen. "Could kind of go for the dick su—" He lurched to a stop as he caught the sparkle of piercings, and the elegant lines of tattoos and hair and arms, suddenly forgetting where he was and what he was doing. *Rory.*

Luka crashed into him from behind, sending them both reeling.

"What the hell?" Luka laughed, grabbing onto Finn so they didn't fall over. "You have to go *all* the way through the door, Finn."

"Sorry," Finn muttered. "I...um..."

Rory looked up at the commotion. "Morning," they said with a small smile.

"Morning, Rory," Luka chirped on his way to the coffee machine.

"M-morning," Finn said, managing to stumble over the one word.

"Finn, right?" Rory asked, when Finn continued to stand there staring.

"Yes. Rory. Hi."

"Hi." Their eyes were the loveliest deep dark brown, framed by beautiful, thick lashes.

Finn tried to swallow. "How are you?"

"I'm good, thank you."

Luka came back with a full mug, eyebrows raised at Finn. Finn ignored him.

"I didn't get a chance to thank you properly for the other night," Rory said.

Unsure what to do with his free hand, Finn tugged at his shirt. "You thanked me at the time." He'd replayed the words in his head a million times.

"I know, but still." Rory's gaze dropped to their coffee.

Fuck, I sound like an ass. "But you're welcome," Finn blurted. "It was no problem."

"The other night?" Luka asked.

"Yeah, at the bar I told you about?" Finn said. "This drunk guy was harassing Rory."

"Finn scared him off pretty good." Rory smiled.

"Sounds right." Luka threw an arm around Finn and squeezed his shoulder. "Nobody wants to mess with *this*."

Finn cleared his throat, cheeks burning. "Right. Well. I should get back to work."

"Don't forget your refill," Luka reminded him, with a helpful nod at the coffee station.

"I should get back too," Rory said, but as they stood, they bumped a stack of files and knocked over their mug. "Shit," they mumbled, yanking the papers off the table before the puddle could reach them.

Without a word, Finn found a dish towel and was on his hands and knees mopping up the mess.

Luka grabbed another handful of paper towels, and the three of them got the spill cleaned up quickly.

As he stood, Finn's pinky finger tingled from when it brushed against Rory's hand.

"Thanks," Rory said, rubbing the back of their neck. "I'm not normally so clumsy."

Finn shrugged. "Accidents happen."

Rory flicked their hair back and smiled with the crinkly eyes again. "Thanks for your help. Have a nice day, you two."

"You too." Finn watched Rory leave, then finally got his coffee and followed Luka back down the hall.

"You okay?" Luka asked after a few beats of silence, giving Finn a sidelong look.

"Yeah, fine, why?" Finn's cheeks were still hot.

"I don't know, you seem...off."

Finn walked faster. "I'm fine. Not off. I'm on."

Luka rolled his eyes. "Yeah, cause that's a normal thing to say."

Finn was thankful for the distraction when he noticed a petite, angular blond man hovering outside Luka's office. "Don't you have some work to do, Moreno? Morgan's waiting for you."

Luka groaned and muttered under his breath, "Of course he is."

"Been around a lot lately. Maybe he likes you." Finn waggled his eyebrows.

Luka sighed. "He does not. Trust me."

Finn left Luka to deal with Morgan, the snippy composer, and tried to calm his thrumming heart. Each beat echoed through his body — *Rory, Rory, Rory.*

* * * *

Arriving home that night, Finn dumped his portfolios and laptop bag onto the kitchen table with a thump and made a beeline for his fridge.

He lived in an older part of town in a sunflower-yellow bungalow that showed the love and attention Finn had put into it since he'd moved to Oakport. The house had been his grandma's and was about the only thing of worth he had inherited from his family, aside from his red hair and artistic abilities. He enjoyed the ritual of mowing the lawn every Saturday morning through the spring and summer, raking the leaves in the fall and even shoveling his front walk and driveway in the winter.

He had redone the inside of the house too, but tried to retain the funky, vintage vibe with wood paneling, an avocado-green couch, ceramic lamps and his grandma's dining room table. His art hung all around the house too, since no one else was going to display it.

The beer went down nice and smooth as he rummaged around for the ingredients for a quinoa salad. He cranked up a seventies playlist and slid into a comforting rhythm, washing, peeling, chopping as his thoughts drifted.

Well, not so much drifted as tornado-ed. *What the fuck is wrong with me? Why am I acting like a fourteen-year-old with a crush around Rory? Why do they make me feel like my heart is about to explode?* Finn was used to being comfortable in any room, around any people. Smoldering sex appeal didn't throw him off—it just made him horny. But there was something about Rory's gentle aura and soft smiles that turned him into an awkward, tongue-tied idiot.

A silly crush, Finn told himself as he fluffed the quinoa. *No big deal. It'll fade. Right?*

Right.

* * * *

"How was your date?" Luka asked Monday morning. The department heads were gathered around the conference room table waiting for a staff meeting to start.

Finn couldn't stop his eyes from flicking over to Rory, who was a couple seats away from him and Luka. "Fine."

Luka huffed. "Fine? That's all I get? 'Fine'?"

"Also…good?" Finn offered.

Luka leaned in to murmur, "Were you right about…?"

Finn raised an eyebrow. "Yup. And I didn't hear his life story." A low chuckle slipped out. It had been a good date. Henry had asked to see him again, and there was no reason to say no. They were going to go out again Wednesday night.

Luka snickered as their boss Ilona clacked in.

"Good morning, everyone," she said, perfect and polished as usual. Raven-black hair cascaded onto her sharp red blazer, lips painted a matching color. "Hope you all had a good weekend. Now, if you'll refer to the agenda I sent out on Friday…"

They were making their way through their files, reviewing the status of their major projects, when Ilona paused, shuffling a stack of papers. "One moment...I'm just trying to find the numbers for the PDF downloads."

"The downloads for the PDF were up by two hundred and five percent," came a small voice in the silence. Heads snapped over. It was Rory. "It was one hundred and twenty percent the previous quarter."

Ilona raised her groomed eyebrow.

Rory squirmed. "I'm pretty sure."

Ilona flipped to the next page and ran her finger down some columns. "That's right." She studied Rory for a moment. "Any chance you know the click-through rate?"

As a matter of fact, Rory did know. They proceeded to rattle off any number Ilona could ask about.

"Um." Ilona put the papers down. "Thank you, Rory."

Finn picked his jaw up off the table. So. Eidetic memory. No big deal. What else was going on behind those deep brown eyes?

"Before I let you go," Ilona added after the file review, "I wanted to let you know that I heard from head office this morning, and they are sending a VP to head the Sartini file. Thomas Badgley will be joining us in about two weeks." Sartini was a prestigious wine label that had recently expanded into the fine-dining business and had chosen Breakpoint as their new advertising firm. It was a huge client and would take up a lot of their time and energy.

Finn knew that name. "The Big Bad Wolf is coming here?"

Ilona narrowed her eyes. "I can only assume, Finn, that you will refrain from using that nickname again, particularly when Mr. Badgley is in our office?"

"Er, of course, boss." Finn mimed zipping his lips shut.

"The Big Bad Wolf?" Rory asked as they filed out of the room. "What's that nickname about?"

"Well, he's big and bad." Finn laughed. "That's all I know."

"He's apparently a little scary," Luka added. "He's huge, wears expensive suits. They send him in for the really big clients."

"Another suit telling me about art." Finn rolled his eyes. "Can't wait."

"They say he's helpful." Luka shrugged. "Maybe it'll be a good thing." He checked his watch. "Damn it, I'm supposed to meet Morgan. Catch you later." He waved and disappeared down the hall.

The silence stretched out between Finn and Rory. "Well—" Finn said, at the same time Rory started talking.

"What are some good lunch places around here?" Rory asked. "I couldn't face my leftovers this morning."

"Uh, there's a great deli just down the street. It's my favorite lunch spot."

"Sounds great. I'll give it a try. Would you care to join me?"

"Oh." Finn's stomach twisted. "I brought a lunch."

"Okay, ano—"

"Sure," Finn blurted. "Yes. I don't want to eat my leftovers either."

Rory's eyes crinkled. "Great. I'll meet you in the foyer at twelve?"

"See you then."

* * * *

Finn sat at his desk. *Did Rory ask me out to lunch?*

No, they were just being polite, he decided, clicking open his latest project.

Oops, wrong file. He clicked open another one.

But still, now I have to eat lunch with Rory...alone... and...talk to them?

Finn got up again and marched back down the hall to Luka's office. Luka was hunched over his laptop, staring at a score, the mass of music notes an incomprehensible jumble to Finn.

Finn rapped on the doorframe. "You want to go for lunch?"

"When do I *not* want to go for lunch?" Luka asked, without looking up. He clicked the mouse a couple times much harder than necessary.

"Perfect. I'm meeting Rory in the foyer at twelve. We're going to Montagu's."

"Wait." Luka spun around. "You're having lunch with Rory?"

"And you."

"Did Rory ask you to lunch?"

"It wasn't like that. They asked for a good lunch place."

"And?" Luka waved his hand looking for more information.

"And then asked if I wanted to come."

"So...they *did* ask you to lunch."

Finn shook his head. "They were just being polite."

"I don't have to c —"

"*Luka.* Please, come for lunch."

"Fine, but if you want me to bail, give me a sign, like —" Luka gave an exaggerated scratch of his nose.

"A sign? Okay, this is not a sitcom. And this is not a date! I'm just going for lunch with my colleagues."

"Hmm. If you say so."

* * * *

Finn rolled into the foyer two minutes early, and Rory was there waiting.

They smiled up at Finn. They looked so cute today, in a black blazer over a star-speckled T-shirt and shiny boots.

"I invited Luka along," Finn said. "I hope that's okay. He never has a lunch. That guy can't cook to save his life."

"Of course."

Again, the silence stretched between them. Finn put his hands in his pockets, then took them out again. "I'm sure he'll be here in a sec. Luka's never late."

"Right." Rory bobbed their head.

"So..." Finn searched for something to say. "Settling in okay? Everyone being nice? Have you met Morgan yet?"

Rory's forehead scrunched. "I think so, I —"

"He's a bit of an ass, isn't he?"

Further scrunching. "Well —"

"Sorry. Maybe he hasn't shown his 'ass' to you yet." The laugh that escaped him sounded like a cat with a hairball. *Shut up, Finn. You're an ass.*

Rory blinked.

Finn cleared this throat. "I mean, like..." *Fuck.* The glimpse he caught in the mirrored 'Breakpoint' sign was devastating. A lumbering troll with a face the same color as his hair, and a serene elfin creature who was clearly regretting their decision to invite the troll along to lunch.

"Hey!" Luka bounced into the foyer, rescuing Finn from his agony. "Sorry! Got hung up on a call." He grabbed Finn's forearm and closed his eyes, inhaling deeply. "When I tell you what my client just said to me, you will perish."

"I have no doubt." Finn smiled at his friend in relief. Luka made everything so much easier.

Luka entertained them with his story as they walked down the busy sidewalk. "First of all, she emailed *seventeen times* over the weekend..."

Finn tried to focus and laugh appropriately, but his brain was screaming about all the times his shoulder brushed Rory's. Especially when Rory pulled off their blazer and tucked it through their elbow. Finn's gaze slid sideways over the vines that wound down Rory's arm. When he looked closer, he realized that each leaf contained a letter in flowering script. He wanted to trace each one with a finger and find out their story.

"And then she *finally* says," Luka said, approaching the punchline, "through her tears, 'when I said *a Grease aesthetic* I meant the *movie*, not the *country*.'" Luka threw his head back with a burst of laughter. "Can you even believe it?"

Finn cackled. "I'm actually surprised you didn't immediately assume the movie." Luka had a deep love of movies, especially musicals.

"I know, right?" Luka sighed. "Anyway, this project just got a lot more fun, at least. And it gives me an idea for my Halloween costume."

"Halloween?" Finn shook his head. "It's August."

"Practically September, and one can never prepare for Halloween too early. Wouldn't you agree, Rory?" Luka generously lobbed a question at Rory, who was silently striding along next to them.

"Oh, absolutely," Rory said. "I like to plan ahead."

"See? Finn does not." Luka laughed. "He gets mad if I mention holidays more than a week in advance."

"Not true." Finn sniffed.

Luka laughed again. "It absolutely is! You do your Christmas shopping on Christmas Eve."

"I just don't like how the holidays seem to start earlier and earlier, and you have to buy your shit then, because when the normal time to shop rolls around, you can't even get it anymore. Sorry if I want to be able to buy a beach towel in July." They were now standing in line at the deli, perusing the giant chalkboard menu.

"Yes, yes," Luka soothed, patting his arm. "Poor Finn. Anyway, the turkey is amazing," he told Rory. "You have to get it with the cranberry bread, it's to die for, and if you like cheese, the smoked gouda." He kissed his fingers. "Heaven."

Finn could not be more thankful for Luka, who chatted easily, filling in the silence before it even existed, being sure to include Rory in the conversation.

"How long have you two been at Breakpoint?" Rory asked once they were seated on the sidewalk patio with their sandwiches.

"About four years," Luka replied. "Finn started just before me."

"Nice to work with friends, isn't it?" Rory asked. They folded one ankle over the other, pants cuffed in an effortlessly stylish way.

"You've got that right," Luka replied. "Finn keeps me grounded, reminds me not to worry about the bullshit."

"And Luka is really good at attracting bullshit," Finn added.

Luka sighed. "I'd smack you, but, unfortunately, you are completely right. Did you have lots of friends at your last job?" he asked Rory.

"Yup. Friends and family. It was my parents' company."

"Oh, cool. What made you leave?" Luka crunched on a potato chip.

"Just" — Rory lifted a shoulder — "ready to do my own thing."

"I get it. I love my parents but it was a relief to move away from Andchester."

Finn was painfully aware that he was mostly observing a conversation between Luka and Rory, but by the time he'd thought of something not stupid to say and his mouth wasn't full of sandwich, they'd moved on. Luka shot him the odd confused look at his unexpected silence. Desperate to say something, Finn rifled through his brain.

"What about outside of work? Are you seeing anyone?" Luka asked.

"No," Rory answered quickly. "Definitely single."

"I have a date with Henry," Finn blurted. "We're going mini-golfing."

There was an awkward pause. "Oh, is Henry your boyfriend?" Rory asked, fiddling with an empty soda can.

"No! I don't have a boyfriend. Or girlfriend. Or partner. I'm just...dating. Casually." Finn's voice got higher and higher as he spoke, the very opposite of casual. Rory's nose piercing had a tiny white bead on it, pearlescent in the sun.

"This guy is a dating monster," Luka said, balling up his sandwich wrapper. "Just wait, Rory. The stories he has — "

Oh, God. "Yes, well." Finn stood, chair screeching, before Luka could say more. "Time to get back." They both stared up at him. *I could not be more awkward if I tried.*

Luka gave him a look like he had an alien growing out of his head. "But we can save those for another time. You all done, Rory?"

"Yup. All done." They smoothed their elegant fingers over their lap and folded them neatly around the soda can—the most beautiful fingers Finn had ever seen.

He met Rory's eyes, lips pressed tight together to hold in the fluttering in this throat that threatened to burst out. *Shit,* Finn thought as Rory smiled at him. *I'm done, too.*

Chapter Three

Thrill Island

Finn threw himself into his work. Sketching, coloring, checking in with his team, calling clients...pretending he didn't see the looks Luka was giving him whenever Rory was in the room. But mostly ignoring the adrenaline crashing through his veins whenever he saw Rory — or thought about Rory.

Trying to ignore it, anyway.

He was standing in a meeting room with a few other designers, watching a competitor's new dog food commercial.

"This is shit," Finn said, hands on hips, tilting his head, trying to get his thoughts around what the fuck they had been thinking. "First of all, that dog isn't even that cute."

"Finn!" Tawney protested.

"What? You can't tell me that's the cutest dog they could find."

"It's cute," Tawney said firmly.

"Debatable. But—" Finn paused the video. "What's with this shot? Why are the dogs eating their dog food on a beach? Who takes a bowl of dog food to the beach? Plus the composition." He shook his head. "It's half sky. Total shit."

Then Rory slipped into the room and it was like hitting a brick wall. "And the, uh..." Finn continued. "The...um..."

"Rory!" Tawney said. "Would you say this dog is cute?"

Rory studied the screen. "Of course. What kind of monster would say this dog isn't cute?"

Tawney snickered. "Finn, actually."

Fuck. His face did its usual searing burn. "I never said it wasn't cute." His tongue tripped over itself. "I just said it...wasn't the cutest."

Rory's eyes twinkled. "Like I said, monster."

The feeling was terrifying, the way his brain short-circuited, rendering him wordless, the way his heart beat so furiously he was worried it was going to give out. And it was all pointless, because Finn knew Rory would never be interested in someone like him.

Rory was quiet—Finn was loud.

Rory was careful—Finn was brash.

Rory was elegant, graceful, delicate. Finn was a blunt edge, smashing his way through life, saying dumb things about dogs when he wasn't tripping over his own tongue. Breakpoint discouraged employees dating anyway, thanks to an ugly situation a few years back, but even if they didn't, the two of them could clearly never happen.

"Hey," Finn mumbled when he had to stop at Rory's office Tuesday morning. It was cool, sleek and tidy, all screens and hidden wires, dim lighting and the scent of lemongrass and sandalwood. Finn's office had more of a post-apocalyptic aesthetic—sketch pads, mock-ups, storyboards, color swatches, fabric samples, splayed throughout in piles of chaos, although Finn knew where everything was…roughly.

Rory looked up from their biggest screen, a dizzying array of numbers, and smiled when they saw Finn.

"I just got a call from Ilona," Finn said. "She asked to see us in her office when we had a moment. Is now good?"

"Oh, sure. Give me one second…" Rory's fingers flew over the keyboard in a satisfying hum, then they locked their screens and stood to follow Finn. "Do you know what she wants?" they asked as they began to make their way to Ilona's office.

Finn shook his head, a whiff of sandalwood following him down the hall. "She said something about a new client."

Ilona's assistant, Sabrina, waved them through when they arrived.

"Finn, Rory, please come in," Ilona said from behind her ruthlessly tidy desk. "How are things, Rory? Feeling settled in?"

"They're great, thanks," Rory said. "Everyone has made me feel really welcome."

"That's wonderful to hear. Now, the reason I called you in… Have you been to Thrill Island lately?"

Finn blinked. Not the direction he was expecting this conversation to take. "Never."

Ilona looked surprised. "You've *never* been to Thrill Island?"

"Nope. I didn't grow up here." He'd never been anywhere as a kid, and his mom certainly couldn't afford a trip to Thrill Island for the family. The old amusement park sat on an actual island near the Oakport harbor, but its best days were behind it. It looked faded and sad to Finn now. He'd thought about checking it out a couple times since arriving, but ultimately the promise of creaky roller coasters and stale popcorn didn't appeal to him.

"How about you, Rory?" Ilona asked.

"Not since I was a teenager," they replied.

"Well, I have a new project that I'd like the two of you to head." She looked at Finn's expression. "I know, I know, you're busy, Sartini is ramping up, but Thomas will be here soon to help with the load, and I think this one will actually be a lot of fun. Thrill Island is rebranding. Admissions have been way down, their website launch failed and they've reached out to us. They want a new look, new app, better online experience for customers. They've really fallen behind and are paying for it. So" — she smiled brightly — "I would like the two of you to spend the day there. Tomorrow, if you can. Take it all in, get inspired, see what's missing and find the spark that's going to get families to show up. Yeah?"

Finn pictured the teetering stack of files on his desk...then imagined working closely with Rory, beginning with a paid day at an amusement park. "You bet. Sounds fun."

Rory nodded too. "Of course."

"Terrific. Connect with Sabrina, and she'll give you your tickets and a credit card for expenses. We'll talk when you get back. Can't wait to hear your ideas!"

* * * *

Finn met Rory at the central station downtown Wednesday morning to hop onto the line that would take them to Thrill Island. It was a warm day, another gasp of late summer, so Finn wore a forest-green tank top and long gray shorts, paired with slip-on running shoes. Rory was — as expected — all in black. A low-cut

V-neck tee, black jeans, black boots and the same glimmer of silver piercings in their ears and nose. A tattoo curled over Rory's delicate collarbone, feathers or a wing of some sort. The vines wound down their left arm. The other arm had a sword peeking out from under their sleeve, and script along their inner forearm that read 'You feel it, don't you?'

"You look hot," was the first thing Finn said. "I mean, not *hot* — shit. You look like you'll *be* hot. Not that you're not hot. Fuck."

Rory laughed. "Hi. You look hot, slash not hot, too." Their eyes crinkled. "Nice and cool in that shirt, I mean."

"Oh." Finn looked down at this tank top. It was the fourth shirt he had tried on that morning. Luka said he looked good in that shade of green. "Thanks." *God, why did I say 'thanks — 'that was not actually a compliment.* He resisted the urge to facepalm.

They made their way through the tail end of the morning commute crowd to their gate. Their ride wouldn't be long, but the train was fairly busy, as office buildings stretched all the way from the downtown core along to the eastern side of the harbor before giving way to industrial buildings.

"So, four years at Breakpoint," Rory said once they settled, knee only an inch away from Finn's. "And you're happy there?"

"Yeah." The train lurched into motion. Finn tried to ignore the jolt when their knees bumped. "Mostly. I mean, I love the design part of it. The art. Sometimes the clients not so much."

Rory chuckled. "I'll bet."

"You know, when you recommend *this* font, but they insist they want *that* font, then once they see it, they want the one you suggested in the first place? Or they get mad cause you didn't read their mind or they didn't actually know what fucking color 'cyan' is?"

Rory laughed. "I don't have to deal with clients much, usually. I'm the one in the back Quasimodo-ing over my keyboards. I was kind of excited to be sent 'into the field,' as they say."

This time their shoulders brushed over a particularly uneven corner. Finn's heart skittered.

"And how long have you been in Oakport?" Rory asked.

"Just over four years. I moved here when my grandma died. She left me her house. And then Ilona hired me."

"I'm sorry about your grandma."

An unexpected pang hit Finn. "Thanks. I didn't see her much—my mom was…is pretty toxic…" He trailed off, not wanting to peel off that particular scab in front of Rory. "Anyway. What about you?"

"Born and raised, actually. I've been working for my parents doing IT and data analysis since I was about twelve. I was ready to move on."

"Were they okay with you leaving?"

Rory gave a rueful chuckle. "They said they understood, but…I think they were sad. And it was hard to walk away, to be honest. Pretty much the whole family works there."

Another shoulder bump, with a whiff of sandalwood. "Do you have a big family?"

"Yup. Mom, dad, two brothers and a sister, plus tons of aunts and uncles and cousins. My parents both come from big families, and they almost all still live here."

Finn nodded, wondering what that would be like. Growing up, it had been him, his mom and his sister. His mom had pissed off or otherwise cut off every other living relative they had, not that there were a lot of them out there. He'd never even met his dad.

The train rattled, and this time their shoulders and their knees brushed together. But when the train shifted again, their knees stayed touching. Finn started sweating. The tank top was not cool enough.

"What made you choose Breakpoint?" Finn asked, happy he managed to ask a normal question despite his dancing heart.

"My parents' plant makes rebar. Not the most exciting thing, you know? I liked the idea of working for a company with a creative side, with lots of types of people working there. Artists and such. Like you."

"Oh, well..." Finn blushed. "I'm not exactly an artist."

Rory shot him a surprised look. "Of course you are. Designing is art. Plus, I'll bet you do other stuff outside of work."

"I just...paint, a little."

Rory's smile sparkled. "Sounds like an artist to me, Finn. What kind of painting?"

Finn's face got hotter. He didn't talk to a lot of people about his art anymore. "Er, acrylic on canvas, mostly. Abstract expressionism."

Rory looked absolutely enchanted for some reason. "I'd love to see your work someday."

"Oh, uh. It's only..." The only place his art hung was his house. *Shit. Do I invite them over? Is that weird?* "I'm not that good."

They were saved by the doors sliding open and a gang trooping in, two women with a stroller each and five small kids, squealing and giggling and climbing on the seats.

Finn wondered, briefly, what his sister's kids would think of Thrill Island, then pushed that thought from his mind. "Wouldn't it be cool," Finn said instead, "if the Thrill Island experience began on the train? Like there's a countdown— 'three stops until the thrill begins' or something."

"That's a great idea," Rory said. "Build up the excitement."

Finn pulled out his phone to take some notes, and they bounced ideas back and forth a little longer until the train pulled into their station. They hopped off with the moms and their pack, and only a trickle of other people. Granted, it was a Wednesday and school was back in session, but Finn had still been expecting decent crowds.

The first thing they saw was the front gates. 'THRILL ISLAND' the sign screamed at them, in a cheesy 'slasher' font with faded red letters. Otherwise, the entrance was unremarkable. The view of the harbor was wasted—nothing but lampposts, garbage cans and railings leading up to the ticket booth, and a few dreary gulls circling in the breeze.

"So." Finn blew out a breath. "There's work to do."

"It should be exciting when they get off the train," Rory agreed.

"Imagine, like, a selfie-station…signs for the rides, those things where you put your face in the cutout, all with the ocean view behind you." Finn took a few pictures and added to his notes.

Once they were inside, it didn't get much more impressive.

"They went for 'thrill' as in 'scary' with the logo, but once you get inside, nothing is really 'thrilling,' is it?" Rory asked.

"Not really." Finn shook his head as he took a few more photos. "What should we do first?"

"I don't know," Rory said, turning in a circle. "What do you think?"

"The big rides first? Since those lineups get longer as the day goes on."

"The Thrillcoaster it is!"

The signature roller coaster was a great ride—three loops and plenty of scream-inducing corners and drops. They went on it twice before a line started to form.

"Okay, that was an awesome coaster," Finn said at the exit, heart pounding from the adrenaline instead of Rory, for once.

"Amazing," Rory agreed. "And your hair is awesome, too." They laughed and reached up like they were going to touch it, but paused a few inches away. "It's got even more life than usual."

Finn chuckled and raked his hand through his curls, even though that probably made it worse. "Yeah, there is not enough product in the world for my hair once gravity is no longer working for me."

Rory's eyes glinted. "I like it."

Now the heart pounding was from Rory again. "What's next?"

They tackled the 'Disco Thrill,' a smaller roller coaster that ran partly indoors in the dark, aside from the disco balls and mirrors casting rainbow light across the tracks. Next was the Ferris wheel, a ride that faced the ocean and actually made use of the view. The sun sparkled off the peaks in flashes of white, the far edge of harbor green in the distance, low hills climbing up to a crystal blue sky.

"So beautiful," Finn said, when their car stopped at the top.

"It really is," Rory agreed. "I need to get outside more. I feel like I miss a lot behind my screens all the time."

Finn took a breath, the salt air curling deep into his lungs. "Same. Sometimes I think about, like, finding a cabin in the woods with no Wi-Fi, setting up my easel outside and just painting for days."

"That sounds perfect. You should do that."

Finn turned to look at Rory. Their eyes met, held... "I should."

Then the car jerked into motion again, and they began their descent.

All the rides had lineups now, but the one for the 'The Haunted Lagoon' wasn't too long. The boats wound along a canal through a graveyard, weeping willow tunnels shading them from the heat of the day. Tombstones peeked out from the tall grass, while a few robotic crows perched on top, cawing at them.

"It doesn't feel very haunted, does it?" Rory asked, reaching to trail their fingers in the water speckled with leaves from the trees. "It's sort of...romantic."

Finn pointed. "There's a skeleton arm poking out of that grave."

"I like skeletons," Rory said, gaze following their fingers through the water. "Still romantic."

Finn shifted and took out his phone for more notes. "So...the Haunted Lagoon also needs work."

It was lunchtime when they were back on dry land. "Hope you're hungry," Finn said, flashing the office credit card.

"Extra hungry, in fact." Rory patted their stomach.

They found the food court, which only had one counter offering the basic park food. "We should probably try as much as we can, right? Get a feel for what we're working with?" Finn asked.

"I think it's our responsibility," Rory said.

They got a hot dog, a burger and nachos then split it all in half. Finn got a chocolate milkshake, Rory strawberry. They spread their food out before them on a round metal table under a sun-beaten red-and-white-striped umbrella.

"So whereabouts do you live?" Rory asked, going for the nachos first.

"On Black Bear Drive," Finn said. "Down past the old high school."

"Oh, yeah, I know that area." Rory nodded, wiping their mouth with a napkin. "My aunt lives on Cougar."

Finn picked up his milkshake and snickered. "Cougar, you say?"

"I know." Rory chuckled, reaching for another loaded chip. "She is a bit of a cougar, too. The jokes write themselves."

"Where do you live?" Finn asked.

"An apartment downtown. Well, I say downtown. It's suburb-adjacent. The Southern Horizon buildings?"

"Oh, nice."

"It's okay." Rory shrugged. "My parents tried to pay for a bigger place by the water but I said no thanks."

"Wow." Finn wondered what that would be like, to have parents not only offering to buy their kid an expensive apartment, but giving a shit where they lived in the first place.

"It's small, but there's enough room for me and my gear. Just."

"Gear?"

"Oh, all my computers and stuff."

"Ah, I get it. I have a room full of paintings, plus the garage."

"Are you working on anything right now?"

Finn's phone buzzed. "Sorry, one sec," he said, looking at the screen. His sister was calling. "What the fuck does she want?" he muttered, then stuffed it back in his pocket.

Rory watched him. "You don't want to answer that? I can wait."

"Nope," was all Finn said. *Nope, nope, nope.* Liz only called when she wanted something — money, usually, a logo for her new 'business' or maybe to lay a guilt trip because he hadn't called Mom on her birthday — and he was not in the mood. "It's just my sister, and it's never worth answering."

"Oh. That's too bad."

"Yeah." Finn took a bite of hamburger, trying to push thoughts of her out of his head. Silence fell as they chewed.

"The food is actually pretty good, isn't it?" Rory asked, after swallowing their next bite. "The nachos are yummy."

"Agreed." Finn lifted his cup. "And this milkshake borders on life-changing."

"Maybe we should have done all the spinny rides before lunch, though," Rory said, studying another loaded nacho chip.

"Oof." Finn put his milkshake down again. "Good point. Let's do the Haunted Lagoon again next so we can digest."

They went on every ride at least once, including the Thrilloscope and the Ziller, without incident, then checked out the arcade and gift shop for a burst of mid-afternoon air conditioning. When the sun was dipping toward the horizon, the light thick and golden, they sat on a bench, windswept and sun-warmed, a bag of cotton candy between them.

Finn leaned back, arm along the bench behind Rory, another piece of pink fluff disappearing on his tongue. He closed his eyes, the salt breeze lifting a languid curl off his cheek. The plastic bag rustled as Rory reached for the last piece of cotton candy.

Good day.

His phone and his brain were full of ideas, and his heart was full of Rory. The way they didn't mind waiting in line, limbs loose and patient leaning against a railing. The way their eyes lit up each time gravity released them from its grip. The way they laughed easily and generously at Finn's jokes and silly observations, and…those eyes crinkling, with a warmth and sweetness that reached out and held Finn in a way he'd never felt before.

"Such a fun day," Rory said, with a happy sigh.

Finn opened his eyes to meet Rory's. His heart threatened to burst. "It really was."

Rory studied the pink wisp in their fingers. A pause. A head flick. "I was wondering…did you want to grab some dinner somewhere on the way home? We could keep talking about our ideas while everything is still fresh —"

Finn's phone buzzed, and he had it out of his pocket before Rory's invitation could sink in. "Dinner?" he said. Dinner with *Rory*?

He glanced at his screen as he processed. It was a text. From Henry.

Hey Finn, I'm running a little behind, but I should only be a couple minutes late. Excited for mini-golf! See you soon!

Henry? Finn frowned, then it clicked into place.
Henry!
Fuck.

Chapter Four

The Big Bad Wolf

"Fuck," Finn muttered.

Rory's eyebrows pinched together. "Everything okay?"

"Yes. No. I mean...shit. I have to go." He held up his phone, as if Rory didn't know how texts worked. "I forgot I have a date. Henry."

"Oh." Understanding dawned on Rory's face. "Oh, right. You mentioned. Mini-golf."

"Yeah."

Rory stood, crumpling up the empty cotton candy bag. "Then you'd better get going."

"I'm sorry, I —"

"It's okay." The setting sun streamed around Rory's head like a halo. "I'll see you at work tomorrow."

Finn stood too, self-consciously straightening his wrinkled shorts. Rory still looked immaculate, sleek and cool in all black. "Were you going to catch the train back now, or...?"

"Nah." They tossed the bag into a trash can. "I think I'll go visit my parents instead. They're not far."

"Okay." The day slipped from Finn's fingers.

A breeze teased at Rory's bangs, blowing the long strands aside. "We can schedule something to go over our notes, get some proposals together for Ilona. I'll send you a calendar invite."

"Sounds good," Finn said, even though it was not good.

"Bye, Finn."

Then Rory was only a flash of black in the brightly colored summer crowd, then gone.

* * * *

Finn's date with Henry was...fine. Henry was cute and perfectly likable. Henry kissed him by the windmill, and offered to do quite a lot more behind the windmill, but Finn said no, thank you.

All he could think about was Rory. After he got home, he rinsed the summer salt away in the shower, then stared at his phone. He wanted to text Rory, to say thanks for the day, and suggest maybe they grab that dinner another time soon, but...no. It was nearly eleven, not the time to be texting about work. Plus, what if it didn't really count as work? He didn't want to make Rory feel uncomfortable. Best to wait. He checked his Breakpoint email though, in case Rory had already sent the calendar invite. But they hadn't.

And still no invite when he got up the next morning. Or after his workout, either.

"That's good," Finn said to himself. "Rory has healthy work-life boundaries. I'm sure they'll send it once they get to work."

No invite when he checked his email in the elevator. Or when he got to his office. Still nothing by lunchtime.

On his way to the staff kitchen, he turned left instead of right and happened to wander by Rory's office.

He rapped on the frame and popped his head in.

Rory looked up, then back at the screen. "Hi."

"Hi." Finn leaned against the frame, then realized he probably looked like he was *trying* to lean, and quickly stood again. "How are you?"

"I'm good. What can I help you with?"

"Did you want to meet about the Thrill Island campaign today?"

Rory frowned and glanced over to another screen to pull up their calendar. "I got a little swamped — Ilona wants a bunch of metrics pulled for Sartini, and I have software training this afternoon and tomorrow. But I could maybe fit you in Monday?"

"Oh, okay."

"I'll send you an invite." They went back to their big screen, fingers a blur.

Finn nodded. His stomach dropped as he turned away. Clearly he had been imagining things yesterday. Rory was all business.

Of course they were. Finn shook his head and he picked up speed striding down the hallway. *What were you expecting?* he growled at himself.

A few hours later, the calendar invite came for Monday afternoon. Finn made himself pause before clicking accept, as if there was dignity in those extra six seconds.

* * * *

Finn booked one of the meeting rooms close to his office in case he needed to dash back to grab any other materials. He was a few minutes early, and spread out some of the sketches he had done for Rory to look at.

He had barely seen Rory since they had spoken on Thursday, which was fine. Both of them were busy, and he was there to work, obviously. He didn't need whatever weird electrical thing was going on with him when Rory was near. Like how when he saw Rory arriving on Friday and the humming through his veins was so distracting he nearly walked into a door. Rory's bangs were brushed back, maybe a bit of product in them, so they fell with a curve over one side of their forehead instead of a straight line down the middle. The day was overcast and rainy, and they were wearing a sleek black coat with a high collar that made them look like they belonged in *The Matrix*.

Finn had spent a few free hours that weekend sketching ideas for Thrill Island, and Monday morning had stretched on endlessly before their meeting.

When Rory walked in, laptop under one arm, they froze in their tracks at the sight of Finn's work laid out across the table.

"Finn," Rory breathed, edging forward and reaching out to touch the paper. "These are beautiful."

"Oh…" Goosebumps swept over him at the praise. "You like them?"

Rory leaned over, soaking up the details. "I *love* them."

Finn's cheeks flushed. "Nothing is set in stone, of course. It was just an idea I had."

Finn had turned Thrill Island into a heist movie. Cutouts at the entrance featured genre archetypes — the stakeout trench coat with a fedora and a newspaper, the tuxedo, the slinky evening gown, the hacker, the muscle, the getaway driver. The Thrillcoaster would be a car chase. The Disco Thrill became the diamond heist, laser beams and glittering jewels lighting up the dark.

The Haunted Lagoon was called the Undercover Romantic Boat Ride.

When Rory read those words, eyes sparkling, Finn had to explain. "That's a placeholder title, of course. I couldn't think of a better name yet."

"It's brilliant." Rory shook their head. "All of it. So fun. Ilona is going to adore it."

"Do you think it could be translated into an app?"

"Oh, yes..." Rory slid some papers to the side so they could set down their laptop. Finn reached to help and their fingers bumped. Finn nearly jumped from the spark.

Rory flipped open their laptop and logged in. "I had a few thoughts about the app," they said, fingers flying over the keyboard. "Like a fun user profile, and look, this is perfect." They turned the screen so Finn could see. "Users can upload a picture of their face and it'll generate a most-wanted poster. Or even a fake passport."

"That's awesome." Finn leaned over to watch Rory work, so thrilled that Rory liked his ideas, and even more thrilled about how good Rory smelled and how close they were sitting.

They brainstormed a while longer until there was a pause in the conversation as Finn sketched and Rory typed.

"So...how was your date with Henry?" Rory asked, voice light as they stared at their screen.

"Henry?" Finn blinked, confused. That date seemed like ages and ages ago. "Henry's not—we aren't... I'm not seeing him again."

Rory's fingers paused. "You're not? That's too bad."

Finn shrugged, brushing eraser shavings away. "It's fine. There wasn't anything special there, you know?"

He raised his head to look at Rory, and his heart crashed into his ribcage when they were looking back, eyes wide.

Rory's mouth curled in a small smile. "Yeah, I know."

"Well." Finn cleared his throat. "I, uh, better get going. I have a design meeting to finalize some stuff for the Sartini presentation."

Rory shut their laptop and stood to help Finn collect his papers. Their fingers brushed again, and this time Finn didn't jerk them away. They stood only inches apart as Rory slid a stack into Finn's hands. "Amazing work, Finn." Their eyelashes fluttered.

Something bubbled up Finn's throat — either elation or panic, he couldn't say which. "You too."

"I'll see you later." Rory swayed toward him for a second, bringing a whiff of sandalwood with them, then they collected their laptop and slipped out of the room.

Finn sat down in a chair with a thump. He flipped through his sketches again, the smile on his face stretching wide.

* * * *

Finn had been working so hard with Rory and prepping for Sartini that he realized he had barely talked to Luka the past week. He made a point of popping into Luka's office one morning, the day before Thomas Badgley arrived. "Do you want to grab lunch?"

"Can't," Luka said shortly, rifling through the papers on his desk. "I have to get these storyboards finished before the meeting with Thomas tomorrow."

Finn frowned. "You don't even have time to eat?"

"I have a granola bar somewhere," Luka muttered, shoving that stack aside and moving onto the next one.

"Hey, are you okay?" Finn asked. Luka never missed a meal.

Luka stopped and looked up, smile strained. "I'm good." Then he shifted, noticing the concern on Finn's face. "You know what, a quick lunch would be great, actually. Thanks, Finn."

They went to grab tacos at a food truck up the street that was fast and delicious. They perched on a planter with their lunches while Finn updated Luka on their progress with Thrill Island.

"Rory's been amazing to work with. They have so many good ideas, and you should see how fast they can type when they really get going."

Luka wiped his mouth with a napkin and smiled as he swallowed. "Oh yeah?"

"Yeah."

"Well, that's great. Hey, when's your next date?"

Finn studied his remaining taco. "Don't have one planned."

Luka grinned. "You don't?"

"Nah, work's been so busy." Finn took a big bite.

"Mmhmm."

"What?" Finn mumbled.

"Nothing. Thanks for the lunch break, Finny."

* * * *

The day finally came where they would meet the legend, Thomas Badgley, a.k.a., The Big Bad Wolf, a nickname Finn had promised Ilona he would never use...where she could hear it. Finn slipped into the conference room ready for the meeting a few minutes before nine and scanned the crowd. A seat was open next to Rory.

"Morning," he said, slipping into the chair.

Rory's smile made Finn think of the painting he worked on the night before, a soft curve of pink that hinted at so much more. "Morning," they replied. "How are you?"

"All right. Gotta shit ton of work to do. Hope this is short."

Rory had their 'they/them' T-shirt on again under a crisp blazer. Two of their ear piercings were now connected with a small chain, threaded with delicate stars.

"Did you get that copyright issue sorted out?" Rory asked, as Finn flipped through his Sartini folder to make sure he had everything.

Finn blinked for a second, pushing an unruly curl behind his ear, then remembered mentioning it to Rory before he left last night. "Yeah, I did. Thanks."

Their conversation was cut short when Ilona strode in. "Hello, everyone, we'll get started now."

Rory leaned over to mutter in Finn's ear. "Where's Luka?"

Finn hadn't even noticed his friend wasn't there. He swung his gaze around, searching, then took a quick glance at his phone to see if he had missed a text. He turned his head to reply. Rory's lips were inches away. "I don't know. Not like him to be late."

Then Finn's attention was grabbed by the man who followed Ilona into the room. So *this* was Thomas Badgley. Never had a nickname fit so well. Big Bad Wolf, indeed. He was stunning — there was no denying it — although a little scary-looking. His expensive suit expertly framed his thick shoulders and the rest of his muscles too, all the way down. A killer jaw, dark brown hair pulled back in a manly bun and a smooth, prowling gait completed the package.

When Thomas introduced himself and talked a bit about his background, his deep rumbling voice and stern expression did nothing to challenge Finn's initial assessment. But the man clearly knew his shit, touching on all aspects of the Sartini campaign and delivering information in a smooth, efficient and engaging manner.

Then Thomas' stern brow deepened into a frown when Luka burst in, catastrophically late and visibly sweating. Every head in the room whipped over to stare at him. Luka froze, an agonized smile on his face.

Shit, Finn thought, watching his friend apologize and clamber through the silent room to an open chair next to Tawney. Luka, immaculate at all times, was a disaster. His clothes didn't match, his hair was rumpled and he even had a crust of toothpaste on one corner of his mouth. Finn tried to get his attention to subtly point out the toothpaste if nothing else, but Luka resolutely kept his eyes down. The chair screeched in the silence when he finally, finally sat.

"Well, now that Luka is settled..." Ilona said. "Please go ahead, Thomas."

The rest of the meeting was as painful for Luka as his entrance had been. He didn't seem to be paying attention, and, even worse, his storyboards weren't ready when Ilona asked. Finn tried not to cringe when Luka stammered an excuse about the subway.

"Well," Ilona said, shooting him a disapproving frown, "the design team can meet again later today. But I think the rest of us are clear on next steps. Thanks, everyone."

Luka bolted from the room, Tawney hot on his heels. Finn followed, sticking his head into Luka's office before Tawney could close the door. "Moreno!"

Luka sighed. "Finn."

Finn shook his head, grinning. "Jesus."

"So..." Luka nodded. "It was as bad as I think."

"Worse! First of all..." He put a hand on Luka's shoulder and studied him at arm's length, rubbing his beard. "What the fuck are you wearing?"

Luka looked down at his clothes—a forest-green blazer, burgundy trousers and a crooked yellow button-down dotted with blue flowers, topped off with a coffee stain.

"Second—"

"You know what, you can stop. I was there." Luka yanked his blazer off while Finn snickered.

"It wasn't so bad," Tawney piped up.

The two men turned to stare at her.

"I mean..." she stammered. "We all know that was not usual behavior for you."

Luka fell into his chair with a groan. "Thomas Badgley does not know that. Thomas Badgley thinks I'm a screw-up who dresses like a sloppy clown, shows up late and doesn't meet deadlines. Could it be any worse?"

"You, um"—Tawney cringed—"actually have some toothpaste." She pointed at the corner of her mouth. "Just here."

"I *what*?"

Then Ilona appeared in his doorway, as flawless as ever, thick raven hair cascading perfectly into place.

"You don't even need to say it," Luka told her, wiping at the toothpaste.

She pursed her plum lips. "Design team meeting after lunch." She turned to go, then paused to look at him again. "That means one o'clock sharp. And can you change?"

Finn blew out a breath on Luka's behalf as she whirled away. "What happened, man?"

Luka groaned. "I slept in, then"—he gestured at himself—"did everything else in a blind panic. And then my fucking train broke down."

"It'll be okay," Tawney encouraged him. "You've just got to get it together for the next meeting."

Finn nodded. "Yeah, try not to fuck it up again."

Luka shook his head, chuckling despite himself. "Great advice. Thanks, Finn."

"You're so welcome." Finn's phone buzzed in his pocket and he pulled it out to see a text from Rory.

Is Luka okay?

"What are you smiling at?" Luka asked.

"Oh, nothing. Just…nothing." Finn went off down the hall, whistling, in the general direction of Rory's office.

Chapter Five

Going for a Ride

Finn gathered up his designs and made his way to the conference room for the 'Get It Together, Luka' meeting after lunch. He stopped by Luka's office to make sure he wasn't about to miss it again, and found Tawney doing the same thing. Fortunately, the office was empty.

"Looks like he made it this time," Tawney said.

"We'll see," Finn replied. "Maybe he went for a wank first to calm his nerves."

"Finn!"

"What? It helps! Hey, that reminds me, did I tell you the one about the three friends on a skiing trip who had to share a bed?" He and Tawney had an inappropriate joke exchange going on, and it was his turn.

She laughed. "Not yet!"

He relayed the joke on their way and finished with the punchline as they filed into the conference room. "'Weird,' the guy in the middle says. 'I dreamed I was skiing all night!'"

Tawney rolled her eyes, snickering as they found seats. Finn was relieved that Luka was in fact already there, looking like his usual gorgeous self. He had changed into a light blue dress shirt that coordinated with the burgundy pants and sorted out his hair situation.

Thomas' suit jacket was off and he had rolled up his sleeves to reveal rather prodigious forearms. Morgan was already there too, blabbing away about himself as usual, this time to Thomas. Finn didn't know how Luka managed to spend so much time talking to Morgan without throttling him.

"Thanks for gathering again, everyone," Ilona started, joining Thomas at the head of the table. "Luka?" She wasn't one for preambles.

Luka took a breath as he spread out his designs.

Finn relaxed about ten seconds in. Luka was back, charming and confident...although maybe a little nervous because he was speaking rapidly and kept wiping his hands on his trousers. His ideas were fantastic, and Thomas had to be impressed, although every time Finn snuck a glance at him, his face was unreadable.

Thomas offered only a small nod when Luka was finished. Then it was Morgan's turn. Not that Finn was a musical expert, but he really liked what Morgan had composed. It had an emotional depth that he did not expect Morgan to be capable of reaching. If he had to be an insufferable dick, at least he was good at his job.

"Did you need anything else, Thomas?" Ilona asked when they were finished sharing.

"I'd like to take another look at everything, if you don't mind. I'll find you if I have any questions."

They stared at him. He stared back. "Does anyone have any questions for me?"

When no one said anything, Thomas nodded once. "I appreciate your hard work. We'll meet again soon."

"Thanks, everyone," Ilona dismissed them.

Luka scrambled out of the conference room again. Finn followed him. He was still rattled, Finn supposed. Could probably use a distraction.

"Oh, I didn't tell you, Rory was looking at the data again from the last batch of Sartini surveys? They noticed that the favorables, if you break them down by age, are actually a whole different story..." Finn chattered away until they got back to Luka's office. "Anyway, Rory said they weren't too worried about it, so I figure it will be fine."

"Mmhmm. Are we going to talk about it?" Luka asked, leaning back in his chair with a smile.

Finn scratched his head and leaned against the doorframe. "Talk about what?"

Luka's grin widened. "You want me to say it?"

His heart skipped a beat. "Don't know what the fuck you're talking about."

"Your undying love for Rory."

Finn's stomach shrank into a lump of granite. His face flamed. "I don't... I—what..." he stammered. *Oh shit. How did Luka know?*

"I'm sorry, what now?" Luka cupped a hand around his ear. "You don't...?" He was thoroughly amused.

"Fuck off," Finn mumbled, fighting off an embarrassed smile. He pushed himself off the frame and marched out, eyes on the ground. Luka chuckled behind him.

Okay. So. Luka knew he was losing his shit for Rory. That was fine. Luka was his best friend. Finn could survive some gentle teasing. The concern was that other people might notice too. He had to get the lost shit back together.

Finn rounded a corner and almost crashed full-on into Rory. His hand slid onto Rory's waist to steady them, then he quickly yanked it away when he realized what he was doing.

"Sorry," Finn stammered as Rory apologized too.

"No, my fault. I wasn't paying attention. Are you okay?"

"Totally fine." *Not fine.* "You?"

"Oh, I'm fine too." Rory smoothed their hair and looked up at Finn. Today there was a cuff ring over the helix of their ear with Greek meander lines on it. "What did Luka say?"

Finn's heart tried to escape up his throat. "What?"

"The other meeting? With Thomas... Did Luka recover okay?"

"Oh. Yeah. Yeah, it was fine. He did good." Finn took a deep breath, trying to calm his thrashing heart.

"That's good."

"Yup."

Another awkward pause.

"Well, I'll see you tomorrow morning, I guess?" Rory said, eyelashes fluttering at Finn.

Finn's brain raced. Rory's eyes were so warm, pools of cedar brown he wanted to soak in. *Tomorrow morning...?*

"When we meet with Ilona about Thrill Island?" Rory supplied in the silence.

"Right! Right. Ilona. Yes. I will see you tomorrow."

"Okay. Have a good day, Finn."

Finn nodded and continued down the hall. A sigh burst from his lips that might have been more like a groan.

Shit. Is. Lost.

* * * *

Finn considered the white canvas.

Curves of blush first, easy and rolling.

Then a wedge of ruby red. And another, and another, along the curves, a trail of desire.

Cedar brown, pools of warmth and understanding.

Finally black.

Long, sweeping lines. Smooth, graceful, from the bottom left corner, swirling up into delicate silver swoops.

The painting came to life in his dream that night, more beautiful than anything he could capture on canvas, surrounding him, cradling him, whispering, "Finn…"

A fire built in his chest, from simmer to inferno, an intense longing that stole his breath, and traveled lower, heating his belly, then lower still, thickening —

He woke up with a jolt, sweaty and rock hard. "Fuck," he moaned when he saw it was not even five yet. There was no more sleeping to be had.

A cold shower helped, and since he was up so early, he decided to bike to work and expend some of the jittery energy crawling through his limbs.

The light shifted from night to dawn as he left his house, an inky black to a deep ocean blue, then orange and red over the horizon. The ride helped, letting him pull in deep breaths of cool air, his cells burning through the oxygen instead of his brain burning through thoughts.

When he got to the office, muscles blissfully rubbery, he unclipped his helmet and scrubbed a hand through his sweaty hair, then wheeled his bike inside.

He secured it in the storage locker in the lobby, then clicked over to the elevator in his clip-in biking shoes.

"Good morning, Finn." It was Rory, waiting for the elevator.

Finn swallowed, hard. *Oh my God. I'm in my spandex. I look like such a dork.* "Oh, hi. Morning." Not just spandex, but sweaty and red-faced.

"How was your ride?" Rory asked. They, of course, looked perfect in an asymmetrical top and fitted black jeans topped with a studded leather belt.

"Good. Good ride."

Rory bobbed their head. "That's good. Do you ride often?"

"Not as often as I'd like."

Rory's eyes flicked up and down Finn's body. *Such. A. Dork.* "I know the gear isn't especially flattering," Finn mumbled, resisting the urge to tug at his shorts.

"What? Not at all. I was thinking how" — Rory cleared their throat — "um, fit you look. I mean, you're...in really good shape."

"I—" *Fit.* Mouth dry, he fumbled for his water bottle. "Thanks," he croaked.

The elevator dinged and Finn's mind swirled as they flowed in.

"I haven't been on a bike in years," Rory mused, watching the numbers above the door.

"I could take you for a ride sometime?" Finn offered before he knew what he was saying.

Rory's smile bounced off the mirrored walls and lit up the tiny space. "I would love to go for a ride with you."

"Great." *Holy shit.* He let his mouth keep talking, seemingly independent from his brain. "Maybe this weekend? While the weather is still nice."

Rory nodded. "That sounds like fun. I'm free Sunday?"

"Okay." *This is fine.* "Yeah, me too. Sunday works. Do you have a bike?"

"I think so, if my parents still have it in the garage. Or I can borrow one from my brother, I'm sure."

The elevator dinged and they spilled out into the Breakpoint lobby. Finn's heart pounded. "Awesome. Do you know Lupine Park? It's not far from you. We could meet there."

"Perfect." Rory stopped, holding onto the strap of their bag and so beautiful it hurt.

"Well, I've got to go shower..." Finn said, pointing down the hall in the other direction from Rory's office.

"Right. I'll see you in Ilona's office at nine."

"You bet." He turned to head to the bathroom that had a shower and had a quick scrub—more cold water—then stopped by the kitchen to grab a coffee to go with his protein bar.

Luka and Thomas were there, sitting at a table with coffee and a few files, and Luka was so focused on Thomas that he didn't even notice Finn come in.

He was smiling at something Thomas said—a smile that could melt the remaining polar ice caps. Then he replied, leaning forward and tapping Thomas' forearm to make a point. Finn studied the way they were sitting, shoulders and hips facing each other, knees tipped together, posture open, eyes bright.

Well damn. Finn grinned as he filled his mug. Looked like he wasn't the only one losing their shit at work. He tucked that note away for when a time came along to pull it out.

* * * *

As Finn pulled into the parking lot, Rory was waiting, bike propped against a bench. Lupine Park was a linear path dotted with purple flowers that ran along the river from the south end of the city to the harbor. It was busy with people wheeling and walking, enjoying the September sunshine.

Rory looked absolutely adorable in black shorts and a gray T-shirt. They stood smiling when they saw Finn gliding up on his bike.

"Are you surprised that I own running shoes?" they asked once Finn was within earshot.

Finn grinned as he came to a stop. "A little bit, to be honest." He had his mountain bike today, not a scrap of spandex to be seen, just regular shorts and a T-shirt.

"I think I've had them since high school," Rory said, studying their Nikes.

"They'll do," Finn said.

"No spandex for you today, though?" Rory asked.

"Glad I didn't wear mine." Their eyes twinkled.

Finn laughed. "Not today, I'm afraid."

They took the path down to the ocean, sharing occasional snatches of conversation when they could ride side by side, until they reached the loop at the end and the blue-gray water of the harbor stretched before them, gulls wheeling, air cool with the salty breeze. They had taken off their helmets and found a bench to settle on when Finn's phone buzzed. He had already missed it twice when they were riding, but he knew who it was. She'd been calling all weekend.

And Finn had been ignoring her all weekend — she refused to leave a voicemail or text — yet she couldn't take the hint. Now here she was, ruining his day with Rory.

Pressure built in Finn's throat as he stared at her name on the screen. "I'm sorry, it's my sister...again. I'd better answer or she'll only keep calling."

"Of course," Rory said.

Finn stood and took a few steps away. "What?" he snapped when he answered the call.

"Well, fucking hi to you, too."

Finn watched a wave break on the shore, white and blue, then swallowed by the dark, pebbled sand. "What do you want, Liz?"

"Are you kidding me?" She laughed, as sharp and unforgiving as ever. "That's how you answer the phone?"

"I do when it's you."

"Jesus. Could you be a bigger asshole, Finn?"

He bit back a curse and rubbed his forehead. "As I said, what do you want? I'm busy."

Her sigh was long and deep, the weight of the world on her poor shoulders. "I talked to Mom."

"And?" A little girl squealing in the ankle-deep surf drew Finn's attention. Her mom gripped her hand tight.

"She asked how you were doing."

"For fuck's sake, Liz. Why are you calling?" Finn realized his voice was growing louder. Probably enough that Rory could hear.

"Oh, I don't know, because you're my brother and maybe you should give a fuck about either of us?"

All Finn could do was laugh. "Excuse me if I'm not into being manipulated and lied to every time I talk to you."

"Lied to? If that's what you think — "

Finn hung up. He took a deep breath, eyes on a wave, trying to find a calmness in the rhythm. He took another breath with the next swell, then went to join Rory on the bench again.

"Are you okay?" Rory said after a pause, lying a gentle hand on Finn's arm.

"Yeah." His voice cracked. "Fine."

"Do you want to talk about it?"

His curls bounced as he shook his head. "My sister…" Another breath, in and out. "Do you get along with your siblings?"

Rory answered without hesitation. "Yes. They're my best friends. Even when my brother can sometimes be a bit…"

"That's great." Finn studied his shorts.

Rory moved their hand to Finn's. "I'm sorry you don't have that."

Finn looked up and met Rory's eyes. The compassion he saw nearly broke his heart with its tenderness. "Thank you. I'm glad that you do."

Rory squeezed. They sat for a minute. Finn looked at Rory's hand on his and thought about stroking it with his thumb, then Rory pulled it away and straightened.

"Are you hungry?" they asked.

"Starving."

About halfway back, they found a trendy brewery, the type with vaulted ceilings, rustic beams and large, communal tables.

They each got a flight of beers to sample, then Finn ordered a pulled pork sandwich with coleslaw and Rory got fried chicken with a salad.

"Tell me about your sister and brothers," Finn said when the server left.

"All right." Rory straightened the label on one of their samplers while they thought. "The oldest is

Jackson. He's a VP at the company now. He'll take over when my parents retire. Griffin is younger than me and he does sales. He's…still trying to figure his life out. The youngest is Bailey. She just finished college, and she recently transitioned."

"Good for her," Finn said.

"Yeah. I'm really proud of her."

"Have you always gotten along so well with them?"

"Yeah… I mean, we scrapped a bit as kids. You know, dumb stuff like fighting over the TV or the last of the good cereal."

Finn nodded, the lump in his throat coming back. Rory's childhood was absolutely nothing like his. They had dollar-store cereal that was nowhere near as good, but that was the least of it.

Rory told him more about their family, but didn't pry into Finn's at all. The food was delicious, and they rode slowly back to Finn's truck after, stomachs full. Finn loaded his bike into the back, then turned to face Rory. "Are you sure you don't want a ride?"

"No, it's okay. I'm so close."

Then Rory was hugging him. They fit so snuggly right under Finn's chin. Finn wrapped Rory in his arms, buried his nose in Rory's hair, closed his eyes and let himself sink into it.

It was a long hug.

Then they pulled away. "Thank you for another fun day, Finn."

The electricity humming through his veins was interrupted by his phone buzzing in his pocket again. "Thank *you*."

Rory looked like they had something else to say, but they put their helmet back on, climbed onto their bike, waved then peddled away.

Finn ignored his buzzing phone, insignificant next to his pounding heart.

Chapter Six

5K

There was no getting around it.

Finn wanted Rory.

Craved them. Was, honestly, a bit obsessed with them. Whether he was fiddling with fonts, brushing paint across a canvas, rattling in plastic seats on the train, working up a sweat in the gym or working up a sweat in other ways, Rory was never far from the forefront of his brain.

But it was a ridiculous idea. Obviously. The two of them were nothing alike, and hitting on Rory, putting them in a position where they had to reject a coworker, could only lead to hurt feelings and a painful work environment. Thrill Island? More like Curl Up and Die-land.

But still.

Rory.

Maybe it was okay if this feeling sat in his heart a while. He didn't have to *do* anything about it. It would just be a...respectful infatuation. Subtle. Contained, and quickly, before anyone else figured it out.

He needed to talk to Luka.

Finn's leg bounced under his desk all morning, but he avoided bugging his friend until it was almost lunch time. When he reached to open Luka's office door, it swung wide and he nearly collided with Thomas who was striding out.

"Excuse me," Thomas muttered.

"No problem." Finn scooted in and shut the door in Thomas' face.

"Finn!" Luka seemed flustered, cheeks pink.

"What?" He dropped into his chair. It was the temperature of Thomas' ass. *Blech.*

Luka's brow furrowed. "That was rude."

"Nah." Finn leaned back, running his hands through his hair. "Thomas is a busy, important man, places to be. He's already forgotten it." His brain whirred, trying to find the words he could say to Luka about the mess swirling inside.

Luka continued. "I just don't know if closing the door in the new VP's face is really the best move."

Finn scratched his beard. It wasn't that he really thought Luka would blab to anyone, but what if he was too obvious around Rory with his winks and nudges? What if he actually *said* something to Rory, thinking he was doing Finn a favor? Finn's insides contorted themselves imagining it. Rory would try to be nice when faced with Finn's crush, of course, since they were so sweet, but—

"Can I help you?" Luka asked in the lengthening silence.

"Look." Finn scrubbed his face and plunged in. "About…Rory." His cheeks burned, giving him away yet again.

Luka fought a smile. "Yes?"

"I'm not—It's…" He took a deep breath and smoothed his trousers, then looked up at Luka. "You won't say anything, will you?"

Luka softened. "No. But if you really feel that way, you should."

Finn scoffed. "What would Rory ever want with me? They're so…gentle and quiet and sweet, and I…" He trailed off. *I'm none of those things.* Then he realized Luka was watching him, all smug and shit, and scowled again. "Anyway, like you're one to talk."

"What does that mean?" Luka's voice climbed, fingers jumping to fiddle with a stack of papers.

"Why's *your* face so red, eh?" Finn grinned. "I've seen the way you look at the Wolf."

Luka's jaw dropped, then he snapped it shut. "I don't know what you're talking about. Thomas is my boss. And it's red because I shat the bed and the storyboards are garbage. We have to redo them all." He waved an arm over the pile on his desk.

"What?" Finn furrowed his brow. "Thomas said they were garbage?" If that was the case, there was something seriously wrong with Thomas.

"Well, no."

"What did he say?"

"He said he talked to Aleandro and we need to go in another direction."

"So?" Finn shrugged. Classic Luka. Spiraling for nothing. "You did the work based on the information we had at the time. Now we know more, so we adapt."

Luka blinked at him. "I guess."

"Just means more time working with him," Finn teased.

"*Anyway*," Luka said, blushing further. "Speaking of work…" He gestured to the stacks of paper on his desk.

"Yeah, yeah," Finn muttered, getting to his feet. "I know, 'Fuck off, Finn.'" He paused at the door and turned back, heart swelling with a burst of affection for his friend. "Thanks, Luka."

"Anytime, bud."

* * * *

Work for Sartini piled up now that Thomas was leading full-steam ahead. Their Thrill Island pitch meeting with Ilona had gone well—she loved their ideas—and now there were a few adjustments and some polishing to do before they met with the owner of the amusement park. The big cancer charity fundraiser Finn headed up every year—the 5K for Hope—was approaching too, and he was busy organizing the Breakpoint office team.

With all those things on his plate, he wasn't surprised when he looked up from his desk one evening to see it was after nine.

"Fuck," he muttered, rubbing his eyes. That was more than enough for one day. His stomach growled as he packed up his bag and trudged toward the elevators.

And there was Rory, waiting. The overhead lights were off, but the light from down the hall cast Rory's long neck and sharp jaw in stark relief.

"Hi," Finn said, his throat threatening to close.

Rory tuned at the sound of Finn's voice, tired face lighting up with a smile. "Hi, Finn."

"You're here late," Finn said.

"So are you."

"Yeah." Finn pushed his hair back. "Lots going on."

"That's for sure."

The elevator ride was quiet, and so was the night when they stepped out onto the sidewalk. Finn paused and turned his face up to the cool air, refreshing after so many hours inside.

Rory tilted their head up, too. "What a beautiful night," they said softly. The faint stars that were visible over the city dotted an inky sky, scattered with thin, purple clouds.

Finn's hunger and exhaustion had vanished, replaced only by the desire to stay by Rory's side. "Can I give you a ride home?" he offered. "I drove today. Getting a train this time of night can be tricky." A bolt of worry stabbed through him at the idea of Rory traveling home alone.

"Oh, no." Rory shook their head. "It's totally out of your way."

"Not that far," Finn said. "I'd be happy to drive you."

Rory shifted their bag and looked up at Finn. Their eyes reflected the streetlights, sparks of yellow in bottomless black. "Well, if you're sure."

"I'm sure."

Finn's head spun as Rory climbed into his truck next to him. Fortunately, he had just cleaned it, so the seats were shiny and crumb-free.

"What were you working on so late?" Finn asked as he pulled out of the parking lot.

"Smoothing out a few bugs in the Thrill Island app, crunching some numbers for Thomas, catching up on emails. You?"

"Getting shit together for the 5K for Hope, mostly. Emails for me too, harassing people to sign up."

"Not me though—I registered today!" Rory said proudly.

"I saw." Finn had in fact made an involuntary noise in the lunchroom when Rory's name had popped up in his inbox.

"That's so cool that you're organizing this. How long has the office been participating?"

"Since I arrived, so this is the fifth year."

"That's great, Finn. Good for you."

Finn shrugged. "My grandma was the only one in my family who actually gave a shit about me. When cancer got her, I wanted to do something in her memory."

Rory reached over and touched Finn's knee. Only for a second, but their hand left a searing imprint. "I'm sorry."

"Thank you." Finn gave Rory a sideways smile. "I wish I had known her better, but I like remembering her this way. Plus, I'm living in her house now and it helps me feel more connected to her." Finn told Rory about the work he'd done to update her place, but keep its original seventies vibe.

"Wow, you did all those renovations yourself?" Rory asked.

"Most of them, thanks to online tutorials. I'm good with my hands." Finn's cheeks flamed. "Like, with wood. Uh, building stuff."

"I can't do anything like that." Rory fluttered their lithe fingers. "Kind of useless."

Finn snorted. "Tell that to your keyboard."

He could see Rory smile from the corner of his eye and turn to look at him. "I bet your house looks amazing."

"You'll get to see it if you come to the office Halloween party. I host it every year."

"I'll be there."

Finn dropped Rory off at the front walk of their building and waited for them to get safely inside. Rory turned to wave through the glass door. Finn waved back until Rory had vanished from view.

He smiled the whole way home.

* * * *

At lunch the next day, Luka put his phone down and gave Finn his full attention. "Wait. You drove Rory home last night?"

"Yeah, why?"

Luka chuckled. "You keep saying you and Rory aren't a good fit, but like...you're practically dating, Finn."

"Did you get hit in the head or something? No, we're not!"

"Let me recap this for you real quick," Luka said. "They asked you to lunch —"

"Only 'cause it would have been awkward not to."

"You spent a day at Thrill Island —"

"That was for work."

"—after which they asked you to *dinner*—" Luka paused, waiting for Finn's counter-argument. There was none. "And then you went bike riding all day — how adorable is *that*?"

"It was just a bike ride," Finn mumbled.

Luka's look was withering. "That was a date."

"No, it wasn't!"

Luka ticked off a point on his fingers. "Did you get food?"

"Um..."

Another tick. "Did you hug at the end?"

Finn pressed his lips together. "Maybe."

Luka's grin was massive and annoying. "Did you, or did you not, smell their hair during said hug?"

Finn glared.

"That's what I thought. Dating." Luka took a smug bite of his pasta.

"So are you and Thomas practically dating then?" Finn asked, hoping Luka would take the distraction bait. "You guys are together all day in your tiny little office." Thomas had taken over one arm of Luka's desk instead of getting his own space, and Finn knew for a fact there was an available office by the conference room.

"I do not *want* to date him," Luka said primly. "He is my boss. Plus he is definitely not interested. Which is fine, because I would have to be insane to pursue him. Because he is my boss. So…no."

"I've never been more convinced," Finn said.

* * * *

At the next staff meeting, there were a few minutes on the agenda for Finn to talk about the upcoming fundraiser. "Don't forget, the '5K for Hope' is this Sunday," he announced from the head of the table. "If you have any donations that weren't online, you can bring the cash and pledge forms with you. The run itself starts at nine, so please try to be there by eight-thirty. I'll have your shirts for you tomorrow. And" — he turned to Luka — "I need to congratulate Moreno who, once again, has raised the most money in the office."

"Oh." Luka hunched his shoulders as the room applauded. "It's nothing."

"It's definitely not nothing," Finn insisted, resisting the urge to check and make sure Thomas was listening. "That money will make a difference to people with cancer. You did a great job." Luka's charm was a highly effective fundraising tool.

"Do you need any help with anything?" Rory asked him after the meeting. "Now, or on Sunday or...?"

"Sure." Finn's heart fluttered. "If it's not too much trouble, I could use some help with setup or takedown?"

"I can do both. What time do you want me?"

Finn coughed. "Seven-thirty would be great."

* * * *

Sunday dawned bright and clear, although a late September chill frosted the grass. The leaves were a dance of autumnal colors, gold and burnt orange and apple red against the cloudless sky. Finn carried a bin of supplies from his truck over to their assigned team table, then began unpacking, trying to focus on the task and not looking around to see if Rory had arrived yet.

Then there they were, in sunglasses and damp hair, walking over from the parking lot carrying two coffees. Rory wore their usual jeans, plus a cozy black hoodie Finn hadn't seen before, featuring a band he'd never heard of.

"You've got me in my running shoes again, Finn," they said, handing over one of the cups. "That's twice in as many weeks. Who even am I anymore?"

Finn chuckled. "Thanks," he said, toasting Rory with the cup. "Maybe next week we can play racquetball."

Rory laughed. "How'd you know? My favorite of all the racquet sports."

Finn smiled and took a slow sip, savoring the warmth and rich flavor. "Mmm, this is good."

"Dark roast, black," Rory said.

"Thanks so much." Brain spinning with so many things to remember that morning, he had forgotten to bring coffee with him. Luckily, Rory seemed to know his order.

"You're welcome. So, put me to work."

They carried the fold-up tent from Finn's truck and set it up over the table, then added a pop-up Breakpoint sign and a tablecloth to match their logo.

"How do you feel about clipboards?" Finn asked, holding up the team list and a pencil.

"Huge fan," Rory said.

"Could you please double-check that everyone is here? If their name is highlighted, they didn't get their shirt yet. Their size is listed in this column and the extra shirts are in the bin."

"Got it." Their fingers touched when Rory took the clipboard.

As the park filled up around them, Finn started making the rounds through their team, greeting his coworkers and their families and handing out stickers and balloons to the kids. He waved at Tawney and Ilona, rolled his eyes at Morgan who was wearing sweatbands and the whitest shoes ever to have graced the planet and smirked at Luka drooling over Thomas in his admittedly very flattering running tights.

When it was almost time for the official opening ceremonies, he climbed on a chair and got his team's attention. "Welcome to Breakpoint's fifth annual 5K for Hope!" He paused for a round of hooting and clapping.

"Thanks to your fundraising efforts and a last-minute anonymous donation, we have smashed our previous best, for a total of just over twenty-six-thousand dollars!"

The cheering grew louder.

Finn took a breath and pushed aside a thought about his grandma. "You're all making a real impact. Don't forget to stay for the closing ceremony, drink lots of water and have fun out there!"

A pair of bouncing blondes skipped onto the main stage to lead the participants in a warmup. Finn hopped off his chair and started copying their moves.

"So I guess you'll be running at the front of the pack?" Rory asked, doing the cutest arm circles ever in their hoodie and jeans.

"I'll do my best, anyway," Finn said.

"Well, I'll be with the strollers at the back." Rory chuckled. "But good luck."

With the starting horn, Finn set a brisk pace and stayed near the front throughout, finishing in a hair under twenty-two minutes. He waved to Rory on the loop back — they were indeed deep in stroller territory, chatting with Sabrina and her wife and kids.

The walkers were still returning when the closing ceremonies began. He went up on stage with Ilona to accept the award for top corporate fundraising team. There was a team photo after, then a barbecue for everyone. Finn tracked down a hot dog and took it back to lean against their table next to their plaque. He was finishing his last bite when Rory came over.

"Congratulations, Finn," they said. "Your grandma would be so proud of you."

The emotion that Finn had been holding back all morning hit him without warning. "Thanks," he said, tears welling, chest aching.

Rory stepped closer and rested their hand on Finn's arm but didn't say anything for a moment. "If you want to talk about it, I can listen. But it's fine if you don't."

Finn wiped at the tear that escaped and let the memory bubble up. "We used to visit her for the holidays when I was little." He closed his eyes. "I remember the way she smelled, like flowers and fresh baking." He smiled and sniffled. "She made the best cookies. They were as big as my head."

"She must have loved baking for you."

Another tear. "Jesus." Finn laughed, embarrassed, dabbing at it with his napkin. "I'm sorry. Yeah, I hope she did."

Rory leaned next to Finn, shoulders touching, and tilted their head up to the flawless blue sky. "She did. And she'll be with you, always. She's in your heart, you know?"

Finn took a deep breath. "I know. Thanks, Rory. And thank you for your help today."

"It's my pleasure. Whenever you need me."

It sounded like they really meant it. Finn bumped their shoulder with his.

Chapter Seven

Open Table

Finn's stomach swooped when he looked up from his desk Tuesday morning. Rory was framed in the doorway, in an outfit Finn hadn't seen before – black pants with silver-buckled leather straps down one side, and a half kilt wrapped around the other side. Their beautiful eyes, crinkling at Finn, were lined with a touch of smoky eyeliner. Impossibly hot.

"You look nice," Finn choked out. He quickly looked back down at this sketch, knowing his eyes were much too wide. "Big date tonight?"

Rory chuckled. "Ha, no. Dinner out with my parents." The answer reassured Finn more than it had any right to. "It's their anniversary. I try to step it up a notch."

"Well, you, uh – you did." Finn cleared his throat. "Several notches. And happy anniversary to them."

"Thanks, I'll pass that on." Rory fiddled with one of the straps on their thigh for a second, cheeks flushing a faint pink. Then they gave their belt a tug and straightened their shoulders. "Did you see that email from Markos? He confirmed our meeting for next week."

"Terrific." So far they had only exchanged a few emails with the owner of Thrill Island, but Markos seemed like a nice enough guy who was excited to work with them. "Do you want to meet one more time before that to make sure we're ready?"

"That would be great." Rory pulled out their phone and they made a plan to meet Friday at two o'clock. Finn spent the rest of the day with visions floating through his head of him walking into a restaurant with Rory on his arm dressed like that.

* * * *

You can do it, Finn. Just ask Rory to go for a drink. A simple drink. It was four o'clock on Friday and they'd been huddled together in Finn's office putting the finishing touches on their presentation for Thrill Island for the last two hours.

"We still need a better name than 'Undercover Romantic Boat Ride' for the Haunted Lagoon," Finn said, tapping his chin.

"I know, why is it so hard?" Rory replied.

"What about..." Finn frowned, trying to think of a suitable boat pun "...Taking the *Sea*-nic Route?"

Rory half-laughed, half-groaned. "I don't think that's it."

"Hmm... okay," Finn continued, undeterred. "Ferry-tale Ending?"

"Finn. Stop," Rory said with mock seriousness. Then they grinned. "Harbor-ing Strong Feelings?"

"A-boat Time?"

"Feeling Nauti!"

And so it went, until their shoulders shook with laughter, and their knees bumped together under the table.

"Okay, seriously," Rory breathed, wiping a tear threatening to escape. "Maybe boats aren't the angle here. Back to heists..." They flicked their bangs back, eyes alight. "And the romance angle. I don't care what anyone says, drifting along together in a boat is romantic. How about...Stolen Kisses?"

Finn blinked. "I love that! It's brilliant."

Rory's eyelashes fluttered as they looked down. "Thanks."

Finn dug through the stack of mock-ups, found the one for the lagoon ride and got to work sketching out the new sign.

Rory leaned over to watch, arm brushing against Finn's. "That looks great," they murmured as it took shape under Finn's pencil.

Their breath smelled like mint. Goosebumps swept over the back of Finn's neck. His heart was a bird beating its wings madly against his ribcage, desperate to take flight. Then the bird busted right out. "Do you want to go grab a drink tonight?" Finn asked.

Rory looked up, eyebrows bunched. "A drink?"

Oh fuck. They look confused. Because obviously, why would he ask that? *Fuck fuck fuck.* "We should round everyone up, head over to the Exchange after work," Finn covered quickly.

"Sure." Rory relaxed. "Yeah, sounds good."

Ass, Finn scolded himself as he got back to work on his drawing. *Rory doesn't want to go out with you.* He had to let go of that stupid idea. But at least their time together today wasn't ending just yet.

* * * *

Finn tracked down Tawney, who was stoked to go for drinks, and got to texting a few others. Then he ran into Thomas refilling his water bottle in the kitchen. Once again, Finn considered how appropriate Thomas' nickname was, watching him move around in his gray suit, smooth and powerful, with a calm dignity.

"Hey, Wolf," Finn said, then froze. *Shit.* It slipped out.

"That's okay," Thomas said with a hint of a lip curl when he saw Finn's panic. "I don't mind the nickname. I've certainly been called worse."

"Haven't we all," Finn said, relaxing. "Hey, a bunch of us are heading for a drink after work. The Bitter Exchange, just down the block, if you haven't been yet."

"Mmm," Thomas said, glancing at his watch. "I'm not sure…"

"You should come," Finn said. "Get to know everyone a little better." *Like Luka.* "It'll be fun."

Thomas considered a moment longer, then nodded once. "Yes, thank you. I have a few things to finish up here, then I'll come for a drink."

Finn tidied up his desk a little—very little—then barged into Luka's office at 5:01, shrugging on his jacket. "Moreno! It's quitting time."

Luka didn't look up, in the middle of madly scribbling notes in the margins of a report. "I just have to—"

"Nope!" Finn snatched the papers out from under his pencil and held them aloft. Luka would work all weekend if you let him. "Everyone's going for drinks."

"Finn!" Luka reached for his work, then paused. "Everyone?" he asked, in the most obvious way possible.

"Everyone," Finn said, trying to rein in his smirk.

Luka chewed his lip and eyed his monitor. "Okay." He stood and grabbed the papers back so he could file them away. "Where are we going? Do not say Exchange."

Finn grinned. He had to admit, as the Bitter Exchange had become the usual afterwork hangout, it was rather amusing how much Kazio, the owner, seemed to actively dislike Luka — handsome, charming and liked by literally everyone else.

"Why do we have to go there?" Luka groaned.

Finn clapped him on the back. "Ten-dollar pitchers and the best wings in town! What's not to like?"

"Were you wanting a list, or…?"

With a playful shove, Finn turned to charge out. "Last one there buys the first round!" He didn't want to keep Rory waiting.

* * * *

Finn and Rory walked to the pub with Tawney. It was her turn for a joke — "Why do walruses love a Tupperware party?" — then they grabbed a few tables in the corner. The place buzzed with the usual Friday crowd, and their tables filled up with Breakpoint coworkers. Luka arrived, giving them a wave and heading straight to the bar to battle with Kazio.

Finn was draining the last of his first beer, feeling pleasantly warm and admiring Rory's exquisite profile, when his phone rang.

It was his mom.

Mel was all the Caller ID said.

What the fuck? She never called.

His finger twitched over the screen, a whispered curse escaping his lips. There was no way he was going to answer.

Except, fuck. She *never* called.

"Excuse me," he muttered to Rory.

He swiped to answer and pressed the phone to his ear. "Hello?" he said, wiggling between tables to slip out through the front door.

There was a pause, entirely too long, coming from the person who had placed the call. "Finn," his mother finally said.

"Mel," he replied, already tired of her bullshit.

"How are you?" she asked.

Finn leaned against the brick wall of the pub. Wow, acting like she cared and everything.

"Busy," he answered. "What do you want?"

"Liz was saying you're a hard guy to get a hold of."

"Yeah, well…" Finn shook his head, wanting to laugh. "Here I am."

"Look, Finn. I just wanted to tell you…" She paused again, the silence on the line louder than the traffic rolling by at the end of the block. "Things haven't been great for Liz lately."

A twinge in Finn's gut. "What do you mean?"

"She's splitting from Neil. He's dragging it through court. She's a mess, so are the kids."

"Pretty sure I said not to marry that asshole."

"Christ, Finn. What good does that do anyone right now?"

Finn closed his eyes and took a deep breath. "What do you want, Mel?"

"I wanted you to know about Liz. Maybe you should reach out. She could use some support. So could her kids."

Finn's eyes snapped open. *No. There's no way...* "Are you asking me for *money?*"

"Your sister needs some help, Finn. You got the house, no kids—"

A laugh choked from his throat. "Which you both love to remind me, endlessly."

"Well, it's true."

"You are un-fucking-believable. The last time I saw Liz in person she told me I was a selfish prick, and you—I've gotta go, Mel."

"Finn—"

He hung up.

He was going to need a lot more beer.

When he got back to their tables, it looked like everyone was there now. Luka and Tawney were throwing darts, and Morgan was throwing himself at Thomas.

"Everything okay?" Rory asked, watching Finn grab the pitcher and slosh another round into his glass.

Finn took a long pull, heart racing. "Yeah," he said, once he had thumped his glass back down. "Fine." And another drink.

"It's just that... I don't mean to pry, but you don't really look okay."

Finn drained that glass and poured another. "Yeah." He shook his head, then jammed a curl behind his ear. "That was my mom."

"Oh." Rory didn't say anything else, just waited.

The words bubbled up his throat. "Remember how I said things weren't great with my sister? My mom is like...a whole lot worse than that." He took a gulp of his beer. "She was barely around, she never gave a shit about me and Liz but Liz was always on her side, like I was the one being a dick and I—" He shook his head. Another gulp. "I try to keep them out of my life now."

"That's fair," Rory said softly. "It's up to you who you want in your life."

"Right. I want people...who care, you know?" He looked up to meet Rory's eyes. They were soft and warm and he tumbled right into them.

"I know," Rory said. They placed their hand on Finn's forearm and squeezed.

Finn had to look away when the eye contact threatened to send his heart throbbing right out of his chest and into a quivering pile on the table. As his gaze wandered, he caught sight of something new in the back corner behind the bar.

"You like pool?" he asked Rory.

"I'm not great, but yeah," Rory said, turning to see what Finn was looking at.

Finn got to his feet, clutching his glass and maybe swaying a bit. He eyed Luka and Thomas, huddled together over at the bar looking cozy as fuck. "I've got an idea." Finn barreled across the pub and threw his arm around Luka.

"We challenge you, Big Bad Wolf!" he bellowed, waving his beer at Thomas.

"We challenge him to what, darling?" Luka asked, a wary eye on the sloshing liquid.

"Pool!" Finn announced. Now he pointed his beer at the new table. "Me and you versus Thomas and Rory! We'll crush them."

Luka laughed. "If you say so." He looked at Thomas, who appeared skeptical. "What do you say, Thomas?"

Thomas frowned. "Probably not a good idea."

"Why not?" Finn squinted at him. Thomas was a little blurry. And apparently not much fun at all.

"I don't want to listen to you whining when you lose," Thomas said, completely straight-faced.

Finn blinked at him then burst out laughing. *Oh, yes. I knew I was gonna like him.* "Loser buys the next round, pretty boy."

Thomas' eyes twinkled. "Deal."

Finn went to collect Rory and a pitcher, then carefully topped up his glass while Luka racked up the balls.

The call from his mom was a distant memory. Or it would be, soon enough.

"You guys can break," Finn said to Thomas and Rory, ever the gentleman, even several beers in.

"Go ahead." Thomas gestured to Rory when the balls were ready.

Rory approached the table much like a deer — timid, lithe, eyes liquid and steps careful.

"Give us a good spread!" Finn called as Rory lined up their shot. The way they bent over, aimed so carefully... Finn tugged on his collar, like one of those cartoon characters releasing a burst of steam.

The triangle of balls exploded and clattered all around the table, but none went in. Rory groaned.

"Excellent work, Rory!" Finn tore his eyes away from their lovely ass. "Open table." He squeezed his cue and admonished himself to focus, skittering around the table like an idiot. If Rory was a deer, Finn was a baby giraffe, all flapping limbs and knobby knees. "Three, corner pocket," he decided. He breathed a sigh of relief when he sank it. "We're solids. Don't let me down, Moreno." He picked up his pint and collapsed onto a stool, happy his turn was over and he had managed to look competent.

Luka, however… He lined up his shot, then flinched for absolutely no reason whatsoever, and the cue slipped off his hand and bumped a nearby ball.

"Are you kidding me right now?" Finn asked after a moment of incredulous silence.

"Sorry," Luka said sheepishly, rubbing the back of his neck.

Finn shook his head. "Brutal." A little *too* brutal. He watched Luka, whose gaze flicked to Thomas, pulse jumping in his throat. *Oh. He is* gone, Finn decided, smiling into his pint. *Head over fucking heels.* His gaze danced over to Rory, stomach swirling. Who was more pathetic, him or Luka?

"I guess it's me," Thomas rumbled. With the precision of a sniper's bullet, a striped ball slammed into a pocket.

"Ah, fuck. I picked the wrong partner," Finn moaned, as if it wasn't apparent to all of them.

"Mmm," Thomas agreed.

Luka didn't even bother to argue.

Thomas and Rory won the game easily.

"All right, all right," Finn muttered, signaling their server for another pitcher. "Rematch. Get it together, Moreno! You're breaking. I swear to God…" He took a swig, hoping Luka wouldn't embarrass himself too badly.

Luka's break didn't have much power, but he managed to sink a stripe.

"That's my boy!" Finn cried, proud of his friend. He slapped Luka on the back.

"Well done, Luka." Thomas nodded. "You were bound to sink one eventually."

Luka gasped. "How dare you, sir? Just for that, we're going to destroy you!"

"Starting when?" The corner of Thomas' mouth twitched.

Luka's cheeks were pink. "Just you wait!"

Too fucking cute, Finn thought, brain fuzzier than the green table felt. He sank another ball and an easy shot was waiting for Luka that he managed not to mess up.

"Scared yet?" Luka asked the other two as Finn lined up his next shot.

Rory perched on a stool in the corner of Finn's eye, pant cuff sliding up, revealing an exquisite ankle. "Fuck!" Finn swore as the cue ball followed the other into a pocket.

Rory grinned. "Nope. Good try, though, Finny."

His stomach fucking packed a bag and began hiking up his esophagus at the nickname. "It's still early. I'm not worried," he choked out. Finn pushed his curls off his forehead and reclined against the table, willing his heart to calm down.

"Well, I'm going to need you to move," Rory said, pointing at a shot.

"What if I don't want to move?" Finn asked, cranking a wretchedly bold eyebrow at Rory.

"I could make you move." Rory took a step closer, eyes glimmering with amusement.

Make me, Finn wanted to say, picturing Rory grabbing him, hands soft and yet firm... But his courage faded. He cleared his throat and stepped aside. "Still going to beat you," he mumbled.

Rory slammed another ball home. "We'll see."

Rory and Thomas won again. They high-fived each other.

"Good game." Rory smiled at Finn, offering a hand.

Finn took it. Their eyes met. His heart got into a kick line with the rest of his internal organs. Rory's grip was as firm as he imagined it, but with impossibly smooth skin. Their hand was warm, nail beds pink and shining. Rory's hand flexed as they leaned a little closer, a smile soft on their lips.

Finn took a deep breath, inhaling Rory's scent. "Good game," he said, with a nearly imperceptible shake to his voice.

He didn't want the shake to end but he forced himself to let go when Rory stepped back.

Thomas cleared his throat. "Thanks, everyone. I think I'll be heading home."

Luka nodded. "Have a good weekend."

"You too." Thomas headed to the bar to settle his tab before making his way out into the night. Luka stared after him wistfully.

"Wanna play again?" Finn asked Luka.

"Nah, I think I'll head home, too. You two enjoy your weekend."

Rory watched him go, head tilted. "Is it just me, or are they totally into each other?"

Finn snorted. "Oh, absolutely. I'm wondering how much time those two idiots will waste pining after each other."

"Yeah," Rory said with a chuckle. "Me too."

Chapter Eight

Godstrike

Ilona sighed, tapping her nails on the table. "Anything yet?"

Finn checked his email again. "Nothing."

Finn and Rory were waiting with Ilona in the conference room Monday morning for Markos Palamarou, the owner of Thrill Island, to arrive. He was twenty minutes late.

Ilona stood, smoothing her skirt. "Text me if you hear from him." She clacked out and the door thumped shut behind her.

Rory stretched in their chair, long and lazy, neck a pale expanse of skin, a pure —

"How was the rest of your weekend?" they asked.

Finn jumped. *Fuck.* He fluttered his hands over the sketches, ensuring they were laid out with parallel edges, for the fourth time, at least. "Fine," he said. "Slept off all those beers Saturday morning." It had been a blurry train ride home. He remembered the games of pool though, remembered their handshake at the end. "Did some yard cleanup, painted, hit the gym. The usual. You?"

"It was my niece's birthday party on Saturday. It was pretty fun—cake, piñata, a clown making balloon animals. You know, that whole thing."

Finn didn't really know. A hollow spot in his chest gave a twinge. "Sounds fun."

"Yeah, it was. My niece is a cutie. She just turned four. You want to see some pictures?"

"Sure."

Finn leaned over to see Rory's phone as they scrolled. A smiling newly four-year-old with curly brown hair with a streak of vanilla icing on her cheek. The same girl swinging at a cupcake piñata, this time with a streak of determination. Then in Rory's arms, both in ridiculous balloon hats, laughing at each other, faces alight with joy. Finn breathed out, trying not to let the hollow spot get bigger. "What's her name?"

"Minnie."

"She is a cutie."

"Yeah." Rory smiled softly at their screen, then tucked their phone away. "Anyway, Sunday I sat around in my pajamas all day binging the first season of *Godstrike*. Have you seen it?"

Finn shook his head. "Never heard of it."

"Oh, you *have* to watch it." Rory leaned forward, eyes shining. "It's super cheesy but so fun. There's these gods, right, like a Mount Olympus-type situation, waging war, messing with mortals, doing all the normal god stuff, but also most of them are queer and it's like a soap opera, with all the drama and sleeping around and so on." Rory laughed at the skeptical expression on Finn's face and reached over to touch his arm. "Trust me! Give it a try, then we can talk about it after."

Finn looked at Rory's hand pressed to his bare skin, and noted the goosebumps rise as Rory pulled their hand away. *Yup. Watching it.* "Sure, I'll check it out."

"Yay! You're going to love it."

"If it's shit, though, you owe me."

Rory's eyes crinkled. "Deal."

The door clicked open and Ilona came back in, leading a man who could only be described as 'large' — tall and thick, huge forearms, ample belly, wide nose, with a thick cul-de-sac of black hair and matching beard. Finn and Rory stood to greet him.

"Mr. Palamarou, this is Finn Owens and Rory Barrett."

"Finn, Rory!" Markos pumped their arms like he was trying to put out a fire. "So great to meet you in person."

"Likewise, Mr. Palamarou," Finn said, glad when he got his hand back.

"Please, please, call me Markos. I don't like titles." He pulled out a chair and got himself comfortable, gaze darting around the room. "So sorry I'm late! I wish I had a better reason. Sometimes I lose track of time. I was fixing a leak — that damn boat ride, I tell you."

"It's no problem," Ilona said smoothly. "Thank you so much for coming to meet us."

"I can't wait to see what you've come up with!" The big man clapped his hands together and rubbed them with anticipation. "Let's have it!"

* * * *

The meeting could not have gone better. Markos loved the heist angle, and chortled at the redesigned ride names. "You want to keep the boat ride, do you?" he said with distaste.

"Absolutely!" Rory jumped in. "It's terrific, really takes advantage of all those beautiful willows, and nice to have a few quieter rides for your guests. Plus, who doesn't love that vibe—gliding through the water, scent of magnolias in the air, breeze in your hair—"

"Scraping slime off the floor in the pump room, pulling wet garbage out of the reeds," Markos continued, chuckling. "But you're right, Rory, you're right. People love that one. I like how you two made it romantic. Something for the couples."

Finn's and Rory's eyes met, and Finn swore Rory's cheeks flushed a little.

"Exactly," Rory said, scratching their nose.

They left with Markos' enthusiastic approval and a rough timeline for the redesign. It was a massive project, for Markos and for them, and the weight of it sat on Finn's shoulders a little heavier now. But more importantly…

"Who did he remind you of?" Finn asked once Markos and Ilona had left the room.

"I know, it's been bugging me." Rory paused stacking their drawings and frowned. "For some reason I feel like it's a cartoon character?"

Finn paused too, the name dancing at the edges of his brain until he managed to grab hold. "Oh my God, I know! It's the bad guy in *Pinocchio*! The puppet-master dude."

Rory blinked then threw back their head laughing. "Shit, yes! That's exactly it!"

"Aw, damn it, that's all I'm going to be able to think about when I see him now."

"Same." Rory giggled.

"Hey." Finn held Rory's gaze again. "Great job today. You were amazing."

This time Rory blushed for real, cheeks flushing the sweetest shade of primrose pink. "So were you."

"Thanks." The overwhelming urge to hug Rory swept over him. Instead, Finn cleared his throat and shut his laptop. "I guess we'd better get to work."

* * * *

Later that night, Finn sent Rory a text.

I watched the first two episodes.

Rory replied immediately.

You did??? And????

Well, the guy with the crown is hot, I'll give him that, but he seems too attached to his snake.

That's Colios. Yeah, crazy hot, but…he's got issues, and that's putting it mildly!

Wait…he's not in love with his snake, is he?

No spoilers!

The snake thing is a spoiler???

Rory sent the zipper-mouth emoji.

What did you think of Ophy?

They texted back and forth the rest of the night, in between tidying the kitchen, a quick set of push-ups, brushing his teeth, and undressing and climbing into bed. Cozy under the comforter in his boxers, Finn picked up his phone again. A message from Rory waited.

So you're gonna keep watching it, right?

For sure.

You have to keep texting me your thoughts!

Finn resisted the urge to kick his feet in glee.

I will. Hope I didn't bug you too much all night though.

Definitely not.

His heart fluttered. Then another message from Rory popped up.

But I should get to sleep.

Me too. I'm already in bed, in fact.

So am I.

Finn's heart stopped entirely. Rory. In bed. *Fuck. Deep breath, Finn.* He fought the indecent thoughts he was having as he sent one more text.

Goodnight, Rory.

Goodnight, Finn.

He put his phone down and burrowed into the blankets, smiling so big it hurt his cheeks. *Oh, I'm watching* the fuck *out of this show.*

* * * *

The workdays went by in a blur. Finn scaled up plans for the new Thrill Island signage, while Rory got to work on the website and app design in earnest. Markos would hire a contractor for the actual work in the park, but Finn had the entire marketing campaign to worry about too, so he began building his Breakpoint team. On top of all that, there was the Sartini file taking up a large chunk of his time and energy. Most of the office was in a frenzy about that one, especially as the first meeting with Aleandro Sartini approached. Not to mention, Halloween was close, and he had to start thinking about the party he was hosting.

Tawney leaned on the doorway to Finn's office the day before the big meeting. "Hey, I'm looking for the final proofs for the Sartini magazine campaign?"

Finn was just about literally buried in paint samples, finalizing colors for the new Thrill Island motif. He looked up at her and scrubbed at his hair. "What now?"

"Sorry, bud." Her gaze darted to his head. "Did you have those proofs?"

He scowled and smoothed the offending curls. "Gimme an hour."

"Yeah?"

"Or two."

Tawney gave him a knowing head tilt. "I'll be back in three."

No problem. He had this all under control.

* * * *

Okay, I have to warn you about season two.

Rory texted that night, after they had finished discussing the season one finale.

I'm a couple episodes in, and it's…more. A lot more. Of everything. In fact, I'm not sure I can recommend you keep watching.

What?

Finn flopped onto his bed.

I'm sure as hell not quitting now, not with that cliffhanger! I need to know what happens with the snake!

Fair enough, but…it gets a little over the top.

Rory, we're so far past the top already we're back to the bottom.

His cheeks flared realizing he had sent the word 'bottom' to Rory, but it was too late now.
There was a pause that nearly killed him, then Rory's reply came.

Phrasing.

Finn cackled.

My bad. Still, I've gotta give it a try.

Okay, fine, but don't say I didn't warn you!

* * * *

The premiere of season two was still worse than Finn had been expecting. He couldn't wait a whole day to watch it, so he turned it on for his morning treadmill run. The wigs were somehow worse this season, and the dialogue even clunkier. Characters changed alliances without so much as a whisper of logic or motivation, and another one was nonsensically written out of the show — death by stampede. The actor must have been unhappy with the creative direction, and Finn couldn't blame them. Finn didn't text Rory on his way into the office though — he decided to wait and talk about it in person, plus he wanted to go over his notes for the Sartini presentation on the train.

His heart gave a little skip when he saw Rory sitting in the staff kitchen. Rory looked up and smiled. Finn realized the first smile of the day from Rory was what he looked forward to the most.

"Hey," he said, joining Rory at the table with a full cup of coffee.

"Morning, Finn." Rory looked a little tired, face pale and eyes puffy.

"You okay?" Finn asked, noticing their blazer was a little crumpled too.

"Oh, I'm fine." Rory rubbed their eyes. "Just tired. Was up late working on the website coding. How are you?"

"Tired, too. I didn't sleep great either."

"Are you nervous about today?"

Yes. "Nah."

"Well, we should go to bed early tonight."

Finn's stomach dropped. *We should what now?*

"I mean—" Rory's eyes widened. "We should both—each—at home—at our houses—"

A snicker escaped from Finn. "It's fine. I know what you meant."

Rory palmed their forehead. "Fuck. I am *really* tired."

"I watched the first episode of season two on the treadmill this morning," Finn said, thankful for the easy topic change. "And can I just say, what the fuck? Why would Ophy go anywhere near those wildebeests?"

"I told you!" Rory laughed. "It goes right off the rails in the second season."

Finn grinned. "You're right. I should have listened to you. But it started off so good!"

Rory nodded with a deep sigh. "Think of the time we've both wasted now. Maybe if we turned it into a drinking game..."

"Every time someone's wig changes mid-scene."

"Every time Colios pets his snake..."

"Every time Colios pets his *other* snake..."

They were both doing what could only be described as giggling when Luka wandered into the kitchen in search of coffee.

"Moreno!" Finn called. "Ready for the big day?"

"As ready as I can be." Luka topped up his coffee and filled another mug from the cupboard. He looked a little tired, too.

"We've got this. Aleandro is going to love it," Finn said.

"'Course he will!" Rory chimed in. "You're both brilliant artists."

Finn looked down at his shoes, cheeks flushing.

"Thanks, Rory. I guess we'll find out soon!" Luka smiled and left with his coffee.

Rory leaned over to whisper, "He got a mug for Thomas, too. Cute."

"Yeah, he's pretty smitten."

Rory picked up their coffee, eyes sparkling. "Anyway, text me when you're watching episode two."

"I will." *Just try to stop me.*

* * * *

Aleandro Sartini was a warm, grandfatherly figure, straight out of a post-war English manor house—three-piece suit, pocket watch and everything—with dramatic Dracula-style black hair streaked with gray. His wife Penelope was a little cooler, beautiful but straight-faced with her hair pulled back in a firm twist. A third woman with long, wavy strawberry-blonde hair, who Ilona introduced as Georgia Black, the head of marketing for Sartini Wines, was with them.

Finn felt like he pulled off his presentation okay. He knew his team was strong, and even if he was a little scattered himself lately—a large portion of his brain filled with Thrill Island, not to mention a muscly god and his slinky python—the work spoke for itself.

Luka was awesome—*man*, that guy was good at getting people excited about his ideas. And Rory was brilliant, of course, rattling off an insane array of marketing figures from memory. Aleandro was clearly impressed, and the office got back to work after the meeting, happily abuzz.

Finn got a text from Tawney after lunch, and he headed straight to Luka's office. "I hear congrats are in order?" he said. Tawney had let him know that Luka was officially co-leading the Sartini campaign with Thomas.

"Oh, yeah, thanks." Luka tried to look modest, but was beaming.

"Good for you, bud. That's great." Finn looked at Thomas' empty chair. "So things are going good working with him?"

"Mmhmm," Luka squeaked. "Good. Great. I mean, fine. Yup." He cleared his throat. "Hey, I've been meaning to ask. What's your Halloween costume this year?"

Finn shrugged. "Don't know yet." He usually picked up something last minute from a costume shop that they still had in his size.

"What? Your party is a week away!"

"I'll figure something out. What are you dressing up as?"

"Tawney and I are going as Danny and Sandy."

Finn smirked. "You're Sandy, obviously."

"Obviously."

"Poodle skirt or spandex?"

Luka sighed. "Spandex, even though..."

"Even though her transformation is super problematic?"

The next sigh was louder. "Yes, Finn. Let me have this. I look fucking hot in my costume."

"I have no doubt. Is it...is it crazy if I ask Rory to do a costume with me?"

"The only thing crazy is how late it is to be finding a costume, to be honest."

Finn imagined Rory frowning in confusion again when he proposed the idea. "No. I can't. It'll freak them out."

Luka raised an eyebrow. "No, it won't. You two are friends, right?"

Finn considered the question. All the texting lately, the way Rory was so happy to see him every morning... "Yeah, we're friends."

"If you could see the dumb smile on your face right now."

Finn's jaw flapped. "Fuck right off, Moreno!" was the best he could do before he stormed out of Luka's office, leaving that asshole cackling to himself.

Chapter Nine

Maverick and Goose

Finn threw himself into the chair in Luka's office. "I'm gonna do it." He was. For sure. He had spent the weekend pep-talking himself while drinking scotch and carving inappropriate jack-o-lanterns for the party.

Luka tore his gaze from his computer screen. "Do what?"

"Ask Rory to wear a couples costume with me." Finn's heart pounded at the words.

Luka pressed his lips together for a moment. "That's a great idea. Or you could just ask them out."

Finn shook his head, drumming on his thighs. "No, this is okay. This is good. This is a step."

"If you say so," Luka said, smirking. "What costumes were you thinking?"

Finn rubbed his face. "I have no idea." In between jack-o-lanterns, he had searched 'couples costumes' and checked out delivery times. It was slim pickings. "Maybe crayons?"

"Good God, please, no." Luka frowned for a minute. "Daenerys and Jon Snow? You'd rock the blond wig, and Rory would look sexy in that cloak."

"Fuck, no! Too coupley!" Finn waved the idea away. "And I can't support that show after what they did to Dany… The Mandalorian and Grogu?"

Luka wrinkled his nose. "I'm thinking maybe no to the parent-child vibe? Plus those costumes would be crazy expensive if you're going to get good ones. How about a classic — Batman and Robin?"

Finn shook his head firmly. "No tights."

"Fine. What about *Dirty Dancing*? Baby and Johnny?"

Finn raised an eyebrow. "And who's going to want to wear those tiny shorts, me or Rory?"

"Good point." Luka sighed and scrunched his face. "Goose and Maverick?"

Finn blinked at him, then a slow smile spread over his face. "You are a fucking genius! Flight suits are sexy, the inherent homoeroticism of *Top Gun*… I love it!"

Luka offered a head tilt. "At your service."

"Okay." Finn stood and took a deep breath. "Now I gotta go ask them."

"You can do it, Finn. You're just suggesting costumes, not proposing." Then Luka's face clouded over. "Oh, and hey, if something does happen, make sure you go to HR right away."

"Well, of course." Finn rolled his eyes. "I'm not an idiot." He didn't need Luka to get uptight about Breakpoint's strict employee dating policy. Besides, that was the least of his worries right now — first, he had to jump off a cliff. Finn took another breath, feeling it curl into the depths of his lungs. "You're right, I can do it. Okay, here I go." *Oh God oh God oh God.* What if Rory said no? What if Rory laughed at him and such a ridiculous idea?

"Finn?"

"Yeah?"

"You're still here."

"Fuck." Finn shook himself and plunged out of Luka's office while he had the momentum. He didn't remember a thing about his journey through the halls until he was barging into Rory's office.

Rory looked up and smiled.

Of course they did.

Finn's mouth dried out and his foot twitched like it wanted to turn around, but Luka's words came back to him. *It's just costumes.* "Do you have a Halloween costume yet?" he blurted, with zero preamble.

Surprise flashed over Rory's face for a split second, and who could blame them, the way Finn burst in, hair surely as wild as his eyes, then they shrugged. "I was thinking of going as maybe a spreadsheet or something, like columns and rows of numbers on me..." Rory faded off, studying Finn's face with concern. "Are you okay?"

"Me?" Finn gasped, aware of the sweat forming on his hairline. "I'm fine. Great. Sorry, I was just... I was wondering—do you want to do a costume with me? Like, we dress up together? In costumes that match?"

"Oh."

In that 'oh' Finn died a thousand deaths—suffocated, bled, choked, crawled across the desert sand until the winds carried away his desiccated skeleton.

Then Rory relaxed, a smile curling the edges of their mouth like daisy petals in the sun. "Sure. That sounds fun."

Finn fell against the doorframe before his legs could fail him. "Great. Um. I was thinking *Top Gun*? Maverick and Goose? You know, flight suits, aviators..."

Now Rory's face was a sunflower, bright and wide. "Love it. As long as I'm Goose."

Finn forced a swallow down his parched throat as his heart soared higher than Maverick's F-14. "Of course."

* * * *

The morning of his Halloween party, Finn was wide awake at six, followed by a workout, beard trim, shower and protein shake. Eight hours later — furniture pushed back, karaoke machine hooked up, bowls heaped with candy, drinks buried in ice — Rory's arrival was looming.

The two flight suits he had ordered arrived just in time. Finn laid them both out on his bed, smoothing the wrinkles while his stomach danced. The way Rory had smiled at him when Finn appeared in their office, the way they stood close, tilted their head up to him, touched his arm when they spoke... Yesterday in the busy staff kitchen, Rory had brushed behind him, long, elegant body against his for one blissful second. There was something there. Maybe. If he allowed himself to dream.

"Don't fuck this up, Finn," he muttered, studying himself in the mirror as he zipped up his suit. "Don't say anything stupid. Just...be normal. You can do this."

A knock.

Rory's knock.

He hurried down the hall, tugging the zipper down a little. Too much. Back up a hair. He took one last look around. His house could not be more perfect.

Finn emptied his lungs in a whoosh and opened the door.

The setting autumn sun haloed around Rory in a thick amber light. They wore brutally sexy aviators and a leather jacket over a white tank top. *Amazing.*

"Hey, Goose," Finn greeted them, resisting the urge to pull Rory in for a hug.

Rory tipped down the sunglasses and gave him an adorable grin. "Maverick."

"Come on in."

"You look fantastic," Rory said, taking in Finn from head to toe. "A flight suit agrees with you."

Finn flushed like a teenager. "Thanks. Oh, leave your shoes on."

Rory nodded, following Finn past the wide doorway that led into the living room. "Wow, your place is so cool." They stopped at the large painting at the end of the hall, eyes wide. "Finn…"

The fire banked in Finn's cheeks. He hung his art so the people he invited into his home could see it, but having Rory study it so intently made him feel naked. "It's called *Home*. It was the first thing I painted when I moved in."

Rory's head tilted. "I love it. It's very warm. It reminds me of…" They lifted a hand, traced the shape of the curve in the air "…a really good hug."

"Yeah." Finn rubbed the back of his neck. "Thanks, I—Thanks."

"Do you have any more art I can see?"

"Yeah, sure. There's one in my bedroom." He led Rory down the hall, heart rate climbing. Finn had, of course, made sure his room was impeccably tidy, but his eyes still darted around, trying to see it as Rory would. There was only one framed photograph—him and Luka accepting the corporate fundraising award from the first year they did the 5K for Hope. And tucked in the corner of the frame was a picture of him and his niece and nephew when they were small. He had straightened the 'To Be Read' pile of books on his bedside table, but maybe he should have put them away. The pile was embarrassingly large. Wait, was that a sock poking out from under his bed?

Rory was staring, but not at the sock.

They were staring at the huge painting above Finn's headboard. It was one of Finn's favorites—long stretches of skin, hints of lips and hands. An open mouth, head thrown back, maybe. Two bodies as one.

"Absolutely stunning, Finn," Rory breathed.

Finn pushed his hair back. "Thanks."

Rory shifted, gaze still locked on the canvas. "What is this one called?"

"*Temptation.*" Finn fiddled with his zipper.

"Wow." Rory shook their head. "It's beautiful. Have you ever shown your work anywhere?"

"Um, I tried, once, in college. Didn't go well." He waved at Rory's flight suit spread out on his bed. "You can change in here." Finn bolted into the hall, dizzy from the compliments and from the fact that Rory was standing in his bedroom staring at his painting of two people having sex. He headed back into the living room and found some cushions to fluff, but the dizziness only got worse as he imagined Rory now undressing in his bedroom in front of his sex painting.

Then, thankfully before Finn's imagination could go too crazy, Rory appeared in the living room in their flight suit. Finn had to hold back a groan of appreciation. *So fucking sexy.* Anthony Edwards had nothing on them. "You look amazing," Finn said.

They popped their aviators on and smiled. "Yeah, we do. Hey, let's take a picture." Rory pulled out their phone and held it up, sliding their arm around Finn's waist. They tucked so nicely under Finn's shoulder. He inhaled the scent of Rory's hair as he put his arm around them and smiled for the camera. Their ear-to-ear grins matched exactly.

Rory sent Finn the picture then tucked their phone away, surveying the living room. The kitchen was at the back, partially visible through a pass-through window. A bar was on the counter on this side of the sill, with the table of snacks and candy along the far wall. "What can I help with?" Rory asked.

Finn ignored the buzz of Rory's text in his pocket, even though he so badly wanted to stare at that photo. "Just a few more appies."

They pulled the trays of sausage rolls and mini-quiches from the oven and set out some veggies and dip, until, right on schedule, their coworkers began arriving.

Rory stuck to Finn's side as the house filled. "You two look great!" they heard over and over, and Finn couldn't get enough of it. "Thanks," he said, wanting to pull Rory closer, kiss the top of their head. Instead, he shared a smile and settled for picking a stray thread off of Rory's arm.

"Oh, there's Luka and Thomas," Finn said when he spotted them in the crowd — together, of course. Luka did indeed look fucking hot as Sandy, black spandex clinging to his lanky frame, calves especially shapely in his red heels. Tawney was nowhere in sight but, somehow, Thomas was dressed as Danny instead, all in black, beautifully aged leather jacket perfectly hugging his wide shoulders. As a pair, they were hot enough to melt the bowl of bite-sized chocolate bars on the table behind them.

"You crazy kids!" Finn called in greeting, clapping Luka and Thomas on the shoulders. "Welcome! First question—why don't you have a drink yet?"

"Danny and Sandy!" Rory exclaimed when they came up behind Finn. "You guys look great!"

Luka and Thomas looked at each other in surprise.

"Wow." Luka laughed. "Actually, Tawney was supposed to be Danny, but she's sick."

"And I'm the Terminator," Thomas added.

"Oh," Rory chuckled. "That's funny. You go together like rama-lama-lama."

God, Rory is so fucking cute.

"Yeah, I guess that works out for me, then," Luka said. "You two look great, too!"

Rory and Finn grinned at each other.

"I feel the need..." Finn began.

"The need...for speed!" Rory finished. They high-fived each other, cackling.

"Adorable." The only word that could be used to describe Luka's expression was smug.

"Not adorable. Badass," Finn corrected, sliding his sunglasses on. "Bar's over there. Get on it." He pointed at Luka. "And there's karaoke later. I'd better see your ass up there, Sandy."

The house got louder and hotter as it filled. Finn had left some windows open, but the cool night air was quickly swallowed by the fuzzy creatures, spooky witches and sweaty pop culture icons. They greeted Aleandro and Penelope when they came in—an old-school vampire, which was perfect, given Aleandro's Dracula hair, and a sorceress, in a glamorous high-collared blood-red dress—and Georgia, their head of marketing, who was a princess, in a lavender dress with a long blonde braid. Morgan strutted in with the confidence of Freddie Mercury himself in pale blue jeans, a white tank top and a black studded leather belt with a matching armband.

Finn's beers went down quickly, a pleasant haze settling over him as the room filled and the noise level grew. And Rory. Rory was always there. Hand brushing his as they collected empties, steadying fingers on his hip as he tripped past a dragon with huge cardboard wings.

Every time Finn turned around, Thomas and Luka were there, too. Huddled together, leaning over to talk into the other's ear, laughing, meaningful glances shared, seemingly a couple in all ways but officially.

"How much longer can they drag this out?" Finn wondered, watching Luka and Thomas through the pass-through window as he added more carrots to the veggie platter. "It's so obvious they like each other."

Rory cleared their throat from their spot at the counter next to Finn. "Maybe it's not obvious to them."

"Maybe, but...look at them." Luka and Thomas were mere inches apart, eyes locked and gleaming, faces wide open and smiling. When Luka tipped his head back to laugh, Finn could read Thomas' desire from across the living room.

There was no reply from Rory aside from the rhythmic *chop, chop, chop* as they cut up a red pepper. "So...do you think Maverick and Goose ever hooked up?" Rory asked, breaking the silence.

Finn looked over at Rory, who had paused their chopping. They put down their knife and turned, leaning a hip against the counter and waiting for Finn's answer.

Finn's stomach twisted into a knot, the electricity between them crackling. *Is this...?* "Oh, for sure," he scratched out. "Please, you could cut the sexual tension with a knife between those two."

A spark flickered in Rory's eyes. "Which one would have made the first move, do you think?" They took a half step closer.

"Goose, obviously." Finn's throat threatened to close, the room suddenly oppressively hot. *Run,* his brain stem told him. "I just need to grab a drink..." And he turned and bolted from the kitchen. He found Luka digging through the cooler, finally without Thomas. Finn threw his arm around Luka's shoulders and gripped his anchor. "Luka!" he hissed.

"Buddy," said Luka, endlessly patient. "What's up?"

"Umm..." Finn looked around the room to make sure no one was listening, then leaned to whisper into Luka's ear. "I think Rory might like me."

"You don't say?" Luka smothered a laugh. "What happened?"

"Well, we were in the kitchen talking, and they asked me, out of nowhere, if I thought Maverick and Goose ever hooked up."

"And what did you say?"

"I said for sure, and then they asked which one I thought would have made the first move." Finn raked a hand through his hair.

"Goose, obviously."

"Right."

"So? What did they say to that?"

"Well, then I came out here."

Luka blinked at him. "And they're just waiting in there still?

"Yeah."

"Get back in there, you *absolute moron*. Go fucking kiss them." Luka shoved Finn in the direction of the kitchen. "Now," he added before Finn could protest.

Go fucking kiss them. Finn stumbled back into the kitchen, thoughts an indecipherable blur. Rory hadn't moved. Their beautiful dark eyes widened as Finn stopped in front of them.

Go fucking kiss them. "Actually..." Finn cleared this throat. "I think Maverick could have made the first move."

Rory let the words hang in the air, a slow smile spreading across their face. Finn pushed his hair back. Then he took a step forward, closing the distance.

And he kissed Rory.

He fucking kissed them.

Chapter Ten

And Then

Rory's lips were even softer than Finn had imagined. They sighed into the kiss and slid their long fingers into Finn's hair like it was their sole purpose in life—like they'd been waiting to explore that territory since the minute they'd met.

Finn leaned Rory back against the counter, pressing their bodies together. His lips parted, and he was home. The kitchen vanished. The party disappeared. Finn's house, his art, his obscene jack-o-lanterns, all gone.

There was only Rory.

The kiss went on and on, until he was dizzy and they had to break apart for air. He pulled in a deep breath, oxygen flooding his cells like the joy flooding his soul.

"Thank God," Rory murmured, hands gentle but very present on the back of Finn's neck.

"Thank God what?" Finn asked, brushing another kiss to Rory's lips, his little kitchen a sparkling disco ball of euphoria around him.

"I mean"—Rory sucked in a small gasp of pleasure as Finn's nose dragged along their jaw. Their fingers were back in Finn's hair again—"thank God you like me back."

"Are you serious?" Finn tried not to snort as he cocked an eyebrow at Rory. "Thank God *you* like *me* back!"

"What?" Rory laughed, thumb now leaving a trail of goosebumps as it stroked Finn's neck. "I've sort of had a thing for you since the moment I saw you."

Finn rocked back onto his heels. "You...what? Really? Rory, I—I've wanted you this whole time, too."

Now it was Rory's turn to be shocked. "You did? I thought maybe you liked Luka."

Finn threw back his head with a bark of laughter. "That princess? Nah, he's my best friend but you... Rory, you..." He kissed them again, his tongue urgent as it found its counterpart.

God, *fuck,* if he could do nothing but kiss Rory for the rest of his—

"Oh, sorry." The words ripped them apart. Georgia stood in the doorway, an empty chip bowl in each hand. "I'm *so* sorry. I did not mean to interrupt...anything."

"It's fine." Finn straightened his flight suit, aware he was desperately short of breath, and desperately aroused. "Sorry." *Well, not that sorry.*

Rory cleared their throat and smoothed their hair.

"Oh, don't be sorry." Georgia set her bowls on the counter. "It's just a little quieter in here, is all."

Suddenly Finn was very aware of the sound of Morgan pretending he was Freddie Mercury, voice rattling the windows at the top of his register. Apparently, the karaoke had started. Finn cringed. "This is *quieter?*"

Georgia chuckled as she refilled the chips. "I'm afraid so. I think he's almost done, though." She collected the bowls with a sheepish grin. "I'll get out of your way."

Finn meant to reassure her that it was fine, but she was gone before he could get the words out. He stared at Rory again. Fuck, they looked so hot, lips pink and swollen, tongue darting out to moisten them. Finn took hold of Rory's hips.

"We should probably join the party," Rory said, seeking Finn's lips again.

"Why did I agree to host a party?" Finn muttered, eyes closed. "So stupid."

"At least it got us here," Rory murmured in reply before their tongues touched.

Finn's hands slipped down Rory's waist and gripped their neat little backside. "I'm kicking out every last one of them right this minute."

Rory laughed. "You can't do that."

Finn sighed, pulling Rory closer, inhaling their scent like it was the only thing he needed to survive. "All right, fine. But, then..." Another kiss, searing and urgent.

"Yes," Rory whispered, sending more goosebumps rippling over Finn's skin. "Then."

With great difficulty—more difficulty than he had ever experienced doing anything in his life—he let go of Rory and got back to restocking the veggie platter. The noise coming from the living room had lessened, and the soft, pleasant sound of Georgia singing drifted in as they chopped and stacked the veggies in brightly colored piles.

But everything was different now. Now Finn's soul was singing. Now he was floating ten feet off the ground. Now he could take Rory's hand and kiss them if he wanted. And he did. So he did.

"Mmmm," Rory moaned, jar of ranch dip in their hand forgotten as they returned the kiss. "By the way, you look so fucking hot in your costume, Maverick." Rory tilted their lips up to his, impossibly tantalizing.

"You have *no idea* how sexy you are in yours, Goose," Finn replied, stealing yet another kiss.

The oven dinged.

"Leave us alone," Finn murmured, holding Rory tight.

"Come on, the pigs are all toasty in their blankets," Rory said, giving Finn a gentle push toward the oven.

Finn sighed. "Right. Food." He dumped the sausages onto a plate and followed Rory with the veggies out to the snack table.

They set down the refreshed food and were collecting a few stray napkins and candy wrappers when Finn saw who was singing now.

"Oh my God." He grinned. Rory turned to look. Luka and Thomas were performing a duet of *Summer Nights* from Grease.

"Aw, look at them! So cute!" Rory said.

"So fucking cute." Finn shook his head, watching them all blushy and unable to hold prolonged eye contact. He hoped he hadn't been that obvious around Rory. Then again, what did it matter now?

Morgan stomped by like a drunken storm cloud. "You're out of ice," he snapped at Finn on his way to the bar.

Finn bit back a retort and instead looked at Rory. "Help me grab a few bags from the garage?"

Rory nodded and followed Finn back into the kitchen and through the door into the garage.

Finn paused before he turned the light on. "Don't judge me."

Just about every painting Finn had ever done was in the garage. Even his work as a kid that his grandma insisted on keeping was there, clumsy and unskilled but fiercely passionate. Finn couldn't bear to throw them away now. Dust covers turned most of them into rectangular ghosts, leaning in piles against the walls, wedged next to broken easels and blank canvases still wrapped in paper, plus boxes of brushes and paint, and some of his grandma's belongings he hadn't been able to part with. Plus, of course, his weight bench and treadmill in one corner. There wasn't room for even a toy car in this garage.

Rory took it in politely. "Wow," they said, running a hand along a painting entitled *Fear* that Finn had jammed in there right before the party, losing his nerve to leave it hanging in the living room. "Look what you've made."

"A fucking mess? Yeah, I know. I just don't know what to do with all of them."

"No, not a mess." Rory drew lines in the air. "A gallery."

Finn snorted. "You haven't been to many galleries."

"You could fill one, I mean. With all of this."

"Nah." Finn yanked open the door of the deep freeze. "I already tried that. I didn't sell a thing and the gallery director made me pay for the custodial crew after my opening. Here." He handed Rory a bag of ice and took another two more for himself. "We'd better get back in there before Morgan files a complaint with HR."

Rory ignored him. "What is this one called? It's...got an ache to it."

"Uh...*Fear.*"

Rory studied him a moment before swinging back to examine the painting again, bag of ice forgotten. A figure was curled in one corner of the canvas, surrounded by dark, oppressive shapes. "What are you afraid of?"

"Morgan singing another song." Finn offered his hand to Rory, smiling. "Come on."

"All right." Rory took Finn's hand. "I'll let you change the subject for now...if you'll sing a song with me."

"I cannot sing. Like, at all."

"Don't care. I want to sing with you, Maverick." Rory waited, but when an answer didn't come, their eyes turned back to the canvas. "So, *Fear*, huh?"

"Damn it," Finn grumbled. "Fine. I'll sing with you."

He was somewhat mollified when Rory beamed and kissed him on the cheek. "Yay! Let's go before the ice melts."

The accountants were singing *Ghostbusters* when they went back inside to dump their ice in the drink tubs.

"There's Luka and Thomas," Finn said, nodding at them over in the hall by the bathroom. "Let's go say hi." He wanted to see Luka's reaction when he took Rory's hand.

As they approached, Finn noticed that Morgan was there too, slumped against Thomas, face green and fake mustache gone. "Everything all right?" Finn asked. Morgan did not look all right.

"Morgan needs to go home," Thomas grumbled. "I can take him, make sure he gets there okay."

Finn's concern for Morgan was tempered by the sparks sent along his arm when Rory's hand brushed against his.

"That's nice of you," Luka said, although he clearly didn't mean it.

Morgan groaned again.

Don't you dare puke on my carpet was Finn's main thought.

"Do you have a plastic bag or two we can take with us?" Thomas asked Finn.

Finn rushed to the kitchen and came back with a handful of grocery bags and two bottles of water. "Here. Make him drink these before he passes out."

"Thanks." Thomas collected the items and hefted Morgan upright. "Well..." He looked at Luka. "I guess I'll see you Monday."

"Yeah."

The disappointment on Luka's face was clear. Finn felt bad for his friend, especially when his own heart was soaring.

Morgan's cheeks bulged. "Air," he burbled, lurching toward the front door.

"Have a good night," Thomas mumbled, then they left.

Luka stared at the door, bereft.

"Sorry, man. That sucks," Finn said.

Luka forced a smile onto his face. "Yeah. But..." He looked at Finn and Rory's fingers now laced together and the smile shifted into a genuine one. "Let's enjoy the party."

"Has she lost that loving feeling?" Rory asked Finn, nodding toward the microphone.

"Fuck, no. That song's too sad. I have a better idea." Finn pulled Rory over to the karaoke machine, the touch lingering as they flipped through the song choices.

"Something to keep in mind," Finn said, pointing at his suggestion and leaning over to whisper in Rory's ear. "As bad as I am at singing?" He dropped his voice even lower. "That's how good I am in bed."

Rory giggled, a blush spreading over their cheeks. "God, I hope you're awful at singing."

Finn raised a confident eyebrow at them. "You're about to find out."

Luckily for Rory, they sang — or "sang," in Finn's case — *You're the One That I Want*, Danny and Sandy's happy ending song, and Finn was indeed truly terrible.

Luka was more his usual self as the night went on, insisting that Finn's singing was not that bad — "When you actually hit the note, your tone is not the worst I've ever heard," he said — and complimenting Georgia on her delicious purple Jell-O shots. And he sang. Oh, did he ever. Finn had never heard Luka sing so much. Usually, he had to be coaxed to do even one song for Finn, but he had clearly found a comfort zone at the party. He even busted out some of Britney's choreo to *Toxic*, at which point Finn started sending Luka Britney GIFs, snickering into Rory's shoulder, completely and perfectly content.

But when Finn closed the door behind the last person to leave, the click was a cannon, a thunderbolt, a gong announcing a profound shift. He turned. Rory was watching.

"Hi," they said, smile knowing and vulnerable all at once.

"Hi," Finn said.

Finn wasn't sure if he moved first or Rory did, then they were one, lips devouring, desperate and hungry.

"Rory," Finn panted when they paused for air, foreheads touching.

"Yeah?" Rory replied, nimble fingers making quick work of Finn's costume zipper.

"I just..."

Rory slid their hands inside his suit, around his waist and up his back and Finn lost the ability to form words. He shrugged his arms out of the sleeves and wound them around Rory, pulling them tight to his body. The kiss heated, erupted and roared white hot behind Finn's eyes. Then they were moving toward Finn's bedroom, Rory stumbling backward, Finn holding them up with strong hands around their small waist.

They banged through the bedroom door and Rory peeled their own flight suit off, revealing a tight white tank top and underwear.

"God, you're sexy," Finn muttered, eyes drinking in the sight, hands reaching, lips searching. Finn pressed them to Rory's neck, dragging along their jaw to their lips, then they fell onto the bed, limbs winding.

"Finn," Rory moaned as their hips rocked together. "Please..."

Finn paused, pushed the hair off Rory's forehead, stared deep into their liquid eyes. "Yeah?" He couldn't tell if the pounding in his chest was his heartbeat or Rory's.

"I'm yours, Finn. Take me," Rory whispered.

So he did.

* * * *

A while later, they lay together spent, naked and sweaty, limbs liquid, a river of contentment under the blankets.

Rory propped themselves up on an elbow and twisted one of Finn's curls around a finger. "The number of times I've thought about doing this..." they murmured.

Finn closed his eyes. "Do it some more, please."

Rory smiled, pushing their long fingers through Finn's locks, leaving a trail of goosebumps across Finn's scalp. "Your hair is a wonder," Rory said. "You don't know how beautiful it is."

Finn's heart was near bursting. "This feels amazing," he murmured.

Rory leaned forward and kissed his nose. "I'll run my fingers through your hair all fucking day if you want, Finn."

Finn reached up to brush his thumb along Rory's cheek, then kissed them again. This kiss was slower, gentler, the kind that went with the delicate teasing of ginger curls, twirled around long, clever fingers. They fell asleep, and the night drifted away.

* * * *

"What are you up to today?" Rory asked. The sun was doing its best to poke through Finn's thick bedroom drapes, but with Rory still tucked firmly against his side, Finn had no desire to acknowledge its existence.

"Today?" Finn frowned in fake concentration. "Let me think. Busy day. First, I was planning to hold you for a while." He lifted Rory's hand and kissed their knuckles. "Second, fuck you into the mattress again." The skin of Rory's inner wrist was soft against his lips. "Then we could shower. I am an excellent back scrubber." He kissed Rory's palm. "I'll make you breakfast and tell you how amazing you are for a while, then maybe I'll fuck you again." He blinked innocently. "Why, what do you have planned?"

Rory's sigh was the sound of angel wings fluttering, like the ones tattooed on their collarbone. "That. Exactly that."

* * * *

At some point in the middle of those plans, they were back in bed. Finn traced a finger along the vines on Rory's arm. "What are the letters?" he asked.

"My family's initials," they said. "My dad, Jonathan. My mom, Lainey. My brothers, Jackson and Griffin, my sister, Bailey." That letter was thicker than the rest, and a little swirlier, like another letter had been covered up. "And then Jackson's wife Amy, plus Minnie and their baby Fiona."

"And what's this?" Finn leaned down to kiss the script on Rory's ribcage. "'Let it out and let it in'?"

Rory smiled down at Finn, whose nose was traveling toward their hip, leaving kisses along the way. Rory rolled onto their back, sliding their fingers into Finn's curls. "Just breathe," they whispered. "Just breathe."

* * * *

"You play the guitar?" Rory asked, eyeing Finn's Gibson sitting on a stand in the corner of the living room. They were on the couch, after Rory insisted on helping clean up from the party, eating leftover candy.

"Not really," Finn replied. "I only know a handful of chords. I just mess around, really. You should hear Luka, though. He's incredible."

Rory got up and retrieved the guitar, bringing it back to Finn with a plaintive smile. "Will you play me something? Please?"

Finn already knew he was going to have trouble ever saying no to that face. "I guess, if you want to hear me scratch a few things out."

"I do." Rory handed it over with a kiss.

Finn strummed a couple of his easier favorites — *Have You Ever Seen the Rain?* and *Love Me Do* — then let his fingers wander. Rory watched it all with a soft smile on their face.

F major seven, F seven, B flat... The last chord hung in the air as Finn realized what phrase he'd been playing. *"Let it out and let it in."*

"You're amazing." Rory said it like it was an undisputed fact.

"Nah." Finn flushed. "Like I said, I just mess around."

Rory took the guitar away and climbed into Finn's lap in its spot. "I mean *you* are amazing, Finn. You." Their lips brushed over Finn's brow, then his cheek, then found his lips.

Finn slid his hands over Rory's back and held them close. "Was there anything else you wanted me to do for you today?" he murmured.

"Yeah." Rory's hips rocked in a lazy circle. "I can think of a few things."

* * * *

"Don't go."

Rory laughed. "I have to, Finn."

"You can borrow my clothes!" They were standing on his front step, his hands wrapped around Rory's waist.

Rory raised an eyebrow at Finn's tall, broad frame. "Oh? Do you have any from when you were fourteen?"

"I have a sewing machine. I'll take them in."

126

"You have a sewing machine?"

"It was my grandma's. I'm not bad at hemming."

Rory leaned forward to peck his nose. "I'll miss you, too. But I need my laptop and stuff for work, and we'll be at the office together all day tomorrow."

Finn groaned. "One more kiss then."

"One more now. The rest later," Rory promised.

Finn watched Rory climb into their car, and stayed on the step until it disappeared around a corner. He went back inside and shut the door behind him. The smile on his face put the fucking sun to shame.

Chapter Eleven

Love

Walking on air, floating on cloud nine—all the happy meteorological metaphors applied to Finn Monday morning. He got to work early and went straight to Rory's office, nearly running into them as they were coming out. Rory was even more stunning than Finn had been picturing all night, eyes rimmed with impossibly thick lashes, hair hanging over their forehead, begging to be brushed aside, and a sweet blush warming their cheeks.

Everything in him screamed to grab Rory and never let go. "Hi," he said, fingers twitching. He stole a glance down the empty hall before leaning in for a kiss.

Rory hauled Finn back into their office and offered another, more thorough, kiss.

"Our appointment's not until two," Finn mumbled around Rory's lower lip. He had wasted no time emailing HR yesterday evening after Rory had left. "So I'm not sure yet, but I don't think we're supposed to do this at work."

Rory's fingers found Finn's hair. "Well, until they tell us otherwise…"

Fuck, they tasted so good, and the way Rory melted under his hands drove Finn absolutely wild. In fact, it had been all he thought about since they hung up the phone last night. About three seconds after the HR email, he had texted Rory. *I miss you,* he said, and only had time for a flicker of nervousness that it was too much before Rory replied,

I miss you too.

Don't text and drive, Finn admonished, heart singing.

Don't text me then, silly. (I'm at a red light.)

Let me know when you get home, Finn said.

They did the whole cliché thing, talking until late in the night with phones on the pillow next to them. Never did Finn think he ever would have engaged in "you hang up, no, *you* hang up," but there he was. And now, here he was, Rory perched on the edge of their desk, Finn's tongue down their throat.

"Okay," Finn gasped at the next oxygen break. "We'd better stop."

"Right. Yes." Rory straightened their shirt, short of breath. So cute how flustered they were.

"You want to grab dinner tonight?" Finn asked, smoothing their hair for them.

"Sure." Rory hopped off the desk. "What were you thinking?"

"Takeout on my couch?"

"Sounds perfect." Their eyes crinkled. "I packed an overnight bag."

* * * *

When Finn finally tore himself away, he headed straight for Luka's office. His brain and heart and nerves were alight. His cheeks were hot. A laugh nearly bubbled out of his throat, there, alone in the middle of the hallway. He got a weird look from one of the sales reps. *Oh my God,* Finn thought, fanning his face. *This is...something.*

He appeared in Luka's doorway, smiling so big it hurt his face.

Luka grinned back. "And how was the rest of your weekend?"

"Good. So fucking good, Luka." Finn collapsed into his chair, damn near ready to cry with happiness.

"Look at you," Luka mused. "You're...completely in love."

Love. Was that the word? Fuck. *Fuck.* "Maybe," he said, only because it was Luka. Anyone else would have gotten a denial.

"That's great, Finn. I'm so happy for you two."

"Thanks. We already made our appointment with HR." Finn sighed, visions of Rory twisted in his bedsheets floating behind his eyes. "Rory is amazing. And the sex... God."

Luka shook his head and laughed. "Congratulations."

"Right? All weekend, man, like—"

Thomas strode in, his face a thundercloud. His scowl deepened when he saw Finn.

Finn did his best to tone down his grin, but couldn't manage to erase it completely as he got to his feet. "Morning, Wolf. Did you get Morgan's drunk ass home okay the other night?"

"Yes," Thomas said, dumping his briefcase on his desk with considerable force.

The room was silent as they waited for Thomas to say more. He did not.

"Well, okay, then. See you guys later." Finn shot Luka a look and eased out of the door. *What the fuck happened there?* He'd have to check in with Luka later. In the meantime…he tried to think of a good reason to wander in the direction of Rory's office.

* * * *

Work. I need to do some actual work today, Finn scolded himself, logging into his laptop to face the barrage of emails that was no doubt waiting for him. He hadn't checked his work email a single time since…since Rory.

And 'barrage' was fairly accurate. Markos had emailed four times over the weekend, plus two more that morning, and a few other emails from his Thrill Island and Sartini teams had piled up. He got to work, with only a few pauses here and there to look at the costumed selfie of him and Rory. And to send Rory a couple of texts. Okay, five texts.

They had arranged to have lunch together, of course, and it was heaven to step into the brisk November air, Rory's hand in his. They had lunch at Montagu's again, but this time, their legs wound together under the table, with Rory's hand on his thigh.

Finn insisted on paying. Rory's eyes glimmered as they tucked their wallet away. "Is this our first official date?" they asked with an adorable head tilt.

Finn leaned forward to give Rory a kiss. "Sure is."

When Rory went to the washroom — *damn*, that ass though — Finn texted Luka.

Hey, everything okay with Thomas?

Luka replied right away. *Yeah, why?*

He seemed pissed off this morning. Did something happen with him and Morgan?

The next reply was short. *Don't know, none of my business.*

It seemed Thomas wasn't the only pissy one. Luka never missed an opportunity to bitch about Morgan. But if he didn't want to talk about it...

All right, man. Good luck with your shoot tomorrow.

Thanks.

He forgot about Luka's shortness when Rory slipped back into their chair and returned their hand to his thigh, sliding it a little higher than before and adding a squeeze for good measure.

"Maybe don't do that in front of HR," Finn rumbled, lifting Rory's other hand to kiss their knuckles. "Otherwise, never stop."

It was slightly awkward discussing their burgeoning relationship with the suits in Human Resources, but the training mostly consisted of several online modules and a stack of forms to sign. Finn didn't mind if it meant he got to be with Rory. He'd do those courses and sign that paperwork every day for the rest of his life if he had to.

"Big day for us," Rory said on their way out of the office. "First date, first pledge against sexual harassment... What's next?"

Finn laughed. "First takeout? You like Chinese?"

Rory didn't kiss him this time, but the smile was enough. "Sounds perfect."

* * * *

Finn pulled Rory in after him, slamming the kitchen door shut while their bags cascaded to the ground. Their clothes followed on their way to Finn's bedroom.

"Oh my God" — Finn ripped his shirt off then went for Rory's — "I've been dreaming about undressing you all day."

Rory's gaze drifted over Finn's shoulders and torso as they undid his belt. "Same."

Fucking Rory only got better each time, as they each learned the other's body, shared whispered requests and check-ins, sighs and moans noted and filed away for future use.

As Finn pressed inside Rory, the words 'I love you' gathered on his tongue, but he bit them back. Too early. Rory would think he was insane. So instead — "You're beautiful," he whispered, brushing his lips against Rory's eyelids. "So beautiful."

Rory said nothing, just kissed him again as their bodies moved together in the shadows.

* * * *

Finn handed Rory a pair of chopsticks and flopped next to them on the couch. "You know what dropped tonight?"

"Season three of *Godstrike*!" Rory squealed. "Do we dare?"

"We can't stop now." Finn picked up his plate. "Is Ophy back from the dead? Will the snake get its revenge? How many times will Colios' wig change? We need to know!"

Rory laughed. "It can't be any worse than season two, right?"

It was worse, but in a glorious, delicious, satisfying way. The producers had clearly listened to feedback, and had leaned right into the absurdity. The costumes were skimpier, the snake was bigger and Ophy was indeed back from the dead — something about how the wildebeest hooves had only made her stronger. It didn't really matter.

They laughed and cheered, rolled their eyes and crunched on egg rolls, and it was the most perfect night of Finn's life.

* * * *

They fell into an easy rhythm, cooking dinner at Finn's house together most nights, watching an episode of *Godstrike* before giving each other a mind-blowing orgasm or two, then curling up for the night in a cocoon of bliss. But that wasn't all — he still got to look forward to waking up with Rory, having breakfast with them and leaving for work hand in hand. Rory spent the odd night at their own place, to swap clothes, pick up a warmer winter coat, collect their mail and water their plants, et cetera. Finn missed them terribly when they weren't there.

Work was better, too, getting to spend so much time with Rory on the Thrill Island project. It was fun seeing their vision become a reality. The park had closed for the season now, the remodel was underway and Finn's attention had shifted to the marketing campaign. Markos' emails were a little like his personality — sort of in his face, although friendly — but so far, all was on track.

The weird blip with Luka and Thomas seemed to have passed as well. Luka didn't mention it again, and Finn was glad to see them back to Obviously Totally Into Each Other But in Denial About It territory. The four of them had lunch together one day, and the cuteness factor was through the roof.

Luka was telling them about their near-disaster commercial shoot in his dramatic Luka way — no heat in the building, the wrong furniture was delivered and there was some mix-up at the agency and half the extras didn't show up.

"I was totally panicking," Luka said, turning to beam at Thomas. "But Thomas kept it all together. He fully saved the day."

"*We* saved the day," Thomas corrected. "You were right there with me."

Luka's smile only grew. "And they put us in the commercial, like we were on a date. Can you imagine!" His laugh was music. "Anyway, the whole thing ended up being a total triumph. I even convinced Thomas to eat some ice cream after in celebration, six-pack be damned."

Finn shared a look with Rory. "Sounds like you two had a great time."

Life continued on that way, until one mid-November night on the couch.

"So… Thanksgiving is coming up," Rory said, once they had finished their salmon and rice.

The holiday was barely on Finn's radar, since he had no family around to celebrate with. He'd had a few dinners with Luka over the years, but last year Luka had traveled to Andchester to see his parents, so Finn had ordered pizza and watched an action movie marathon by himself.

"My family does the whole thing on the Thursday," Rory continued. "Dinner starts at one o'clock, everyone is there — aunts, uncles, cousins, everyone." They fiddled with their napkin. "And, I mean, you're totally invited, but…it might be a lot to meet my entire family at Thanksgiving for the first time, you know?"

To be honest, the idea of meeting Rory's huge family even in small doses was terrifying. He was not good at families. "Yeah, no, that's fine. That would be…a lot."

"But why don't we cook a Thanksgiving dinner for ourselves, too?" Rory said, sitting up excitedly. "On the Saturday. We could even invite Luka, if he's available. Ooh, and Thomas! He doesn't have any family here either. Or anyone else at the office who needs somewhere to go."

"That's a great idea." Finn leaned over to give Rory a kiss. *Phew.* Family gathering avoided. He'd have to meet Rory's family eventually, though. He'd sort of forgotten about that part.

He'd mostly forgotten about his own family too, aside from a few idle wonderings here and there about how Liz's divorce was going. Then, a few nights later, his phone buzzed.

He stared at his sister's name.

"Are you going to answer that?" Rory asked gently.

"No," Finn said, thumb hovering over the answer button.

"I know things with her are shitty," Rory said, rubbing Finn's knee, "and it's totally your choice. But I don't think it'll ever get better unless you talk to her."

Finn took a deep breath and answered the call. "Hi, Liz."

"Well, hello, baby brother. How are you?"

"I'm fine." He studied Rory's calm, encouraging face. "How are things with you?"

She let out a humorless chuckle. "They're shit. They're absolute shit, Finn."

"Neil's being a prick?"

"You wouldn't believe. Him and the fucking lawyers."

Rory squeezed his knee. Finn plunged on. "How are Cali and Bryson doing?"

"It's been really hard on them, of course. All the mind games Neil is playing. That's sort of why I'm calling, actually."

Here it is. Of course. Every fucking time. Finn had tried to help her out where he could over the years, but he was tapped out. It never went well, and it was somehow always his fault. He rubbed his forehead, waiting for the latest ask. "And?"

She sighed. "And I was wondering if maybe they could come stay with you for Thanksgiving?"

Finn's hand dropped to his lap. "What?"

"Neil took the good car, of course, that asshole. Doesn't care that I have to get the kids around, too. And my car is a piece of shit, needs to go in the shop, so I can't drive them to Oakport, but I could put them on a bus Wednesday and that way they—"

"You want to send them *here*? To *me*?" The kids hadn't seen him for years now. He'd basically be a stranger to them. *Who sends their kids on a bus to a person they don't even know?*

Rory's brow pinched in concern.

"They need to get away from the chaos, Finn. They need a break. And I just need a few goddamn days to figure some shit out. I've been trying to pick up extra shifts, but we have a court date the Tuesday after and I'm drowning in all the legal BS."

Finn's jaw dropped. So she wanted a babysitter. "You...are unbelievable."

She paused. "I thought you'd be happy to see your niece and nephew."

Now Finn's jaw clenched into a hard line, rage gathering in his chest. "Don't you dare make this about guilting me, Liz."

Her voice climbed. "I'm not trying to guilt you, Finn, for Christ's sake, I—" She stopped. The distance between them yawned. "You know what? Forget it. I knew this was a bad idea. Happy Thanksgiving." She hung up.

Finn put his phone down, limbs shaking. Once again, his fault.

Rory grasped Finn's hands between theirs. "I'm sorry."

Finn shook his head, thoughts a blur. "Don't be sorry."

"I'm proud of you for trying." Rory climbed into Finn's lap.

Finn wrapped them in his arms and held on tight, burying his nose in their neck. "She wanted me to have them here for Thanksgiving."

"I heard." Rory stroked his hair.

"I mean...I haven't even seen them since I moved here! It's absurd. They're *kids*... I doubt Bryson would even remember me at all. And she's going to put them on a bus to stay here? What the hell is wrong with her?"

"I know, babe," Rory murmured. "It's okay." Finn's scalp tingled under their fingers. "Just breathe."

He inhaled deeply, centering himself in the weight and warmth and scent in his lap. Rory was an anchor and a lighthouse all at once, holding him down, lighting his way. His heart gradually calmed, and his next words came on an exhale. "I love you."

There was no chance to hold them back, but he didn't care.

Rory leaned away to meet Finn's eyes. Theirs were wet, same as his. Rory brushed a tear off of Finn's cheek. "I love you, too, Finn."

Another tear fell. Finn stood and carried Rory into his bedroom.

Chapter Twelve

Thankful

Finn forced himself out of bed at five a.m. the next day. He had gotten way too used to lazy mornings snuggled under the blankets with Rory, and his workout schedule had suffered accordingly. It took a herculean effort to leave the warm, slumbering form next to him, but it was time to get back on track. He went for a run and did some lifting in his garage. When he got out of the shower almost two hours later, his hair dripped over pleasantly fatigued muscles.

Rory had his oatmeal waiting. Finn could not remember the last time someone had made him breakfast. He gave Rory a kiss and dug in.

"What should we make for Thanksgiving dinner?" Rory asked when they were finishing up.

Finn swallowed his last bite, admiring the subtle purple marks on Rory's neck that his lips and teeth had left the night before. "Whatever you want, love."

"You want to do a turkey?"

"Sure."

"Okay." Rory stood to take their plate to the dishwasher. "And what do you like with turkey?"

"Anything is fine."

"Finn!" Rory propped a hip against the counter. "Help me decide. Usually people have very strong feelings about what is included in Thanksgiving dinner."

Finn waggled his eyebrows. "It's hard for me to think when I'm staring at your perfect face and long, delicious neck."

Rory snorted but ran a hand along Finn's shoulders on their way to the coffee maker. "Nice try. Mashed potatoes? Candied yams? Stuffing? What did you have growing up?"

"Um, peanut-butter sandwiches?" Finn shrugged, fiddling with his spoon. "My mom was always working. I remember dinner with my grandma, once. I think we had sweet potato casserole."

Rory kissed the top of Finn's head while the coffee machine hummed. "Then sweet potato casserole it is."

* * * *

Rory left early for their parents' house on Thanksgiving, so Finn was home alone that morning prepping a canvas when the doorbell rang. He grabbed a rag to wipe his hands and was surprised to see a familiar, dignified face smiling at him when he opened the door.

"Aleandro!" Finn said. "I wasn't expecting to see you here."

"Finn." Aleandro gestured to a case of wine at his feet. "Forgive me for showing up unannounced. Penelope and I are on our way to Camarillo with Ilona, but I heard you and Rory were hosting Luka and Thomas for dinner this weekend and I wanted to drop this off for you to enjoy. I hope the Chéreau will be to your liking?"

Finn's tastebuds watered. "Are you kidding? That's amazing. Thank you so much."

"It's my pleasure. I hope the four of you enjoy it."

Finn waved as Aleandro climbed back into his car then hauled the wine into the kitchen, stashing four bottles in the fridge and tucking the case away into the garage chaos before heading back to his studio. He thought about texting Rory roughly four thousand times before he finally caved.

Miss you, he sent, when the first layer was drying.

Rory replied right away. *Miss you too.*

Finn hummed over his paint colors.

* * * *

Rory got home — or rather, back to Finn's house — late that night, smelling like grease and cinnamon.

"How was it?" Finn asked as Rory fell onto the couch next to him.

"Oh, fine." They tipped over and laid their head in Finn's lap. "The usual. Loud, busy, fun but exhausting."

Finn slid his fingers into Rory's hair. "Tell me about it."

"Mmm…" Rory closed their eyes and nuzzled into the touch before starting to talk. "Um, we played Charades first. My team won — quite proud of my performance on *Die Hard*, to be honest."

Finn chuckled. "Did you do Hans falling off the tower?"

Rory smiled up at him, eyes crinkled. "Sure did. Then it was dinner, and Minnie wanted to help set the table. Not sure who thought it would be a good idea to have her carry the cranberry sauce, but she spilled it on the rug, so the first half hour of dinner included a lot of crying. Then, after dinner, one of my cousin's kids, Leo, broke a vase."

"Oh no! Was it an accident?"

"Nah, he pushed his brother into it. So then my cousin was shrieking at him and told him to wash dishes to help 'pay' for it. But my mom gave him some candy and sent him to go play."

"Oof."

"Yeah. That didn't go over well with my cousin. Otherwise, my great aunt managed not to say anything too racist, and overall, conflict was at a minimum. Well, except I caused a bit of an incident when my uncle commented that the actress who plays Ophy put on a lot of weight in season three."

"What?"

"I know, it's insane. She's gorgeous and talented and on a hit TV show, and he wants to talk about her weight? Maddening."

Finn scratched his nails along the shaved part of Rory's scalp. "Ophy is beautiful no matter what, and so are you."

Rory shivered. "I missed you."

"I missed you, too."

"What did you get up to?" Their eyes drifted closed.

"Not much. I painted, worked out, made a salad. And my mom called again."

Rory's eyes snapped open. "She did? How did that go?"

"I didn't answer it."

"You didn't? Finn."

"What?"

Rory sat up. "I know this family stuff is hard and super complicated, but...your mom and sister are clearly trying to patch things up."

Finn stiffened. "'Patch things up'? 'Clearly'? I basically had to raise myself and now they do fuck all but ask me for things. That's all they've ever done. I'm only useful to them when I'm...useful. You have no idea what it was like growing up with them."

Rory paused. "You're right, I don't know."

Finn slung an arm around Rory and pulled them up against his side. They settled back against the couch, feet on the coffee table.

"You could tell me, though, if you want," Rory said, sliding a big toe along Finn's ankle.

Finn puffed up his cheeks and blew out a breath. "Oh yeah? Let's see... You want to hear how I mowed lawns all summer when I was thirteen so I could buy a bike, and my mom stole my cash so she could take a trip with some shitty boyfriend? Not that she ever took me on any trips. Or how about when I was in college, she kept asking for one of my paintings, and I thought for a few fucking seconds she liked my work — she was maybe even fucking proud of me — but then she tried to sell it online the very next day?"

"That's awful. I'm so sorry." Rory rubbed Finn's arm. "Did she, though?"

"Did she what?"

"Sell it?"

"No. I went onto her computer and deleted the listing. Never gave her a painting again. And she didn't even feel bad about it."

"Hmm." Rory was silent, continuing to slide a hand up and down Finn's arm. "She thought it was good enough to sell, at least."

"No, she didn't. She said people would pay lots of money for, and I'm quoting, 'bullshit art.'"

"Oh, Finn."

Finn snorted. "She was wrong anyway."

"What do you mean? I'd pay for your art. Lots of people would."

"I told you, I tried. It didn't work out. I don't really want to talk about it."

"Aw, come on," Rory said, teasingly. "That's what Thanksgiving is for, isn't it? Reliving family trauma?"

"Trauma? Like spilled cranberry sauce and elderly relatives who say inappropriate things?"

Rory's hand stilled. "No, I—That's not what I meant."

Finn regretted his words before he even finished speaking then. "I know... I didn't mean to make light of—"

"It's okay." Rory curled up against Finn. "How about *Godstrike*?"

"Let's just go to bed," Finn said, taking a deep breath of Rory's scent and willing the tightness in his chest to loosen. "I'm tired."

They didn't have sex that night, but Finn held Rory close enough to feel their heart beating. Rory fell asleep quickly, and Finn wondered late into the night what would have happened if he had answered the phone.

* * * *

Rory went to join their parents again on Friday — they were going for lunch and giving the out-of-town family a tour of the plant. Finn had to admit he was curious to see what it was like, but was still not going to touch Rory's extended family with a one-hundred-foot bundle of rebar.

After the tour, Rory went back to their apartment. "I need to catch up on sleep and laundry and water my plants," they explained that morning. "Plus, my friends have been pestering me for a hangout, and — "

"It's okay," Finn had said, leaning down to kiss away the babbling. "Go. See your friends. We'll have the day together tomorrow."

Finn was not expecting Rory back that night, but there they were at midnight, crawling into bed next to him. Finn fucked them long and slow, their sighs and whimpers mingling into the sweetest song he'd ever heard.

* * * *

"Are these your dishtowels?" Finn asked, hands wet and brow furrowed at the mustard yellow cloth hanging from the oven handle that he had never seen before.

Rory kissed his cheek on the way by. "No, they're yours."

"Mine? I already have dishtowels."

"I know, but these ones match. There's dishcloths, too."

Finn now noticed the same-colored cloth draped over the sink faucet. "Match?"

"Yeah, they all match now." Rory pulled Grandma's gravy boat out of the cabinet. "This pattern is gorgeous."

Finn dried his hands on the new linen and picked up the potato peeler, processing. "But I liked the ones I had."

"I noticed that most of them were getting pretty worn, and I saw this great deal online last week when I was finishing up my Christmas shopping."

Finn's head was spinning. "*Finishing* your Christmas shopping? And…you bought me dish towels?"

"Not as your gift, silly! I just thought you'd like the color. They go with the rest of the kitchen… Why, are you not finished your Christmas shopping?"

"Haven't even started."

"You haven't started? It's after Thanksgiving!"

"It's still November!"

"Doesn't it stress you out not having it even started?"

"This conversation stresses me out," Finn muttered, attacking the potato with the peeler.

Rory, who had gone to stare thoughtfully at the dining room table, didn't appear to hear. "What do you think about napkin swans?"

* * * *

"The table looks beautiful," Finn said, admiring Rory's setup. The gold-trimmed china shimmered in the candlelight, and the napkin swans were immaculate.

"The gravy is way too thin," Rory fretted from the stove, madly stirring with a fork. "Will you pass me the cornstarch, please?"

"It looks delicious to me," Finn said, going over to stand behind Rory.

"It's not—it's like water."

Finn pulled Rory in for a kiss, as instructed by the 'Kiss the Cook' apron he had convinced Rory to put on. "Even if it is, it will be fine."

"I just want you to have the perfect Thanksgiving." They sighed.

"Hey, you're here." Finn brushed Rory's bangs back. "It is perfect."

Before he knew it, Rory gripped him in a tight hug, where they remained until they heard a car pull up out front. Finn disentangled himself and went to peek out of the window in the front door. Luka climbed out of a cab with great care, an apple pie in his hands and a bag of rolls tucked under his arm. Another cab pulled up right behind, discharging Thomas' thick frame. Thomas held a pumpkin pie in one splayed hand and a small potted plant with the other.

Finn watched them flirting awkwardly as they made their way up the walkway and flung open the door before they could knock. "Happy Thanksgiving!" he cried, taking the rolls from Luka. "Get in here, you two. Help me convince Rory the gravy isn't too thin."

"This is for you." Thomas handed the pot to Finn. "I noticed you don't have any plants."

Finn eyed it. "Yeah, I always kill them. But"—he brightened up—"it might have more of a chance now that Rory is around. Thanks, Wolf."

Finn bustled them into the kitchen where they deposited the food they had brought. Rory was still stirring gravy.

"Luka, Thomas," they said warmly, giving each of them a hug. "Thank you for coming."

"Thank you for having us," Luka replied. "Wow, this all looks amazing. Especially the gravy."

Rory swatted Finn with a mustard dish towel. "You told them."

"No, I... Yeah, I may have mentioned something. But the gravy is perfect, love."

Then the dining room caught Luka's attention through the doorway. "Just the four of us?" Luka asked.

"Yup," Finn confirmed. "I asked Ilona, but Aleandro and Penelope had already invited her to Camarillo. Everyone else had plans." *Cozy little double-date*, Finn thought with glee, enjoying the way Luka's cheeks flushed.

"Dinner is almost ready!" Rory announced, turning off the burner. "Why don't you two have a seat? Finn will get you a drink."

"Aleandro dropped off a whole case!" Finn said. "Is the Chéreau okay?" They made their way into the dining room.

"Sounds great." Luka pulled a chair out and sat. "The table is beautiful."

"That's all Rory," Finn said. "For a numbers guru, they fold a mean napkin."

Rory followed them in, dropping off a dish of potatoes. "Thanks, hon."

Finn slid his arm around Rory's waist and planted a kiss on their cheek, so proud of his partner and their seemingly endless list of talents.

Once every remaining inch of the table was covered with food, Finn and Rory settled across from Thomas and Luka. There was turkey, stuffing, mashed potatoes, sweet potato casserole, corn and Brussels sprouts, plus a vat of gravy that was, okay, maybe a touch on the thin side, but would meet their needs just fine. They dove in and loaded their plates, their easy chatter accented by the clink of spoons on china and the glug of pouring wine.

Thomas told stories about some of the other Breakpoint branches he'd worked at, and Finn shared one from their office. As the evening went on, the sparks between Luka and Thomas were almost visible, the tension rolling off them in waves. Finn could barely stand it anymore.

"Speaking of sleeping around," Finn said at the end of his story, helping himself to another slice of turkey, "you seeing anyone these days, Luka?"

Luka's cheeks glowed pink in the candlelight. "Nope."

"I don't want to be that person," Rory piped up, "but, you know what? My cousin Dimitri just broke up with his boyfriend. I think you'd like him."

Rory! Finn wanted to facepalm. They had missed the point. But it was sort of fun watching Luka squirm.

"Uh…" Luka's throat bobbed. "No, thanks. I'm good."

"He's cute, too!" Rory added. "I promise. He grew up in Paris, has an accent and everything. He also has like four dogs, but who doesn't like dogs, right?"

"No, it's just—Thanks, but I…" Luka floundered.

"You have your eye on someone else?" Finn finished helpfully.

Luka glared so hard at him. Finn grinned back.

"No," Luka said with gritted teeth. "I'm just not…interested in dating anyone right now."

"Oh. Okay." Rory smiled over at Thomas. "What about you?"

Rory *had* to be trolling. Finn watched Thomas' reaction with great interest.

Thomas froze, eyes the size of his plate. "Um...I don't date much...since I move around so often."

"Don't you get lonely?" Rory asked, leaning forward and frowning with concern.

Brilliant. Finn tried not to laugh.

"Well... I—No. I mean, yes, but..." Now it was Thomas' turn to flounder.

Rory chuckled. "It's okay. You can let me know if you change your mind." They scooped up a forkful of stuffing. "Either of you."

Well, damn. Maybe Rory was genuine. Finn caught their eye and gave them a meaningful headshake.

A glimmer of understanding crossed their face. "Or not," they added, hastily.

Luka gulped the rest of his wine while Thomas focused on scooping another helping of Brussels sprouts onto his plate.

Finn sighed. *These two.*

* * * *

"If they don't hook up soon..." Finn whispered, tilting his head to see if he could get a glimpse of Luka and Thomas washing dishes together in the kitchen.

"Have you talked to Luka about it?" Rory asked, also careful to keep their voice low. The two of them had been banished to the living room with their wine while Luka and Thomas cleaned up.

"Sort of. He just immediately shuts it down. Says he's not interested, Thomas is his boss, et cetera."

"That's too bad. There's nothing better than being in love." They pecked Finn on the nose.

Finn pulled Rory closer. "That's for sure. And thank you for dinner. It was the best Thanksgiving of my life."

Rory rested their head on Finn's shoulder, breath warm on his neck. "You're welcome."

Unexpected tears pricked at Finn's eyes. "I love you so much."

"I love you, too." Rory put their hand on Finn's chest. "You feel it, don't you?"

Chapter Thirteen

Meet the Parents

Finn knew it was coming. It was inevitable.

They were making dinner when Rory said it. Finn was simply chopping cabbage, then...

"I'd really like you to meet my parents."

Finn's heart galloped around his ribcage like a wild stallion in its new pen. "Okay," he said, managing to make the two syllables sound calm and collected.

"Yeah?" Rory turned their face up to Finn's, bright and hopeful.

"Yeah." He tried to give Rory a reassuring smile.

"Perfect." Rory resumed their stirring. "They invited us over for dinner Friday. Does that sound good?"

"Just us and them?"

"Just us and them."

* * * *

"Your parents live in a mansion?" was the first thing Finn said when the house at the end of the drive came into view. He shouldn't have been so surprised – he knew Rory's parents lived near the harbor and they owned a huge, successful manufacturing plant—but good God.

"I wouldn't call it a *mansion*," Rory said, parking at the top of the circular driveway.

"I just fucking did."

"Right, I forgot to mention…" Rory turned off the car and faced Finn. "Could you maybe…try not to…swear in front of them as much? Or, like…at all? My mom is not a fan."

Finn wiped his sweaty palms off on his itchy pants. *Why did I wear these pants?* "Fuck, I'll try." He grinned at Rory's grimace. "That was a joke. I got it. No swearing."

The morning's snowfall, the first of the year, now sat in slushy piles along the side of the walk. Finn watched his feet, careful to avoid the mess, but when he got to the step, he paused and stared up at the house. It was modern and imposing—sleek, gray, lots of glass and square angles—basically the complete opposite of his yellow bungalow.

"Hey." Rory took Finn's hand and smiled. "It's going to be fine. My parents already love you."

"They'd fucking better."

Rory opened their mouth but Finn cut them off. "Just getting the last one out. I'm good now."

Finn half expected a butler to open the door as they approached, but it was Rory's mom and dad, smiling and dressed in the kind of clothing wealthy people wore—muted colors and rich fabrics with a simplicity that screamed *money*. They hugged and patted Rory, then turned their attention to Finn.

"This is my dad, Jonathan," Rory said, "and my mom, Lainey. Mom, Dad, this is Finn."

"Finn!" Lainey took his hand and went in for what Finn thought was going to be a hug, but instead she air-kissed his cheeks. "It is so, so nice to finally meet you."

"You too," Finn said, fully aware that he had fucked up — *er, messed up* — the air kisses.

"Finn." Jonathan shook his hand with a sure, strong grip. "Such a pleasure."

"Likewise."

Both of them were close to Rory's size, significantly shorter than Finn, but Rory took after their mom more, with delicate features and those deep, dark brown eyes.

"Rory has told us so much about you," Lainey said, taking Finn's coat.

"Hasn't shut up about you, really," Jonathan added.

"Dad." Rory grimaced. "We talked about this."

"Oh, please." Lainey waved a hand in the air. "We're allowed to embarrass you a little. Besides, I'm sure Finn would be happy to know that you've told us all about him." Both parents turned to stare at Finn expectantly.

"Uh —" Finn stammered. Which was the correct side to take here?

Rory patted Finn's hand. "You don't have to answer that."

Lainey turned with a dramatic sigh and led them past the massive, curving staircase and out of the white marble foyer. "We thought we'd have drinks on the deck," she said as they passed some sort of study or library, then a formal dining room, and into a living room whose entire back wall was glass and faced the harbor, now only a gray smudge in the fading light.

The deck? Finn wondered. An odd choice, given that it was December and it had snowed. Then again, they probably had heat lamps and a fancy marble fire pit to keep them warm.

Then he saw the deck. He was right about the fancy marble fire pit, but wrong about the heat lamps. Those were not needed, because the 'deck' was essentially a second living room that was slightly less indoors than the first. There was a layer of glass storm doors shut against the night, leading to another actual uncovered deck. Ah, yes, there were the heat lamps.

In the second living room, two curved dark gray couches sat on either side of the round marble firepit, where a flame danced over the shining black stones. A barbecue bigger than Finn's first car sat on one side, gleaming in the firelight. A soothing classical piece played from invisible speakers.

"This is...really nice," Finn said. *'Nice.' Wow, impressive vocabulary, Finn.*

"Thank you." Lainey smoothed her bob. "We had the outer deck added when we did the extension a few years ago and converted this to a transition space."

"It's very nice." *Oh my God.*

"What can I get you to drink, Finn?" Jonathan asked, stopping at the bar in the first living room. "Beer, wine, scotch...?"

"Wine is fine, thank you."

"Ooh, could I talk you into champagne then?" Lainey chimed in. "I've been dying to open the bottle that Dimitri brought us from France."

"Oh, no, don't waste that on m—" Finn started.

"Waste? There's no wasting champagne! It's meant to be enjoyed!" Lainey beamed at him. "You'll have some?" she asked Rory. They nodded as Jonathan pulled the bottle from a wine cooler and arranged four flutes along the bar.

"So, Finn," Lainey said as they settled on the 'patio' furniture that was infinitely nicer than what Finn had grown up with in his one and only living room. She crossed one ankle over the other and rearranged her flowy sweater. "Rory tells us you're an incredible painter."

Finn's mouth dried out. "I, uh —" He flinched when Jonathan popped the cork.

Rory squeezed his knee. "Finn has a really hard time accepting compliments."

"I —" *Goddamn it.* Now his tongue was dry *and* there was a lump in his throat.

"Is there anywhere we could see your work? Jonathan and I have memberships to a few galleries in town..."

A few? "Not really, or I mean, no, I —" He fumbled for one of the flutes Jonathan offered on a tray. "It's just a hobby."

"Oh?"

"He hangs them in his house," Rory offered. "And has a whole gallery's worth in his garage, actually."

"Well...maybe we could see those someday? Cheers!" Lainey offered her glass for clinking.

"Cheers," Finn mumbled, trying to picture Lainey and Jonathan sitting in his tiny living room and failing miserably.

"What do you paint?" Lainey asked.

Finn took a small sip, the bubbles tickling his nostrils until he thought he might sneeze. He wiggled his nose. "Abstract expressionism, mostly. People. And, um...feelings."

"How lovely."

Finn squirmed under her attention and was relieved when Jonathan joined them.

"Oh, Rory, you wouldn't believe who stopped by the plant the other day," Jonathan said as he sat with his drink. "Patrick Harrington!"

Finn didn't know who the fu—fudge Patrick Harrington was, but he was happy the focus was no longer on him. He took another sip. The champagne was delicious, of course. Nice and bright, with a hint of a floral note.

"Who?" Rory asked.

"Oh, you know Patrick Harrington, dear," Lainey said. "Abigail and Hugh's son? The one we tried to set you up with? You went on a date."

"Him?" Rory wheezed. "That was not a date! I talked to him for five seconds at that horrible cocktail party you made me go to. Also, I seriously cannot believe you are bringing it up now."

"Oh, what's the harm? It's not like you two were serious."

"There was no 'you two,' Mom."

Lainey sighed and swirled her drink.

Jonathan continued, put out at having his story interrupted. "Anyway, Patrick has been doing some contracting for Bill Thatcher—you remember him."

"Yes, Dad, I know Bill."

"Well, Bill's been having some trouble with a supplier out of Tulsa, so he got Patrick on the case, and he actually ended up *going* to Tulsa, if you can believe it! Was there for a damn week!"

Finn took another sip. He tried not to look bored while Jonathan went on about Bill and Patrick and other people Finn didn't know. As his thoughts wandered, the giant Christmas tree in the main living room caught his attention—at least ten feet tall and wrapped with gold ribbon and white lights. To be honest, he expected matching designer ornaments, but it looked like many of them were handmade.

Rory nodded along politely to their dad's story as the champagne dwindled, shooting Finn the occasional apologetic look.

Even Lainey got bored eventually, and she got up to refill her flute. "How is work going for you two?" she said as she sat again, taking advantage of Jonathan's pause when he finally took a drink.

"Great," Rory said. "Really busy, but some fun projects."

"Rory has been helping me with the overhaul of a client's brand—they designed a whole new website and app," Finn said proudly.

"*We* designed it," Rory said, squeezing Finn's hand.

Lainey smiled at Rory fondly, then jolted as she remembered something. "Oh! I've been dying to tell you, Stanley found the rubber duck!"

"He did?" Rory dissolved into laughter. "What did he say?"

"He was so confused!" Lainey was tittering too, and even Jonathan joined in. "You should have seen his face when he walked in. 'Mrs. Barrett, I just found this rubber duck glued under my desk...'"

The three of them laughed, until Rory noticed Finn's face. "Oh, Stanley took over my job at the plant. We do this thing with rubber ducks... I'll explain later."

"Can't wait," Finn said, trying not to sound sarcastic.

"I hope you two are hungry," Lainey said, smoothing over the awkwardness. "Hadir has been cooking all day."

"Yum, what did he make?" Rory asked.

"Who's Hadir?" Finn blurted at the same time.

"Our chef," Lainey said, as if Finn was slow. "He's been around for years. He's like family."

"You have a chef?" Finn hadn't meant to add a follow-up question.

The other three all stared at him.

Lainey recovered first. "Sometimes," she breezed. "Mostly dinner, the odd lunch or special event."

"Ah." Finn took a sip only to discover his glass was empty. "How…nice."

Lainey hopped up again. "Let me get you some more champagne."

"Yes, please," Finn said. *Lots more.*

* * * *

Lainey apologized about fifteen times on the way to the kitchen. "I just thought the dining room was too stuffy for the four of us. I hope you don't mind eating at the kitchen table?"

"It's fine, Mom," Rory assured her.

The 'kitchen table' looked like a full-size dining room to Finn, also with windows facing the bay all across the back. A long rustic farmhouse table, no doubt painstakingly handmade, dominated the space. It belonged in a home-decor magazine, with layers and layers of linens, white ceramics everywhere, and pinecones, greenery and goddamn napkin swans.

"I see where you learned to fold napkins," Finn whispered to Rory.

"Oh, yeah," Rory said, sheepishly. "Lenora taught me."

"Who's Lenora?" Finn asked, then instantly wished he hadn't.

"Um. The housekeeper," Rory murmured.

I think that's a 'Rich People' bingo. Jesus.

Hadir had already cleared out, but a mouth-watering meal waited — roasted chicken with peppers and zucchini, sauteed mushrooms and a spinach and quinoa salad.

They were just beginning to serve themselves when there was a banging noise from down the hall. Finn jumped but no one else seemed alarmed.

"Griffin?" Lainey called. Her spoon paused over the mushrooms. "Is that you?"

There was more banging, then, "Mom?" someone called.

"In here, dear!" Lainey called. "It seems Griffin is back," she said to the table, tone unreadable.

Finn steeled himself. The younger brother.

"Goddamn skateboard," Griffin muttered as he stalked into the kitchen. "Bailey's shit is everywhere in the mudroom. Could barely find room for my snowboard. Oh, hey," he said, stopping abruptly at the sight of the elaborate dinner. "Sorry to interrupt." Griffin looked a lot like Rory, but a little taller, more angular. Where Rory was delicate, Griffin was sharp. And he didn't seem the tiniest bit sorry.

"Nonsense." Lainey stood and went to kiss the interloper. "You're not interrupting."

"You kind of are," Rory mumbled.

Griffin flipped a middle finger at Rory behind Lainey's back, then noticed Finn.

"Griffin, this is my partner, Finn," Rory said. "Finn, this is my brother, Griffin."

"Nice to meet you," Finn said, half standing and offering a hand to shake.

"You too," Griffin said, ignoring the proffered hand and wandering over to rummage through the fridge.

"I thought you were getting home tomorrow, Griffin?" Lainey called.

Sorry, Rory mouthed at Finn.

Finn shook his head. *It's fine.*

Griffin emerged from the fridge with a bottle of lager in hand. "I thought so too but Tristan had to come home a day early for some fucking reason, something about his kid's gymnastics meet being changed." He popped the top off and took a long swig.

"Language, please," Lainey said.

"I've been up since five, Mom. Give me a break." Another gulp. "Actually, do you guys mind if I crash here tonight?"

"Well, as I imagine your cab is long gone..." Jonathan said dryly, almost under his breath.

Rory snickered.

"Have you eaten, dear?" Lainey asked, giving her husband and other child a healthy dose of side eye.

"I had a few bites of some dry-ass roast on the plane..." Griffin looked pointedly at their spread.

"Get a plate and join us, won't you?" Lainey patted the empty chair next to her. The table easily fit four chairs on each side.

"Mom..." Rory hissed while Griffin retrieved a plate from the cupboard.

She gave Rory a 'well, what do you want me to do?' shrug.

Griffin squinted at Finn as he sat. "Sorry, who are you?"

"This is my partner, Finn," Rory repeated. "He's just meeting Mom and Dad for the first time."

"And I've crashed the party, haven't I?" Griffin dug into the chicken, chuckling. "So how did you two meet?"

"We work together," Finn replied.

"Huh." Griffin took a bite and studied them some more as he chewed. "I could never work with someone I was banging."

"Griffin!" Lainey scowled. "We are at the dinner table!"

Griffin rolled his eyes and reached for a bun. "We're all adults here, Mom. At least I didn't say 'fucking.'"

Finn tried not to laugh while Lainey glared at Griffin. Jonathan stuffed a rather large bite of salad in his mouth. *Not a bad plan*, Finn decided, and he followed suit.

The rest of the meal passed by with a steady hum around the table. Griffin rattled on about his ski trip, Jonathan talked more about work and Lainey filled them in on their upcoming trip to Tuscany. Rory peppered them all with questions and did their best to draw Finn into the conversation.

Finn had absolutely nothing to add.

* * * *

Finn was coming back from the washroom after dessert, slightly fuzzy from the champagne and full belly, when he nearly ran into Griffin, barreling around a corner in the dim hallway.

"Sorry," Finn muttered, trying to sidestep him, but Griffin planted his feet in the middle of the hallway and jabbed a finger in Finn's chest.

"I hope you're treating Rory good," Griffin said, with his beer breath.

Finn stared at the finger, trying to make sense of this man threatening him. "You're worried about me treating Rory well?"

"Rory is...special. They deserve someone who treats them that way. And if you hurt them, I'll kick your ass."

Finn brushed Griffin's finger away with a smirk. "You should know, Griffin..." He jabbed his own finger in Griffin's chest. "I treat Rory like fucking royalty, and if you threaten me again, I'll kick *your* ass."

Griffin blinked at Finn for a second, then burst into laughter. "Fucking right." He patted Finn on the shoulder and continued on to the washroom, still chuckling. "Fucking right."

* * * *

"Are you sure you don't want to stay over? Your room is always here..."

They were standing in the doorway, bundled into their winter coats and so ready to leave. This was Lainey's fourth offer for them to spend the night, at least.

"No, thanks, Mom." Rory kissed her on the cheek.

"Thank you for an amazing dinner," Finn said again.

She hugged Rory, then Finn. "Please visit again soon, Finn. You'll come for Christmas dinner, won't you? I don't know if your own family will be gathering that day...?"

"Oh, yes—I mean, no," Finn stammered. "I mean, I can come. Thank you."

"I am so sorry about Griffin," Rory said the second they were back in the car. "Trust him to show up. He can be so oblivious sometimes."

"It's fine," Finn said. "He and I... We came to an understanding."

"Oh, did you?"

"I might have threatened to kick his ass."

"Yeah?" Rory started the car and cranked the defrost up to high. "He could probably use an ass kicking. But otherwise...you had fun, right?"

Finn leaned over to kiss Rory. "Right."

As he buckled up his seatbelt, he realized it was the first time he'd lied to them. Because all the dinner had done was remind him that he did not belong in this family. Would he like to fit in, feel comfortable sipping champagne in front of a marble firepit on a covered deck while the chef made dinner and everyone loved and supported everyone else? Sure.

But he never would.

Chapter Fourteen

Roommates

Finn had always known that he and Rory were a bad fit. That was, of course, why it took him so long to get his head out of his ass and make a move in the first place. But he had been completely wrong about *why* they were so incompatible. It was more than just that Rory was quiet and he was loud. Rory was sweet and thoughtful and he was a lumbering buffoon. So much more. It was down to the very fabric of their being — their upbringing, their family, their culture, all woven deep into their DNA. Second living rooms, housekeepers and folded napkins. Marble foyers, snowboards cluttering up the mudroom and champagne actually *from* Champagne.

How long would it take Rory to figure it out?

And when they did…should he fight, or let them go?

By the time they got home, Finn's stomach was in knots. "I ate too much," he muttered, wanting nothing more than to go hide under the covers.

"Yeah, Hadir really outdid himself with that meal." Rory dropped their keys on the counter and stretched.

"Good old Hadir."

Rory noticed the tone and turned to study Finn in the darkened kitchen. The tiny, old kitchen. "What's wrong with Hadir?"

"Nothing." Finn sighed. "Nothing at all. It's...I had no idea. You've literally never mentioned your chef or your housekeeper before, or however many other servants."

Rory's eyes widened and they took a moment to reply. "They're my parents' *employees*, not mine. And I didn't think it mattered if my parents had a chef."

"Yeah." Finn rubbed his face. "It doesn't. I'm sorry, I think I need to go to bed."

"Hey." Rory put a hand on Finn's arm. "Is everything okay?"

"Yeah." Finn gave a weak smile. "Maybe too much champagne. Not used to drinking it."

"Okay." Rory relaxed. "I was going to" —they waved at their laptop on the kitchen table— "for a bit, but if you want me to—"

"No, it's fine." Finn kissed them. "You do your thing."

He went through the motions brushing his teeth and getting ready for bed, but once he hit the mattress, his mind replayed every awkward moment from the evening over and over. It took him a long time to fall asleep, even with the soothing hum of Rory's fingers on their keyboard coming from the living room.

* * * *

"Morning!" Rory chirped when Finn shuffled, bleary-eyed, into the kitchen. "Wow, you must have had a good sleep! I've been keeping some French toast warm for you."

"Not really," Finn replied, heading for the coffee maker. He had tossed and turned half the night. Rory wasn't in bed the first time he'd woken up, but they had been there the second and third times. Then gone again, when, groggy and head pounding, Finn had finally cracked an eye open and found sunlight sneaking through the gaps in the curtains. He slumped at the table with his coffee. The French toast would have to wait.

"Hey, can we talk?" Rory asked, settling in the chair next to him.

Finn's heart dropped into his stomach. *Fuck. This is it. Rory knows it, too. I don't fit with their family. We don't fit. It's over.*

"There's no easy way to say this, but...you really need to start your Christmas shopping," Rory said.

Finn blinked, heart swooping back up in a sickening lurch. "I — What?"

Rory laughed. "I'm kidding, of course. I mean, you do need to start your Christmas shopping, but that's not what I wanted to talk to you about."

The roller coaster plunged again. "Okay."

"So." They fiddled with their coffee mug. "I've been spending a lot of time here..."

And it's too much. I need my space. I'm leaving. "Yeah?" It was a strangled noise.

"And I'm starting to miss —"

My freedom. Being single. Finn's brain skittered through a hundred arguments at once. *Make them stay. Let them go.*

" — my computer."

Your – His brain screeched to a halt. "Your *computer*?"

"I know, I know." Rory chuckled. "I'm a huge geek. But my laptop isn't really cutting it anymore."

"Your laptop?" *Stop repeating everything, Finn.*

"Last night, I was trying to integrate the app with Thrill's database, but they have such bad data, I've been writing a bunch of extra code to handle their issues…" Rory took in the expression on Finn's face. "What's up?"

"Oh, nothing, I'm fine." Finn cleared his throat. Not a drop of moisture left in his mouth. "A little hungover, maybe."

"Been there. My mom's champagne always goes down so easy."

Finn got up to get some water. "Sorry, you were saying?"

"Right, well…" Rory turned to watch Finn fill his glass. "It would be easier with all my gear here. My desktop has so much more RAM, and you know how I love all my monitors. So, I was wondering if it would be okay if I…moved my computer over?"

Finn stopped so suddenly the water sloshed out of his glass. "You want to…move in?"

"Er." Rory scratched their nose. "Not, like, *officially* move. Just my computer. For now. And maybe my plants."

"Um…" Finn tried to tell his racing heart to slow down while his brain processed. *Should I let them get more comfortable here? They'll realize eventually…* "Where would your computer go?" he asked. He'd been to Rory's apartment a few times and had seen the extensive setup. It took up an entire room.

"I know," Rory said sheepishly. "That's a good question. I only...I thought we could maybe figure something out."

Finn sat and chugged his water. Of course, he couldn't say no. He should, but he couldn't. Not when he wanted to spend every possible second with Rory before they realized.

Rory watched him, brow furrowed. "Or not. If you don't think it'll work—"

"No—yes! Yes, it'll work. I... I was just surprised. But of course. Yes."

Rory smiled, relieved. "Great. I mean, no hurry—"

"Let's do it today!"

"Today?"

"Sure! Why don't you go pack it all up and I'll clear out half my studio. There's gotta be more room in the garage somewhere." His laugh was slightly manic.

"Okay. Are you sure you're feeling up to this today, love?"

"Yes! I'll get started right now." Finn stood so fast his chair screeched.

"All right." Rory stood, chuckling, and leaned forward to place a gentle kiss on Finn's lips. "I'll swing by the plant to grab some boxes and see if maybe Griffin or Jackson is around."

"Sounds good."

"Don't forget your French toast," Rory said, fingers already a blur over their phone.

"Right. French toast."

* * * *

"Pick up, pick up, pick up..." Finn muttered as Luka's phone rang. He paced back and forth on the narrow bare strip of floor in his studio.

"Finn?" Luka answered, confused and half-asleep. "Is everything okay?"

"No. I mean, yes. I'm fine, everyone's fine, but...Rory's parents are loaded."

"Hang on." Luka's covers rustled. "Sorry, did you say Rory's parents are loaded?"

"Yes."

"And?"

"And...that's it. They have a chef."

"Sweet. How was the food?"

"Luka!"

"I say this genuinely... What?"

"You know what it was like for me growing up."

"I don't really, you haven't told me that much."

"Well, I didn't have a fucking chef."

"I'm sorry, but other than the *impossible* task of buying Rory's parents a Christmas present, I don't really see the problem. If anything, it's good news."

Finn screeched to a halt, blinking. "*I have to get them a Christmas present?*"

"Oh, Finn." Luka sighed.

"And listen." Finn resumed his pacing, raking a hand through his hair. "Rory has gone to pack up their computer. To move it over here."

Luka let out a low whistle. "Well, that is serious."

"I can't tell if you're mocking me or not."

"I am, but only a little. Because you are freaking out right now, and I want you to know that it's all okay. It's great, actually."

"But—"

"It's great that Rory's parents are rich, and it's great that Rory wants their computer at your place. Aren't they basically there all the time anyway?"

"Yeah." Finn's reply was muffled as he rubbed his beard. He stopped to stare out of the window. It was snowing again, in big fat uneven flakes that had already covered the grass and were now sticking to the sides of the road.

"So. This is your partner wanting to spend even more time with you."

Finn nodded, then remembered Luka couldn't see him. "Right. You're right."

"Do you love Rory?" Luka's voice was clear as day now.

"Yes."

"Do they love you?"

"Yes." Goosebumps swept over Finn's skin when he realized how quickly and certainly he could answer that question. He exhaled. "Thanks."

"You are so welcome."

Finn pressed his forehead to the window. "How's your day going?"

"Well, I was sleeping until my friend called me complaining that his partner who loves him wants to move in. Otherwise, good."

"Fuck you. How's Thomas?" Thomas had been staying at Luka's place for the week while the heating in his condo was fixed, a fact that delighted and amused Finn.

Luka sucked in a breath. "That's fair. Thomas is…good. And unfairly, devastatingly, gut-wrenchingly attractive."

Finn snickered. "So, you had a good week?"

"I saw him practically naked, Finn. *In a towel. Do you know what that did to me?*"

"You're yelling."

"You'd yell too if you saw him." Luka groaned. "Be honest, am I as pathetic as I sound?"

"Oh, Luka. So much worse."

Luka sniffed. "You're welcome for being an amazing best friend and even taking your call."

Finn laughed. "All right, I gotta go. I have to make some room for Rory's hard drives or whatever."

"Yes, do that. And pretend I said something witty about hard drives. I don't know, I just woke up."

"Thanks, Luka."

* * * *

Finn worked all day cleaning out his studio. Another stack of canvases had to go into the garage, encroaching on his workout space, and he reorganized his shelves and packed up the excess supplies strewn about the room. Those boxes teetered high on the existing piles near the freezer.

How's it going? he texted Rory when he paused for some food around three.

Good! Griffin didn't answer my messages but Jackson came over to help. We're almost done. How's it going for you?

For me? Good. For the garage? Not so much.

Lol. That poor garage. It's stuffed full.

Maybe I'll stuff you full later.

Promise?

Finn grinned. He had an idea.

* * * *

A couple of hours later, he was ready. He had dusted, vacuumed and mopped the empty half of his studio, then laid down a thick plaid blanket and a few cushions and set up a romantic candlelit picnic. He didn't have a ton of time to cook, but he whipped up some mini-quiches, and there was chocolate caramel ice cream in the freezer, Rory's favorite. When he heard Rory pull into the driveway, he lit the candles. Then he flung open the back door and ran to help unload the boxes.

"Hey," Finn said, pouncing on Rory the minute they climbed out of his truck.

"Hey—" Rory tried to say, but it was cut off by Finn's lips pressing to theirs.

When Finn pulled away, Rory laughed. "I missed you too."

Finn peered through the window. The computer was in the cab, and Rory's desk in the truck bed. "Alright. Let's get this bad boy inside."

Rory handed him the heaviest box. "Here you go, muscles."

Finn was bursting to show Rory the picnic. "I have a surprise for you," he said as soon as they got in the back door.

"Do you now?" Rory followed Finn inside and plopped their box onto the kitchen table, then reached for their phone. Their face clouded over as they stared at the screen. "Shit. I have to go."

"What?" Finn hefted his box onto the floor.

"I'm sorry." Rory typed madly as they spoke. "It's Griffin. He's... He's having some trouble. I need to go talk to him."

Finn pinched his brows together. "Is he okay? Is he safe right now?"

"Yes, he's at my parents'. He's safe, but not really okay. He sometimes...shuts down."

"I don't mean to sound like a dick, but can't your parents deal with this? Griffin is an adult."

Rory shook their head, jaw tight. "Griffin responds better to me. I need to be there for him."

"But I spent the whole day making room for you. The surprise..." Finn trailed off lamely.

"I know, Finn. But I have to go. You wouldn't really understand."

It was like a bucket of cold water. "I wouldn't understand?"

"You never have to be there for your family —"

"What?"

Rory sighed. "I just mean —"

"No, what did you say? I'm never there for my family?"

"That's not what I said."

"Sounded like it to me."

"Well...you're not, are you?"

Finn stared at Rory, wordless.

"Fuck, I'm sorry, Finn." Rory sagged. "I didn't mean... I'm just worried about Griffin and —"

"Yeah. You'd better get going. Your brother needs you."

"Finn, don't —" Rory paused and studied him. "Do you want to come with me?"

"Do I want to come? Seriously?"

"Yeah. Seriously. You should. I'd like you to."

Finn pictured the waiting picnic. He pictured sitting in his dark house, eating mini-quiches alone on the couch. There were two options here — pout, or step up for his partner. "Give me a second." He ran to the studio, blew out the candles, grabbed the plate of quiches then hustled back to the kitchen where he dumped them into a Tupperware container. "Here, you can eat in the car. I'll drive."

* * * *

"Griffin?" Rory called. They were standing at the door to the main floor powder room in the Barretts' house. Lainey and Jonathan didn't look quite as put together as they had at dinner the night before. Lainey was in yoga pants, not a hint of makeup, and Jonathan's ragged sweater had a hole on the elbow. They hadn't been surprised to see Finn at all, and simply pointed them in the direction of the closed door.

There was no reply.

Rory tried again. "Are you okay, Griffin? Talk to me, please." The lines on Rory's face were drawn. They rested their palm on the door. "Please, Griff."

Then they heard it. A low mutter. "I'm okay."

Rory sighed with relief. "What's up, Griffin? Tell me what's going on."

There was another long pause, then he spoke again. "Bryn broke up with me."

"Shit. I'm so sorry."

"I told her it would be different this time."

"I know."

"But I'm never different, am I? I'm always the same. I'm gonna be alone forever." The last words were hard to hear, fading away into nothing.

"You're not!" Rory said. "There's no way."

There was no response this time.

"Griffin, will you come out of there? Let's grab some food and talk. Have you eaten anything today?"

Still nothing.

Finn stepped closer and cleared his throat. "I know how you feel," he said to the door. "About being alone forever. You feel like you're wrong somehow, like you'll never fit. It's so hard. I get it."

Rory took Finn's hand and leaned their head on his shoulder.

"And I wish I could tell you the right person will come along. And they might. But it doesn't matter, you know? What matters is all the people who do love you. And I know Rory loves you so much..."

Rory blinked at Finn with welling eyes.

"...and so does the rest of your family. So much, Griffin. Can you come out so they can talk to you?"

The door cracked open.

* * * *

It was late when they got home, and they still had to unload Rory's desk and the rest of their boxes and plants. Then Finn took Rory's hand and showed them the picnic he had set up. Rory sniffled and buried themselves in Finn's arms. They spent the night on the blanket.

Chapter Fifteen

Gifting

It was a little cozy, but Rory's desk and all their gear fit into half of Finn's studio. Finn loved painting with the patter of Rory's keyboard next to him. The bungalow was more cheerful with the addition of Rory's plants, and the one Thomas had brought didn't look so lonely anymore.

But Finn's favorite place to be was snuggled up under the blanket watching *Godstrike* with Rory while the snow piled up outside.

He really had to get his Christmas shopping started, though.

"What do I get Rory for Christmas?" Finn asked, tumbling into his chair in Luka's office. Thomas was there too, but he and Luka were basically a package deal now. Thomas knew all the ins and outs of his relationship with Rory.

Luka tapped his chin. "I mean, technically, nothing, unless you draw their name."

Finn stared at him. God, Luka could be insufferable sometimes. Of course, he would try to apply the rules of the office gift exchange here. "You're joking, right?"

"What? These are the rules! You're only supposed to get a gift for someone at work if you have them for Secret Santa." His smirk indicated he was being annoying on purpose.

Finn turned to Thomas. "What do you think I should get them, Wolf?"

Thomas froze, gaze flicking between Luka and Finn. "Uh, do they need a new wallet?"

"Thanks, guys," Finn said, getting back to his feet with a thigh slap. "Big help."

* * * *

Later that day, Tawney popped into Finn's office carrying a Santa hat. "Ho, ho, ho! It's time to pick your Secret Santa! And no telling who you got." Tawney shook the hat and held it out for him.

"No promises," Finn said, reaching.

Tawney scowled and pulled the hat away. "Finn!"

"Kidding, kidding. I won't tell anyone." He stuck his hand in the hat. "Except Rory."

"You —" Tawney pursed her lips.

Finn glanced at the name he'd pulled and grinned at her. "Hey, why does Santa always land on the roof?"

"Why?"

"Because he likes it on top."

Tawney snorted. "Good for him."

As soon as Tawney left, Finn texted Rory.

Do you want to do some shopping with me after work?

Yes!! I can get something for my Secret Santa.

Who did you get?

We're not supposed to tell.

Finn sighed. *What is with all the rule-followers around here! It doesn't count for partners.*

Okay, fine. I got Ilona. You?

I can't believe you caved.

What! Finn!!

Lol, I'm kidding. I got Thomas. See you soon xo

* * * *

When Finn popped into Rory's office at the end of the day, they were typing madly.

"You know," Finn said, leaning against the doorframe. "I'm starting to get turned on by this. Those fingers. They're so...long."

Rory grinned but didn't look away from the screen. "I think that counts as workplace harassment."

"No, it doesn't!" Finn protested.

"Yes, it does. I need to get this done and you're harassing me."

"We have a date." Finn came and stood next to Rory's chair, pretending he was examining the incomprehensible code on the screen, but was really trying to get his groin in Rory's eyeline.

It worked. Rory's fingers froze.

"It's fine." Finn sighed. "You're busy. You know what, I'll start my shopping another day."

Rory gave Finn a playful glare. "You fight dirty."

"I like it dirty." Finn leaned down to kiss Rory on the nose. "Let's go!"

* * * *

They crunched along the sidewalk, wispy flakes twirling down from the night sky and Rory holding tight to Finn's arm.

Rory giggled. "I still can't believe you got that tank top for Thomas."

Finn smiled down at them, admiring the flakes twinkling in Rory's hair. "You cannot tell him it was me."

"My lips are sealed. So, who else do you have to shop for?"

"Not many. You, Luka, something for your parents—"

Rory interrupted, waving a hand. "Oh, you don't need to get anything for my parents."

"I don't?"

"Nah."

"But...I can't walk in empty-handed on Christmas!"

"You can, I swear!"

"What are you getting them?"

"Um, the four of us kids are going in to send them to Camarillo for a wine-tasting weekend in the summer."

"Mmhmm. And everyone else in your family will show up with a gift, right?"

"Er...yes."

Finn threw Rory a wry look.

Rory chuckled. "Okay, fine. I'll help you pick something out for them."

"Thank you. So." Finn continued with his list. "Something for your parents, and I always send something to Cali and Bryson."

"You do?"

"Yeah, why?"

"No reason. That's kind of you."

Finn shrugged. "Not their fault their mom sucks."

"True." Rory squeezed his arm. "And you don't need to get me anything, for real. I've already got you."

"That's true, I *am* a gift…" Finn mused.

Rory laughed and swatted at Finn's shoulder as they came to a stop in front of a men's clothing store. "All right, let's look in here, unless your head is too big to fit through the doorway."

* * * *

Over the course of their outing, Finn picked out a sweater for Luka, a wine and cheese gift basket for Lainey and Jonathan and Lego sets for Cali and Bryson. He also carefully noted the items that Rory 'oohed' and 'ahhed' over as they shopped.

The next day at lunch, Finn took the kids' gifts to the post office and popped back into the men's clothing store where Rory had admired a wallet. As much as he hated to admit it, Thomas had made a good suggestion. Wallets were practical, but he could splurge on a really nice one, and Rory would think about him every time they used it. However, Finn also ordered an extra something special online for Rory too, the kind of gift that would arrive in discreet packaging and spice up their holiday.

The day before the office party, Finn stopped in at Luka's office to give him his present.

"You shouldn't have!" Luka exclaimed when Finn handed him the elaborately wrapped box. He held it up, admiring it from all angles. "Your wrapping, Finn, I swear... Should I open it now?"

Finn loved to wrap presents. He went a little over the top, maybe, with foil paper, cloth ribbons and fancy bows. Half of his bedroom closet was crammed with gift-wrapping supplies. "Fuck yes."

Luka carefully picked at the tape on one end.

"Don't be precious about it, Moreno." Finn reached forward and ripped a chunk of paper off.

"Finn! I was going to save that." Luka opened the box, shaking his head. He pulled out a pale pink cable-knit sweater with a huge smile. "Oh... It's gorgeous! I love it! Thank you so much!"

"Thought it would look good on you," Finn said.

"I feel bad because I didn't get you anyth — Kidding, yes, I did!" Luka reached under his desk and handed Finn a gift bag with gold tissue poking out.

"I thought the rule was gifts for Secret Santas only?" Finn teased.

Luka grinned. "Shut up and open it."

They both cackled when Finn pulled out another cable-knit sweater, but this one in British racing green.

"Thanks, man. I love it."

"Clearly, we both have excellent taste." Luka set aside his sweater, face growing serious. "So, you're finally meeting the rest of Rory's family... Are you nervous?"

Finn groaned. The Christmas Eve gathering at the Barretts' loomed. "No."

"Ha!"

Finn glowered at him. "Fine. I'm nervous as fuck, all right?"

"It's going to be great. You can wear your new sweater! And just be yourself."

Finn huffed in amusement as his insides swirled. "Be myself, surrounded by Rory's whole fucking family? Right. What could go wrong?"

"Okay, well...be yourself but maybe don't swear as much."

Finn sighed. "That's what Rory said, too. Fuck."

* * * *

They woke up late on Christmas Eve, Rory plastered to Finn's back, arm over his waist. Finn wiggled around and planted a kiss on Rory's forehead.

"Morning," Rory mumbled.

"Morning." Finn ran his fingers down Rory's arm and sighed.

Rory nuzzled him. "What's up?"

"Can we just stay here all day?" Finn asked.

Rory lifted their head to look at the clock. "We're supposed to be at my parents' in an hour." But their hand drifted down from Finn's hip and took him in a firm grip.

Finn growled as he pulled Rory closer. "Give me five minutes then."

Rory smirked. "Make it ten."

* * * *

"Are you nervous?" Rory asked, chewing a fingernail as they pulled to a stop at the top of the driveway.

Today's brunch was at least limited to Rory's immediate family. The extended family would descend tomorrow for Christmas Day. Finn was still fucking terrified. "A little. Are you?"

"No." Rory smiled broadly as they climbed out of the truck. "They're all going to love you."

"Finn!" someone bellowed, flinging open the door before they were even up the step. Griffin, huge smile on his face, bounded down the step in his sock feet and threw his arms around Finn.

"Hey, Griffin," Finn said, embarrassed at the attention, while Rory beamed at them both. "How's it going?"

"Good, man. Good. You're here just in time. Jackson's trying to talk about work."

"Griffin, you aren't wearing shoes. Honestly..." Lainey stood in the door holding a beverage that appeared to be a mimosa. "Hello, darling. Hello, Finn. How nice to see you again." She air-kissed their cheeks and ushered them into the house. "Davis will take your coats."

An older man in a white shirt and black vest was by their side before Finn could blink.

"Davis, how are you?" Rory asked, handing him their coat.

"I'm well, thank you, Rory," Davis replied smoothly. "How are you?"

"I'm great. Davis, this is my partner, Finn Owens."

"It's a pleasure to meet you...?" Davis trailed off, eyebrow raised.

"'Mister' is fine," Rory supplied. "Finn uses he/him."

" —Mr. Owens," Davis finished with a polite head-bob.

"Er...you too," Finn stammered. *Davis? 'Mr. Owens?'*

They followed Lainey and Griffin toward the living room, the latter leaving wet footprints on the marble while the former tutted.

Finn leaned over to murmur in Rory's ear. "So that's..."

"Yup."

"...the butler."

"The butler."

Finn nodded. *The butler.* Of course there was a butler. But no time to dwell on that, he was about to...

"Ro-ro!" came the high-pitched squeal, as a tiny human flung herself into Rory's arms the moment they entered the living room.

Rory didn't miss a beat, scooping her up and tossing her in the air. "Min-min!"

Lainey chuckled, heading to the bar to top up her beverage. Griffin flopped onto the sectional.

Damn, Minnie was even cuter in person in her red reindeer sweater and shining brown curls. She wrapped her arms tight around Rory's neck.

"Minnie," Rory said solemnly, holding the little girl so she could see Finn. "I would like to introduce you to someone really special. This is my partner, Finn."

Minnie leveled her serious brown eyes at him. "It's nice to meet you," she intoned, measuring out the words with care.

"The pleasure is all mine, Minnie," Finn replied. "Ro-ro has told me so many good things about you."

She scrunched up her face as Rory set her down. "Like what?"

"Like...how you always beat them at Snakes and Ladders."

"That's true, I do," she said, brushing her curls back. "Ro-ro is pretty bad at Snakes and Ladders. They always land on the snakes and I always get the ladders."

Rory gasped with mock outrage. "I beat you once!"

"I let you win that time, Ro-ro." Minnie giggled.

Rory ruffled her hair. "You munchkin. I'm going to beat you today."

A heavier-set man clutching a bottle of beer came in. His reindeer sweater matched Minnie's. "Amy is just putting the baby down," he said to Lainey. "Oh, hey Rory."

"Jackson," Rory said, taking Finn's arm, "this is my partner, Finn."

Jackson eyed Finn up, and Finn instantly didn't like him — something about his cold eyes and defiant jaw. He hoped his instinct was wrong.

"Great to finally meet you, Finn," Jackson said. His grip nearly crushed Finn's hand.

"You too," Finn said, doing his best to crush right back.

Their gazes met. *You'll have to squeeze harder than that,* Finn thought.

"Grab me another beer, would you, Ro-ro?" Jackson asked. He let go of Finn's hand and sat next to Griffin on the sectional.

Rory poured mimosas for the two of them, fetched a beer for Jackson then settled on the couch with Finn. Minnie went back to her coloring on the floor.

Jackson crossed his legs and examined Finn. "Now, you two work together, correct? What's the place called again?"

"Breakpoint Advertising," Finn supplied.

"Right. So you're an advertiser?"

"Designer."

"Ah. And remind me what is it you do there, Rory?"

Griffin scoffed. "What do you think they do, Jackson?"

Rory's body was laced with tension as they replied to Jackson. "IT."

Jackson chuckled. "Obviously IT. But what do you actually *do*?"

"A lot of coding for the firm, and our clients. I analyze the —"

Jackson was distracted by his buzzing phone and rolled his eyes at the screen. "Goddamn it, Stanley," he muttered.

"Language," tisked Lainey.

Rory faltered, since Jackson was clearly not listening.

"I don't know, Rory," Jackson said, tucking his phone away as if Rory hadn't stopped in the middle of a sentence. "When you're done messing around, let me know. I'll hire you back at the plant in a second. God knows you're better than Stanley anyway." He laughed, like the room wasn't ice cold.

What the fuck is this guy's problem? Finn bit his lip.

"I'm really happy at Breakpoint," Rory replied, sliding their hand onto Finn's knee.

"Yeah, sure." Jackson leaned back, stretching an arm along the back of the couch. "What are they paying you though? Can't be enough."

Nope. "What the fuck is your problem?" Finn blurted. "Who asks that?"

Four — no, five — wide pairs of eyes stared at him.

Finn gulped. *Whoops.*

Chapter Sixteen

Family Tree

Jackson's face flickered with anger, then his condescending grin was back. He held up his hands in mock surrender. "There's no problem here, Finn. Rory knows I wish they'd come back to the plant."

"Finn," Rory said. "It's fine." They shot a nervous glance at Lainey.

Lainey took an angry sip of her drink.

Finn's stomach curdled. "I apologize for my language," he said. "But—"

"It's okay!" piped up a little voice. Heads snapped over to Minnie. "My dad says that word all the time."

Finn resisted the urge to laugh. "But Rory said they are happy at Breakpoint. It doesn't matter what they get paid."

"Doesn't matter?" Jackson's look of derision narrowed every insecurity Finn had ever had into a single needle point stabbing him in the chest. "Of course it matters, Finn."

Finn imagined punching his smug face, but the needle pinned him to the couch.

Rory cleared their throat. "Where are Dad and Bailey?" they asked Lainey.

Heat flared in Finn's cheeks. How could Rory let Jackson get away with a statement like that?

"He's got a ham on the smoker," Lainey replied, getting up to make her way back to the bar. She added more champagne to her already not-very-orange mimosa. "I told him not to bother, but you know your father. Bailey is helping him, I believe. Either that or she's finally talked Hadir into letting her cook the whole meal."

Jackson was still staring at Finn, swirling the beer in his bottle. "And what does a designer do, Finn?"

This fucking – Finn shifted in his seat, deciding how to answer, aside from 'They design, asshole,' but Griffin started laughing.

"Jesus, Jackson! What crawled up your butt and died?"

"Griffin!" Lainey barked.

"What? I said 'butt'!"

A surge of affection for Griffin eased the sharpness in Finn's chest.

Minnie snickered without pausing her coloring. "Butt."

Jackon widened his eyes. "I just asked Finn about his job, Griff. I think everyone needs to relax a little."

Relax? Finn curled his fingers into a fist.

"Well, I think it's time to eat," Lainey announced, shooting to her feet moments after she had settled down. "This way, everyone."

Rory took Finn's hand, but wouldn't make eye contact as they followed Lainey wobbling down the hall.

* * * *

"Is Jackson always like that?" Finn asked the second the truck door slammed behind him.

"What do you mean?"

"What do I mean? He took digs at me and you every chance he got."

Rory waved a hand. "That's just how Jackson is."

"A dick is how he is?"

"He's not a dick."

"Rory… He said you were wasting your time at Breakpoint."

"He's got tunnel vision about the plant, is all. He gets a little obsessed. I mean, look, he's got his tech guy texting him on Christmas Eve!"

Finn punched the ignition button. "You don't have to do that with me, you know."

"Do what?"

"Make excuses for his shitty behavior." Finn had stopped making excuses for his family about twenty years ago.

"I'm not making excuses!"

Do you really believe how much you get paid doesn't matter? Finn wanted to ask, but he was afraid of where that conversation would go. He rubbed his forehead, thoughts swimming. "Okay. Okay." He put the truck into gear. "Maybe I just need to get to know him better."

Rory nodded, relieved. "I'm sure that's it."

I'm sure.

* * * *

"So, tell me again...who are your mom's brothers?" Rory and Finn were tucked onto the couch eating breakfast casserole Christmas morning. Finn was doing his best to memorize the Barrett family tree before becoming mired in its branches.

Rory drew a line in the air with their fork. "There's Alfie, George, then my mom, then Philip — they're the ones that just moved back here from France."

"And which one is the one that said Ophy put on weight?"

"That was my dad's brother, Frank."

"God..." Finn rubbed his eyes. "I'll never remember them all."

"No one expects you to memorize all the names instantly! It's like forty people — "

"*Forty?* Are you kidding me?"

Rory grimaced. "Close to it, anyway."

Finn set his bowl of casserole down and shot Rory a pleading look. "I can't do this. What if we stay home today and...and use your special present?"

Rory flushed. "As tempting as that sounds, I can't skip my family Christmas... At least Jackson will be lost in the crowd?" Their smile faltered at the expression on Finn's face. "Listen..." Rory put down their bowl and took Finn's face in their hands. "You are smart and sweet and gorgeous and an extremely generous lover..."

That got a chuckle from Finn. "Let's not bring that up today, though?"

Rory smiled and tucked one of Finn's curls behind his ear. "Only if things are going really badly."

* * * *

Davis took their coats again, then Finn was loose in the lion's den. Three small boys came screeching through the foyer wielding toy space weapons, one of which nearly took Finn's eye out.

"That's Leo and Troy, my cousin Steffie's kids, and my cousin Xavier," Rory explained as the boys charged up the stairs.

Finn nodded and filed that away. *Leo, Troy, Steffie, Xavier. Got it.*

A harried woman with pink ends to her long blonde hair appeared in the foyer, watching the boys disappear at the top of the stairs. "*Leo!*" she bellowed. "*What did I just tell you?*"

"Sorry, Mom!" came the faint reply.

The woman groaned, then saw Rory. "Hey, Rory. Merry Christmas!"

"Merry Christmas to you," Rory replied, returning her hug. "Finn, this is my cousin, Steffie. Steffie, this is my partner, Finn."

She hugged Finn too. "Welcome to the family! My wife, Mikala, is somewhere around here, and I'm sure she could commiserate with you about joining this shit show." A crash from above startled them all. "*Leo!*" she hollered again. "I *swear* to *God!*" She sighed. "See you two in a bit." Steffie stormed up the stairs, muttering under her breath.

"Well, okay!" Rory said. "Look at that, you've already met four people!"

Finn gave them a wry look as they made their way into the house. There was a snack buffet set out in the living room where most of the adults appeared to have gathered. Finn waved at Griffin, who was on the couch talking to a few others Finn didn't know yet. Rory's dad was grazing at the table…and he was wearing a dark-green cable-knit sweater almost identical to Finn's.

"Merry Christmas!" Jonathan said when he saw them. He came over carrying a small plate of charcuterie. "Great sweater." He winked at Finn.

Rory hugged him, then Finn shook his hand. "Thank you, sir. Love yours, too."

"Help yourself to a drink," Jonathan said, pointing his plate at the bar. "There's eggnog and mulled cider in the kitchen, too. Make sure you have some. You know how your mother gets if no one drinks the cider."

"Thanks, Dad." Rory took Finn's hand and smiled up at him. "Ready?"

Rory's smile still made his heart flutter. Finn nodded. He could do this. For Rory.

* * * *

Two hours later, Finn's head was spinning. He'd had two glasses of eggnog and one cider, four plates of baking and snacks, met at least twenty people and already forgotten half of their names.

"I need to use the washroom," he told Rory, desperate for a few moments to himself.

Rory could tell. "There's one way down at the far end, by the laundry room. It'll be quieter down there."

Finn left Rory with their Aunt Miriam and a grateful peck on the cheek.

The chatter and bursts of laughter faded behind him as he found his way down the long hall and into the silent reaches of the far wing. Then he heard a low voice from the laundry room. Peeking around the corner, Jackson's frame came into view.

"I don't care what Jonathan told you," Jackson said, hushed but angry. "*I'm* fucking telling you it's not good enough. This better be handled by tomorrow or don't bother coming to work tomorrow." Jackson hung up his phone with a huff. Finn should have ducked past the door into the washroom before Jackson could see him, but he wasn't fast enough.

Jackson raised his eyebrows but didn't seem all that surprised to find Finn watching him. "Secretaries, am I right?" He stuffed his phone in his pocket with a smirk and stepped closer, the smell of beer wafting off him. "So. Finn. I wanted to apologize for yesterday."

Finn blinked. Not what he was expecting. "Oh?"

"Yeah, it was rude of me to talk about money. I know, Amy's always giving me shit about it."

"Well, thanks."

Jackon leaned against the doorway and tilted his head. "Doesn't change anything, though, does it?"

A stone dropped in Finn's stomach. "What do you mean?"

A reptilian smile crept over Jackson's face. "It doesn't change the fact that Rory comes from money, and you don't." His gaze flicked to Finn's sweater, the beautiful gift from Luka. "My dad's sweater probably cost a grand. But it's cute that you tried."

With his heart thudding, Finn's tongue turned to dust while Jackson watched him with glittering eyes. Suddenly, Finn was seven again, going to school in the snow in old running shoes with holes in the bottom and nothing but crackers in his lunch kit. He turned and made a break for the bathroom, face burning with humiliation. He slammed the door behind him and gripped the sides of the counter, trying to take deep breaths to quell the rising nausea. *Did I just…run away from that man? Jesus, Finn.*

A quiet knock at the door a minute later interrupted his panic. "Finn? Finn, are you okay? It's Griffin."

"I'm fine," Finn rasped.

"You sure?"

Finn studied his reflection. *Get it together, Owens. It's fucking Christmas in Rory's house.* "One minute." He splashed water on his face, patted it dry with one of the thick rolled up hand towels and opened the door for Griffin.

"Hey." Griffin's face was a picture of concern. He slipped in and closed the door behind him. "Jackson came out of the hall like the old cat that ate the fucking canary. What did he say to you?"

"Nothing." Finn tossed the towel into the waiting basket.

Griffin threw his hands out. "Fuck Jackson, all right? That guy is a dick."

Finn huffed a ghost of a laugh. "That's what I tried to tell Rory, but they disagreed."

Griffin snorted, leaning against the sink. "Rory is too fucking nice for their own good. Jackson used to put my underwear in the freezer and fart in my face. 'Dick' doesn't even begin to cover it. Come on, what did he say to you?"

Finn shrugged a shoulder. "That I'm not good enough for Rory, basically." He waved at his shirt. "My sweater is cheap."

"God." Griffin shook his head. "Look, Finn. Am I a spoiled brat? Yes. But I admit it. Jackon is a spoiled brat who thinks his shit don't stink. You can't let him get to you."

"He's kind of right, though. Rory is...amazing. And I'm just me."

"Yeah, Rory's all right. But so are you." Griffin grinned and tousled Finn's hair. "Now let's go back to the party. Rory will be wondering where you are."

Right on cue, Rory appeared as soon as they emerged from the bathroom.

"Finn! There you are." They slid an arm around Finn and tucked themselves up against his side. "Everything okay?"

Griffin waited for Finn to answer.

"Yup. Fine. I just ate too much." Finn smiled and patted his stomach.

"Oh, I hear you. Did you have any of Miriam's peanut-butter balls? To die for."

"Nah, those are all for me." Griffin slapped Finn on the shoulder and headed down the hall toward the noise.

"You're sure you're fine?" Rory said, pausing to look up at Finn with their deep, dark eyes.

Finn kissed their nose. "Completely. Let's go wrestle some peanut-butter balls away from Griffin."

* * * *

Finn avoided Jackson like the plague the rest of the afternoon, and he was relieved to find that Lainey had seated Jackson at the opposite end of the dinner table from him and Rory. They were sitting across from Steffie and Mikala, happily child-free, with Leo and Troy at the kids' table in the kitchen. Finn was next to Rory's cousin Dimitri, who was lovely with his French accent and musical laugh.

But Finn knew he was in a funk. Rory shot him at least three concerned glances before the turkey was even served, so he did his best to shake it off and get to know the people around him.

"So," Finn said to Dimitri, "you grew up in France?"

"*Oui*," he replied with a dazzling smile. Dimitri actually reminded him a lot of Luka. "I decided to come with my parents when they moved back to Oakport. We all missed our family."

"Do you miss France, though?" Finn asked, reaching for his wine glass.

"Some things, *peut-être*. But Oakport is a beautiful city and I am happy to be here with *mes chiens*."

"Oh, that's right, Rory mentioned you have four dogs?"

"That is correct." Dimitri laughed. "It is too many, *je sais*. But I love them. Do you have any pets, Finn?"

"No, none for me. There would be animal hair stuck in all my paintings."

"Oh, you are an artist?"

Dimitri asked Finn lots of questions, and the conversation flowed easily in between bites of the best Christmas dinner Finn had ever eaten. Rory was smiling, giving Finn's knee a squeeze under the table every now and then.

It was so pleasant that Finn managed to forget what Jackson said...almost.

* * * *

This time when Finn closed the truck door behind him, he didn't say a word.

"You did so good, babe," Rory said, leaning over the seat to kiss Finn's shoulder. "They all loved you so much."

Jackson's words came roaring back. *It's cute that you tried.*

"Yeah," Finn replied, attempting to smile.

"I told you they would," Rory continued. "Casper even told me how awesome you were."

"Casper?" Finn frowned. "Which one was Casper?"

"You know, my cousin Casper? Andre's son? In the purple sweater?"

Finn's eyes widened. "That was Casper? Noooo."

"What?"

"I called him Cam all night."

"Oh. Um, Cam was the one in the green polo."

"Oh my God. Oh my God, Rory! I called him Cam like five times! Why didn't he correct me?"

Rory tried not to laugh. "He probably didn't want to make you feel bad."

Finn thunked his head on the steering wheel. "Well, now I feel ten times worse."

"Hey, if that's your biggest mistake, you did great." Rory rubbed his back.

Finn groaned. "Can we go back in there and tell them all what a generous lover I am?"

Rory leaned closer to murmur in Finn's ear. "How about we go home and you show me?"

Chapter Seventeen

Big Drama in Little Italy

Finn peeked around the doorframe into their bedroom. Rory was examining their outfit in the full-length mirror—the sexy black pants that were half silver-buckled kilt were making another appearance.

"You look hot," Finn announced, gaze traveling over the curves of Rory's lower half.

Rory's eyes flicked over to meet Finn's in the mirror. "Thanks, love. So do you."

Finn came up behind Rory and wrapped his arms around them, burying his nose under their ear. "You smell good, too." He slid his hands under Rory's shirt.

Laughing, Rory swatted them away. "Hey, none of that. We have a dinner reservation to make."

"I know," Finn grumbled. Not that he wasn't grateful that Rory had planned a special New Year's Eve surprise for him…

Rory chuckled, turning around to give Finn a kiss. "You're going to love it. I promise."

Finn had no idea where they were going, even once their cab took an exit ramp off the highway into downtown.

"Close your eyes!" Rory sang when they rolled up to a traffic light.

"Hmph," Finn muttered, but he did it. A few more turns, and the car stopped.

"Take my hand," Rory said. "I'll help you climb out."

"Seriously?"

"No peeking!" Rory's warm grip was comforting.

When Finn was standing on the sidewalk, eyes scrunched shut and curiosity fully piqued, Rory announced, "Open!"

Finn blinked up at the brick façade, not sure exactly where he was until he saw the sign for the imposing wine bar with black and scarlet walls.

Where we first met.

"Oh," Finn said, at a loss for words, eyes watering in the winter air.

Rory's smile made his heart want to explode. "I thought we could start the new year together at the place...where we started."

Finn blinked away a tear and slung his arm around Rory's shoulders. "Did we start here?"

"Yes," Rory said without missing a beat. "The moment I saw you."

"All right," Finn said, voice gruff. "Let's do it."

The hostess led them to a high-top table and scanned their tickets, which included a buffet dinner, live music, and bottomless sparkling wine.

"I love it," Finn said, once the server dropped off their first glasses of bubbly. "Thank you for planning our New Year's."

"You're welcome," Rory said, tapping their glasses together. "Cheers."

* * * *

"So…" Rory said after dinner, scooping up the last bite of brownie from their plate. "Any New Year's resolutions for you this year?"

Finn shrugged. "I don't usually make them. Damn, this is good." He licked his lips and went for another bite of chocolate mousse. "You?"

Rory paused to suck the last of the icing from their fork. "I'd like to spend more time outside."

"Oh yeah? Doing what?" Finn grinned. "You want to join me on my runs?"

"God, no." Rory laughed. "But that bike ride was fun. I feel like I need more…trees. Nature." Their fork flashed out to stab a raspberry on Finn's plate.

Finn gasped in fake indignation. "Are you stealing my dessert?"

Rory went for another berry. "No. I would never."

Their forks battled as they raced to finish Finn's plate. Finn swallowed his final bite and reached to brush a streak of chocolate off Rory's smiling lip. "Would you like to dance?"

Rory took Finn's hand. "Yes."

They danced for a few numbers on the crowded floor, the band rocking solid Top Forty covers, until a slow song came on. Rory slipped into Finn's arms.

Finn closed his eyes and breathed Rory in, his stomach swirling with the same butterflies he always got when Rory was close.

"So, my mom's birthday is coming up…" Rory said.

Finn opened his eyes. "That's what you want to talk about right now?"

Rory chuckled sheepishly. "Sorry, it just popped into my head that I forgot to call her back earlier. Are you free on the tenth? My parents always host a dinner at their favorite restaurant."

Finn's stomach swirled again but not in a good way. "Man..."

"I know, I know, we just had Christmas... Sorry."

"Will..." *Will Jackson be there?* "Is it the whole family again?"

"No, only my mom's side this time."

'Only.' Finn wanted to want to go so badly. He wished the 'yes' could roll right off his tongue. He wanted to be there for Rory. He wanted to feel comfortable surrounded by a hundred relatives — like he belonged in a family like that.

'It's cute that you tried.'

Finn took a breath. "Would it be the worst thing if I didn't go?"

Rory's face fell. "Birthdays are a really big deal in my family. If you weren't there..."

Fuck. "I'm just not used to celebrating every holiday and milestone with so many people."

"I know, but..." Rory's eyes turned up to max power. "Maybe you can get used to it?"

Fuuuuck.

Rory must have been able to sense Finn's resolve weakening. "So you'll go?" they said hopefully.

Be a grownup, Finn. Be there for Rory. "I'll go."

"You're the best," Rory murmured, snuggling under Finn's chin.

"No, you are," Finn replied.

He held Rory close and they danced.

* * * *

When they got back to their table, the server dropped off another round of drinks.

Finn studied Rory in the dim bar lighting as they lifted the flute to their lips. They were perhaps the most beautiful human alive — gentle, elfin features, eyes bottomless pools, plump lips, piercings shining around the curve of their delicate ears. Finn's heart fizzed like it was overflowing with champagne bubbles. "You want to get out of here?" he asked.

Rory checked the time and laughed. "It's only eleven! We'll miss the countdown. We're supposed to go up to the roof to see the fireworks at midnight."

Finn lifted Rory's hand to his lips and kissed their knuckles. "Yeah, but here's the thing — we can make our own fireworks at midnight."

The color rose in Rory's cheeks. "Then get me the fuck out of here, Finn Owens."

It was easy to get a cab, because what kind of idiot left downtown at eleven on New Year's Eve? They held hands and played footsie in the backseat like teenagers. Then when they got home, they reenacted their first night together, slamming the door behind them and tearing off their clothes on the way to the bedroom. It turned out the buckles on Rory's kilt were only decorative.

And the fireworks that exploded behind Finn's eyes were a thousand times better than the pathetic bursts of color popping over the city.

* * * *

They slept late on New Year's Day, then Finn brought coffee back to bed for Rory. He was just wiggling back under the covers to join the warm Rory bubble when his phone buzzed. His stomach curdled at his sister's name on the screen. But there was no message, only a picture. It was Cali and Bryson, smiling and displaying their Lego creations. Cali held a sign that said 'Thank you, Uncle Finn.'

His heart hurt.

You're welcome, he typed. *Hope you had a good Christmas.*

"Aw, look at them!" Rory said, examining the picture. "So cute! How old are they?"

"Bryson is seven, I think, and Cali must be ten." A thought popped into Finn's head. He turned it over for a moment, then shared it with Rory. "You know what my resolution should be? Maybe I should try to see them."

Rory's eyes shone. "I think that's a great idea, Finn. They would be so happy to see you again, I'm sure."

Finn nodded, pulling Rory against his chest. "Okay. I'll...I'll think about it." They sipped their coffee in silence for a moment. "You want to go for a walk?" Finn asked once he had drained his mug. "Work on that resolution of yours?"

Rory shook their head. "Not at the moment. It's awfully snowy out there."

Finn wanted to laugh, then Rory's mouth was on his, and there was no more talking...at least not about the weather.

* * * *

Back at work after the holiday and headed for a much-needed coffee refill, Finn popped his head into Rory's office. "Did you see the email from Markos?" he asked. "Sorry, the seven emails?"

"Sure did." Rory paused their typing and turned to face Finn. "Did he seem a little…"

"Unhinged?"

Rory laughed. "I was going to say intense, but yeah."

"I mean, remodeling my house was stressful and he's remodeling an entire amusement park. I get it. A lot of moving parts."

Rory clicked open their calendar. "Are you free for a call with him this afternoon? Probably easier than trying to respond to all the emails."

Finn nodded. "Sure. I'll see if he's available." He emailed back to arrange a call at two o'clock and joined Rory in their office again when it was time.

"Markos." An annoyed voice answered the phone.

"Markos, hi. This is Finn Owens from Breakpoint. Thanks so much for fitting us in today. How was your holid—"

"Yeah, it was great, how was yours, good, great. Let me tell you about this fucking boat ride—"

Finn and Rory exchanged a look.

"—You don't mind if I swear, do you? Good. This fucking boat ride—the goddamned pipes burst in that cold snap last week, so now I'm up to my ass in glacier water and I've got a guy coming in tomorrow to rip the whole thing out—"

"You're ripping out the boat ride?" Rory repeated, aghast. "Markos…are you sure you can't fix it?

"I'm on the phone," Markos snapped, a little muffled. "What? No! No, it's not slate, it's *stone*! I ordered fucking stone! Did he—? Goddamn it. Give me a minute." His voice got louder again. "I'm done with it. We'll put in a nice little... I don't know what. Why don't you two figure that out? Listen, I've got another fucking crisis on my hands. Call me when you've got some suggestions." Then he was gone.

Finn and Rory stared at each other.

"Um..." Rory ventured.

"Yeah..." Finn agreed, rubbing his beard.

"I can't believe he wants to get rid of that boat ride." Rory sighed. "It was so romantic, the shadows rippling over your face, the smell of the honeysuckle, the water rippling... I wanted to kiss you so badly."

"You're the cutest ever." Finn couldn't resist leaning over to give Rory a peck on the cheek.

"Oh, stop," Rory said, with an adorable head tilt and nose scrunch. "But I'm not wrong, am I? I wish he would keep it."

"Let's draft an email with the stuff you just said and send it off today. Maybe we can change his mind."

Finn wasn't expecting Markos to reply until the next day at the earliest, but his inbox dinged moments after he hit send, before he even left Rory's office.

I told you to come up with something new. No boat ride.

That was it. No greeting, no sign off, nothing.

"Well, fuck," Finn said, showing the message to Rory.

Rory stuck out their lower lip. "That sucks."

"Yeah. Guess we need to come up with something else!"

"Any ideas?"

"Not yet."

Rory leaned back in their chair. "What about all his emails, too? I thought he wanted to go over all that website design stuff with us and give us some notes on the commercials."

Finn sighed. He had a feeling there were more problems ahead with Markos besides a leaky boat ride.

* * * *

Finn changed his outfit three times, stomach in knots. First, he put on his favorite dress shirt—a soft, long-sleeved navy—then he changed into his most expensive shirt—a designer label he'd gotten at an outlet—then thought *fuck that* and changed back into his favorite.

"I love that color on you," Rory said when they saw Finn getting ready.

"Thanks," Finn said, smoothing curl cream through his hair.

Rory leaned against the bathroom door frame. "Do you want to drive or get a cab? This place has some really amazing wine…"

"I'll drive," Finn said. He wanted to keep his wits about him if Jackson was going to be there.

The Barretts had bought out an entire restaurant in Little Italy for Lainey's birthday. *Of course*, Finn thought when he saw the *Closed for a private function* sign in the window.

A host greeted them and took their coats, and a server offered a glass of champagne from a tray.

Suddenly Finn really wanted a beer. One or two drinks early in the night wouldn't hurt.

"Do you have anything else?" Finn asked her.

Jennifer Moffatt

"Of course, sir," the woman replied. "The menu is posted by the bar."

Finn collected a pint, then he and Rory joined the crowd milling around for drinks and appetizers. It was a relief to find the friendly smiles of Steffie and Mikala in the sea of faces.

"No kids tonight?" Finn asked them.

"Nope! Night out for the moms!" Steffie said gleefully, tapping her glass with Mikala's.

Mikala began a story about the trouble they had finding a babysitter, but Finn didn't hear it, because Jackson walked by. Finn started sweating.

An aunt joined their circle, and once Steffie and Mikala were engaged with her, Rory leaned over to murmur in Finn's ear.

"Is everything okay?" they asked. "You flinched like you took a punch when Jackson appeared."

"Fine," Finn said, avoiding Rory's eyes and taking a long pull of his beer.

"Finn." Rory took Finn's elbow and steered him into a more private corner, then trained their earnest gaze on him. "It's me. What's going on? Is this still about Jackon's money comment?"

Finn laughed, a dry humorless chuckle. "You could say that."

"I thought we sorted this out. He's just obsessed with work."

"It's not that, Rory, it's—" Finn paused and bit his lip.

"Would you just tell me?"

Finn sighed. "I'd rather not. It'll cause problems."

Rory folded their arms. "Well, now you have to tell me. I'm starting to get worried."

"Ugh." Finn rubbed his forehead. "Okay. Remember on Christmas when I went to the washroom and you told me to go down to the one by the laundry room? I ran into Jackson…"

"And?"

"And…he told me I wasn't good enough for you."

"He what?" Rory's eyes flashed. "He fucking *what*? Tell me *exactly* what he said."

Finn recounted the conversation, forcing out the phrase that still haunted him, '*It's cute that you tried.*'

"Oh. Oh *fuck* no." Rory slammed their drink down on a table, spun on their heel and marched straight over to Jackson, who was engaged in conversation with Jonathan and one of Rory's uncles.

"Rory!" Finn whispered, chasing after them. *Fuck.*

They stopped in the center of the circle. "May I speak with you, Jackson?" Rory's voice crackled with barely contained rage.

"Uh…" Jackson cranked an eyebrow up. "I'm in the middle of—"

"Did you actually, *for real*, tell Finn that he's not good enough for me?"

Jonathan and Uncle Alfie—or was it George?—shrank into their collars, eyes wide.

Jackson's gaze flicked to Finn's for a moment, who had come to stand behind Rory's shoulder. Then he frowned and looked back at Rory. "Absolutely not. I never said—"

"Oh, spare me the *bullshit*," Rory spat. "Whatever fucking words you used, did you make Finn feel lesser because of how much *money* we have?"

"I…" Jackson sputtered. "No, I—look, however Finn felt—"

"Fucking *hell*, Jackson. You are the most disgusting, spoiled—"

"Rory!" Lainey appeared at Rory's side, literally clutching her pearls. "What on earth...?"

Rory shook their head. "I'm sorry, Mom. I really am. I know it's your birthday. But I can't even *look* at Jackson right now. I will not sit at the same table as him."

Finn's heart soared.

Jackson rolled his eyes. "Give me a break, Rory. You don't have to be so—"

"So what, Jackson?" Rory whirled on him, eyes blazing. Finn had never seen Rory so pissed, not even close. It was kind of hot. "So *what*? Please tell me."

The whole room had fallen silent. Even the waitstaff had stilled, gripping their trays. Now was not the time to be offering stuffed mushrooms.

"So"—Jackon's jaw flapped—"uptight about it. I only said what Finn already knows." He drew his shoulders up. "Now quit making a scene and go sit at the table like an adult."

Rory rocked back on their heels. "Right." They turned to Lainey. "I'm so sorry, Mom. I need to leave. I hope you have a wonderful night but I can't be here. Let's go." Rory took Finn's hand, then they collected their coats from the rack and fled.

The sound of Griffin laughing followed them out into the snow.

Finn could barely keep up with Rory as they marched back to their car.

"Rory..." Finn breathed. "Hang on a second..."

Rory screeched to a halt and turned to face Finn. Their eyes were wet and blacker than the night.

"I…" Finn took hold of Rory's hands. "I love you so fucking much, Rory."

Rory's eyelashes fluttered as they blinked back tears. "I love you too."

They turned to continue walking, holding hands. "I'm sorry about dinner," Finn said after a few steps, muffled in the fresh snow.

"Fuck dinner. Fuck Jackson." Rory glanced up at Finn. "Why didn't you tell me?"

"I know…" Finn ran a hand through his hair. "I didn't want to cause any drama."

Rory snorted. "Fair. That was pretty dramatic."

"Is your mom going to be mad?" Finn asked after a few more steps.

Rory groaned. "Probably." They stopped again, looking up at a restaurant front. "This place has the best poutine. You hungry?"

Finn smiled and gave Rory a soft kiss. "Starving."

Chapter Eighteen

Mess

Rory's face lit up when Finn walked into their office. "Perfect! I was about to message you!"

Finn leaned over for a kiss then perched on the edge of their desk. "What's up?" The question he came in with could wait.

Rory pointed at a screen. "Here is a list of the most popular rides at the top ten theme parks in the US. This one is a list of the most common rides in the country, and this is the top search engine results for amusement park rides. So I cross-referenced them, and I think Thrill Island needs a VR ride."

"Virtual Reality?" Finn frowned. "Do you think Markos would want to invest in something like that?"

"All the big parks have them now." Rory pulled up more pictures of those rides from around the country to illustrate their point. "If he is really looking for a refresh, I think he should consider it."

Finn studied the screens and nodded. "That makes sense...but can we get it installed in time?"

"Markos can buy the actual physical ride ready-made and just plop it in. The biggest job would be programming the experience and I can outsource that."

If anyone could make it happen in time, it was Rory. "The ride could be like an immersive heist experience," Finn said, seeing it in his head, "as if you're in the movie — sneaking in, defeating the security system, being chased by the guards, the getaway car..."

"Love it." Rory's fingers were already busy. "I'll put together a proposal, estimate some costs and we can see what he thinks. Do you want to do some mock-ups?"

"For sure." Finn watched Rory work, but the question he had come in with wouldn't stay put on his tongue. "I actually came in here to ask... Did you talk to your mom?" Rory had been planning to call their mom over the lunch break. It had been three days since the birthday dinner blow-up and they'd been putting it off.

Rory's fingers stopped. "No," they said in a low voice. "But I will tonight. I promise... You have to make me call, okay?"

Finn leaned over to kiss the top of their head. "Okay."

* * * *

Rory got up from the couch when the episode of *Godstrike* ended and collected the remnants of dinner from the coffee table. "You want anything for the next episode, babe? A drink? I could make some popcorn?"

Finn tilted his head. "You have to call her, love."

Rory groaned and plunked their plates back on the table. "I don't want to."

"I know, but..."

"But I have to." They took a deep breath and picked up their phone.

"Proud of you," Finn said, doing his best to sound gentle yet encouraging.

"Ugh." Rory pressed a button and started pacing while it rang, raking a hand through their hair. "Hi, Mom... I'm fine, how are you?"

The rise and fall of Lainey's voice reached Finn, but not any specific words.

"I know... I know, Mom. I'm sorry, I—" Rory stopped by the door to the kitchen and pinched the bridge of their nose, listening. "Yes. I know. Can I—" They shot a look at Finn, grimacing.

Finn gave a sympathetic grimace back, unable to do much more.

Rory resumed their pacing. The tempo of Lainey's voice increased. "I understand that, Mom, and I'm sorry. I know it was your birthday. But Jackson... Mom... How can you *defend* him when he—" Rory stopped and stared out of the window, shaking their head. "He *did* though, Mom! He *did* mean to belittle the person I love... Yes, of course I love Finn! We are in love, Mom. Are you f—are you *kidding* me right now?"

Despite the anguish on Rory's face, Finn melted a little. *I love you too*, he wanted to whisper.

Rory continued, voice tight. "I will see Jackson again when he apologizes. It's as simple as that... No, he hasn't so much as texted... Mmhmm. That's fine... Well, we'll see, won't we? Okay... Okay. Yeah. Bye."

Rory turned. Their eyes were wet.

Finn opened his arms.

Rory fell into Finn's lap. "She said he's going to call me," they mumbled into Finn's shoulder.

"Okay." Finn smoothed Rory's hair.

"That was so hard. I never fight with my mom."

"I know." Finn's stomach twisted. Rory had stormed out of their mom's birthday party because of him. Rory was arguing with their mom because of *him*. He should never have told Rory what Jackson said. He should never have—

"I hate this feeling. I hope Jackson calls soon." Rory sniffled.

"I hope so too."

"Now can we watch some more *Godstrike*?"

"Yes, love. I'll go make popcorn."

* * * *

"Rory, Finn!" Markos burst into the conference room and shook their hands even more enthusiastically than at their last meeting. Finn pictured him holding a wooden puppet. "Great to see you two. I looked at the proposal you sent over and I love it. *Love* the VR idea." He heaved himself into a chair.

"That's great! We're exc—" Finn started to reply.

Markos steamrolled ahead. "But I also think we need to keep the boat ride."

"You...you what?" Finn's voice squeaked up a register.

"I know, I know." Markos chuckled. "You caught me on a bad day before. That thing drives me crazy, but since I had to get the pipes fixed anyway, I'm doing a full upgrade to the plumbing."

"Well, that's...that's great!" Rory jumped in, beaming, while Finn floundered for a response. "Your guests will be thrilled."

"And don't worry"—Markos waved a hand—"we don't need to use the boat ride space for the VR. I have the perfect spot. The arcade is way past its prime. Let's use that lot for the new ride. We can have an arcade set up in the exit."

"That sounds great!" Rory said, nudging Finn with their foot under the table. "Finn, did you want to show Markos your sketches?"

"Yes. Yup. So…" Finn opened up his portfolio. "It starts with the riders gathering in the tech van—you know the old nondescript, windowless van filled with computer screens where two people sit and support the heist team?"

"I'm with you, Finn." Markos' eyes shone as he studied Finn's drawings. "Tell me all about it."

Before their meeting ended, Markos also approved the TV commercials they'd be running and newspaper ads for the local area. "And we're opening March ninth," he informed them. "I've confirmed that with the contractors and all my suppliers."

"And…when is the *soft* open?" Finn hedged.

"Nah." Markos scoffed. "Not needed. We'll be good to go for the grand opening."

Rory's eyes bulged. "You don't…you don't want to do a few days with friends and family just to make sure—"

"Rory, please. I've been doing this my whole life. I learned to walk in the fucking park. My first word was 'roller coaster.' We'll do a few test runs on the new ride, and Rory will test the app, right? It'll be business as usual."

"I'll definitely test it, but—"

"Perfect. March ninth."

* * * *

When Markos left, Finn propped his head on the table with one hand and rubbed the back of his neck with the other.

"You okay?" Rory asked.

"Yeah, just got some whiplash from the boat ride one-eighty. Not to mention...no soft open?"

"Yeah." Rory grimaced. "I really wish he would do one. Seems like a no-brainer."

Finn groaned. "I have a headache."

"Poor baby," Rory said. "How about I give you a backrub when we get home?"

"Yeah, okay," Finn said, slightly mollified.

"At least we get to keep the boat ride, right?"

Oh, Rory. Ever optimistic. "Yeah, for now, until he changes his mind again."

Rory gave Finn the promised backrub when they got home...but every time their phone made a noise, Rory jumped a mile. As the days passed, Finn could tell it was eating Rory alive.

Because Jackson never called.

* * * *

"Hey, stranger."

Finn looked up from his desk. Luka. For some reason, seeing his friend's bright blue eyes and soft smile in his doorway made Finn want to crumble. "Hey, bud."

"It's *Luka*." Luka frowned and pointed at himself. "Remember me?"

"I know your name, smart-ass."

"Good, good, just making sure you haven't forgotten me. You free for a lunch date?"

"Sure." Finn dropped his pen and shuffled some papers into a stack. "You don't need to eat with Thomas today?"

Luka sniffed. "You don't need to eat with Rory today?"

Finn studied Luka for a moment. "Thomas had a meeting, didn't he?"

"No, he—Yeah, he did."

* * * *

Luka moaned about his shoes getting wrecked through slushy piles of snow the whole way to Montagu's, but as soon as they sat with their sandwiches, he turned his blue gaze onto Finn with an intensity that made the redhead squirm.

"So?" Luka cracked open his soda. "Talk. Something is bothering you."

Not much got by him. "Oh, nothing. Only that Rory's family hates me."

Luka froze, can halfway to his mouth. He set it down again. "Finn. There's no way that is true. Come on, being a drama queen is my thing."

"I'm not being dramatic." He told Luka the whole story—Jackson at Christmas, Lainey's birthday disaster, the follow-up phone call and the deafening lack of a subsequent apology from Jackson. "Rory's family is a mess," he summarized, "and it's all because of me."

Luka put his sandwich down and wiped his mouth. "First of all, Jackson is a fucking prick, obviously. Second, every family's a mess. They'd be fighting over something, whether you were there or not. My mom and sister fight over fruit snacks."

"But this isn't a fight, like I insulted Lainey's china or something, or even that I swear too much. It's that I don't belong in that family."

"Finn." Luka rubbed his forehead. "Listen to me. Fuck Rory's family. Fuck them. They don't matter."

"Yes, they do, they —"

Luka held up a hand. "Oh my God, are we going to do this again? Do you love Rory? Yes. Does Rory love you? Yes. Everything else is bullshit."

Luka looked so certain. Finn wanted to believe him. "I hope you're right."

"Of course I'm right. Have I ever steered you wrong?"

"Well, there was the time —"

"Besides that time!" Luka huffed before Finn could finish his sentence.

Finn grinned. "Thanks, Luka."

"You are welcome, as always."

"So how are things going with Thomas?" Finn had to ask.

"Still no 'things,' because as I keep telling you —"

"Yeah, yeah, he's your boss. But...?"

Luka couldn't fight the smile that took over his face. "We're getting to be pretty good friends. We text and stuff... He actually... He's convinced me to sign up for an open mic night."

"No shit! That's amazing! Good for you."

"I don't know if I can actually get up there though... What if I throw up? What if they throw...muffins at me?"

"Muffins?"

"Oh, it's a coffee shop."

"No one's going to throw muffins at you."

Luka's eyes widened. "You don't think they'll throw *coffee* at me, do you?"

Finn snickered. "No, drama queen. I don't think so."

* * * *

The Breakpoint staff went to the Bitter Exchange after work the next night, and Rory and Finn ended up at a table with Luka and Thomas. The electricity between them made the hairs on Finn's arm stand up.

Thomas, looking so handsome as always in his exquisitely tailored suit, never took his eyes off Luka, and Luka's face radiated such beauty when he smiled at Thomas that Finn could barely look at them. The two of them hooking up had to be only a matter of time.

So, when the news came at the end of January that Thomas' last day in their office would be March first, Finn's stomach dropped. "Shit." He showed the email to Rory in the seat next to him on the train.

Rory gasped. "Oh no. Oh...Luka will be devastated."

"He *has* to say something," Finn said. "He can't let Thomas just leave. They're clearly into each other. He must know that Thomas feels the same."

"I don't think he does though," Rory said. "Sometimes it's not obvious when you're in it, remember?" They winked at Finn.

"Should I talk to him?" Finn asked.

"Maybe." Rory took Finn's arm and tipped their head onto Finn's shoulder. "Let's see how he handles it."

* * * *

He didn't handle it well. Luka moped around the office, head down, sparkle gone from his eyes. His clothes were even more subdued, all blues and grays, not a pink or yellow to be seen. Finn had to step in.

"Are we going to talk about it?" he asked in early February when he found Luka alone in his office. He closed the door behind him.

Luka sighed and pushed back from his desk. "Talk about what?"

Finn shook his head. "Gonna make me say it?"

"I don't know what you're talking about, Finn."

"Your undying love for Thomas." Finn gave him half of a mischievous smirk, gaze still gentle.

Luka closed his eyes. "I don't... We're not— It's not..."

"Yeah, except you do, you are, and it is."

"Fuck." Luka slumped in his chair. "Am I that obvious?"

"Yes, but if it makes you feel any better, Thomas is into you, and it is equally as obvious."

"What?" Luka shook his head. "He is?"

Finn groaned and pinched the bridge of his nose. "Jesus. I knew you were thick. Rory tried to warn me. Look. It's clear as day that he likes you back, just as much as you like him. You gotta say something. You're killing us."

Luka shook his head again. "He's leaving in less than three weeks, and in the meantime, he's still my boss. I can't. Now would be the worst time ever."

Finn wanted to shake him. "Well, you don't gotta marry the guy. Looks like he'd be good in bed."

Luka covered his face and groaned. "I can't even tell you how much I am not about to proposition Thomas for a quick romp in the sack before he leaves."

"Why not? Wait till his last day. If he's leaving, doesn't matter if he says yes or no."

"I don't just want to sleep with him, Finn. I…"

"You what?"

Luka exhaled. "Nothing. Thanks for your help. But I can't."

Finn narrowed his eyes at Luka. "This from the guy who told me to take the plunge with Rory."

"It's totally different!"

"Is it?"

"Of course it is."

Finn shrugged. "Think about it. You don't want him to leave and regret not even trying."

"I appreciate your thoughts, Finn, but… It's complicated."

"All right. Just…think about it, yeah? It might work out. And it might be amazing."

Luka didn't say anything, only gave him a sad smile and went back to work.

Finn wanted his friend to be happy…but… 'It's complicated.' Well, he was right about that. Everything was complicated.

Chapter Nineteen

Hearts

Jackson didn't call, Rory grew more and more miserable and it ate at Finn until his skin felt two sizes too small.

"Since you planned New Year's, can I plan Valentine's Day?" Finn asked one night while they were making dinner.

"Sure," Rory said, staring morosely into the stew as they stirred.

"Great, here's my plan." Finn took their wrist and spun them around, pressing them up against the counter with his hips.

Rory looked up at him, lips parted.

"I'm going to make dinner for you" — Finn rumbled, with a kiss to their neck — "and feed you every bite" — he kissed the other side — "then I'm going to devour *you*." Finn nibbled at Rory's earlobe, then whispered exactly what his lips and teeth and tongue would do to Rory for his Valentine's Day meal.

"That, uh…" Rory stammered, cheeks pink. "That sounds good."

Finn grinned. "I thought so."

* * * *

If Rory was struggling, though, Luka was the picture of misery. They had a staff meeting on Valentine's Day for an update on the Sartini campaign. Luka was literally dressed all in black and spent the entire meeting staring at the bowls of pink and red heart-shaped chocolates Tawney had placed along the center of the table.

"Before we finish up here," Ilona said once they had all checked in, "I have some news." She paused until she had everyone's full attention. "Aleandro has extended our contract for another four months! Congratulations, everyone. You should be proud of your exceptional work."

Finn's attention went straight to Luka, of course, whose head had snapped over to stare at Thomas. Luka's face was aglow, like a dying man given new life. Thomas was looking at his hands, a slow smile spreading across his face.

A wave of claps and small cheers swept through the room.

"Aw, yeah!" Finn crowed as he high-fived Rory. He was celebrating for Luka, of course, although the Sartini thing was nice too.

"Does this mean Thomas is staying?" Rory asked.

Thomas nodded. He looked up at Luka instead of Rory. And, oh, the way they fucking smiled at each other.

* * * *

Finn slapped Luka on the back as they left the conference room. "Congrats, boys. You guys crushed it."

"We all crushed it," Luka corrected him, bouncing on his toes. "We need to celebrate! Who's free for a drink after work?"

Finn laughed. "Sorry, Moreno. Valentine's Day, remember? We've got plans." Finn looked at Rory, thoughts of all the things he planned to do to them flashing through his mind. Rory clearly had the same thoughts, because they blushed furiously.

"Oh. Right. Well, I don't have any plans." Luka looked at Thomas. "Do you?"

Thomas shook his head. "No."

"Okay, this might be crazy, but...do you want to grab a drink anyway?"

Finn rolled his eyes behind Thomas' back, but he was actually proud of Luka for doing *something*.

"Uh..." Thomas looked a little panicked.

"Just to Exchange or something," Luka said, voice climbing.

Thomas nodded. "Sure."

"You two have fun on your date," Finn said, waggling his eyebrows.

"Thanks, Finn," Luka said through his teeth.

"Oh, those two," Finn said, once Luka and Thomas were safely out of earshot.

He started to say more, but Rory pushed him up against the wall and gave him a kiss that made him forget all about Luka and Thomas.

* * * *

As soon as they got home, Finn started putting together the dinner he had planned. With the spring rolls in the oven, he turned to offer Rory some wine. They were scowling at their phone.

"What's up?" Finn asked.

"My mom," Rory muttered. Their gaze dropped to Finn's socked feet. "Doesn't that bother you?" they asked.

Finn looked down. "Doesn't what bother me?"

"Your socks don't match."

"They don't?" Finn frowned and wiggled his toes. "Eh, close enough. They're both black."

"Yeah, but one has stripes around the ankle and one doesn't."

Finn laughed. "It doesn't bother me at all. Does it bother you?"

"No," they said in a way that sounded very much like 'yes.'

"Okay. Do y—"

"Bailey's birthday is coming up." The words tumbled from Rory's lips, their eyes still down.

"Oh." Finn leaned back against the counter. "*Oh*."

"Yeah."

"So…" Finn's heart scrunched into a ball. "You want to go."

"Yes." It was a short, hollow sound.

"Even though Jackson never called," Finn said, needing to say it out loud.

Rory's eyes snapped up to meet Finn's, two pools of emotion. "I have to, Finn. It's killing me."

"I know," Finn said softly. The kitchen was silent around them as they stared at each other. "Do you also get why I can't go?"

"I don't want to go without you, though."

Finn sighed. "I can't, Rory."

"Finn...Jackson is my brother. My brother, okay?" Rory sat up straighter, voice filling the room. "He's in my life forever. I know you've cut off your entire family—"

Finn recoiled like he'd been slapped. "That's not fair."

"Oh no?" Rory spread their arms wide and looked around. "What happened to your New Year's Resolution? Where are they? Where are Cali and Bryson? Your sister? Your mom?"

Acid rose up Finn's throat. He stared at Rory, at a loss for words. "Yeah. I, uh..."

Rory sighed. "Finn—"

"No, you're right. Clearly, I don't get how families work. Listen, I'm not very hungry. The spring rolls will be done in about twenty minutes and there's lemon chicken in the fridge. I'm going to...go for a walk."

Rory didn't stop him on his way out of the door.

* * * *

Finn wandered the darkened streets of his neighborhood a while, imagining every glowing window containing a happy couple enjoying their Valentine's Day. And here he was. Alone. Like an idiot.

He pulled out his phone.

His sister answered right away. "Finn? What—? Are you okay?"

"Hi, Liz. I'm fine."

"Pardon the language...but why the fuck are you calling?"

"Yeah, uh... Sorry to bother you on Valentine's Day."

"Oh, yes, I'm in the middle of some big romantic plans—helping Cali with her math homework while I make chicken noodle soup for Bryson 'cause he's got strep throat."

"Sorry to hear that. I hope he feels better soon."

"Yeah." Her sigh whooshed over Finn like she was standing right next to him. "Same."

"So." Finn pushed his hair behind an ear. "The reason I'm calling…"

"Please. Tell me."

"Well… I was thinking about—er, hoping, that is…"

"Finn. Just say it."

"…Hoping that we could figure something out… Well, I'd like to see your kids."

The two seconds of silence nearly killed him.

"Yeah. Yeah, that would be great." The note of surprise in Liz's voice was hard to ignore. "They would love that."

"I could come visit? Or would you want to—"

"They would love to come to Oakport. They've never been."

Now it was Finn's turn to sigh in a whoosh, shoulders sagging in relief. They talked about a few possible weekends coming up and agreed to check their schedules and connect again tomorrow. Finn hung up and took a steadying breath. He had done it. It was happening. Then he looked around. Where the fuck was he? It took him a second but he'd ended up at a small park not too far from his house. He could take Cali and Bryson here to play. He smiled and turned around to head back.

When he got home, dinner had been cleaned up and the house was dark.

Finn crept to the bedroom. The bed was empty. "Rory?" he called toward the bathroom. Not there either. They weren't anywhere. He went back to the kitchen and found a note on the table. *Went home for the night. Let's talk tomorrow. Rory.*

Finn fell into a kitchen chair, chest hollow. *Rory…left. Rory left?*

He replayed their conversation—fight?—in his mind. All he said was he couldn't go to dinner with Jackson, and Rory left. That was how important their family was to them.

Finn had known all along this was a losing battle. So why did it hurt so much when the inevitable happened?

* * * *

Alarm silenced, Finn rolled over and reached for Rory. Rory was not there. He listened for shower or breakfast noises for about eight seconds before he remembered.

Rory left.

He checked his phone. No texts from Rory.

There was one waiting from Luka, though.

Help, I think I just went on a date with Thomas.

You think? Finn replied.

Luka's next message came right away.

I didn't mean for it to be a date!

Okay, but...you asked him for a drink on Valentine's Day.

I'm such an idiot.

A cute idiot though. Did you guys have a good time?

Yes. Fuck. And please do not tell me to hook up with him again.

Finn sent the zipper-mouth emoji

How was your night? Luka asked, with the sly emoji.

Finn tapped the edges of his phone with his thumbs. He didn't want to lie to Luka, but he also didn't want to tell him he spent the night wandering the streets of his neighborhood while Rory abandoned him. Another zipper-mouth emoji would have to do it.

Luka sent a winky face. *Gotcha. See you at work.*

Work. Fuck. He thought about calling in sick to avoid seeing Rory for a hot second, but his inbox was also busting with things he had to do for Sartini and Thrill Island, and taking a day off to feel sorry for himself at home was not really an option. Besides, it was Rory. He shouldn't have to hide from them.

Right?

His heart was not convinced, and by the time he got to work, it was threatening to punch through his ribcage. Despite the nerves, his feet took him straight to Rory's office, because he couldn't imagine sitting in his office working while Rory sat in theirs.

And there they were...typing. Finn knocked on the doorframe.

Rory's face crumpled when they saw Finn. "Hi."

"Hey. Can we talk?" Finn asked.

Rory pushed back from their keyboard. "Of course."

Finn shut the door behind him. "So...you left."

"No..." Rory frowned. "*You* left."

Well...Finn hadn't considered that. "I—I guess I did. I came back though."

Rory shrugged and ran their fingers along the edge of their desk. "I thought you didn't want me there anymore."

"Of course I want you there." Finn resisted the urge to scoop Rory into his arms.

Rory looked up, lower lip trembling. "But you won't go to Bailey's birthday with me?"

And here we are again. "What about Jackson?"

"Things are not done with Jackson, trust me, but I can't punish Bailey for that. She's already been through so much."

"Of course, and I want to support her, too. But I can't go to her party, Rory. I'm not wanted there."

"But—" Rory was interrupted by a sharp rap on the door. "Come in?" they said, blinking rapidly.

The door opened and Ilona's raven head popped into the room. "Finn, Rory, just who I wanted to talk to. I saw the latest email from Markos and the park is looking amazing!"

"Yeah," Finn said, doing his best to ignore the two deep black pools of emotion on Rory's face and flip his brain into work mode. "We're a little behind now since we added the VR ride, but I think the rest of the remodel is about done. Just a few finishing touches."

"Excellent. How about the app, Rory?"

"It's great. I'm scheduling our testing now. I think we should have the user experience team go through the registration flow one more time, and get a group from QA to start some bug testing. I'm still waiting to hear back about API integration with their POS but they gave me a data dump of available fields to put in staging."

Damn, it's hot when they talk like that, Finn's groin observed, despite the turmoil that his heart was in.

The two of them answered a few more of Ilona's questions, then she requested an update in a few days and clacked off down the hall.

They stared at each other, recognizing they had made exactly zero progress. "I should send my notes to Markos," Finn said, chest aching.

"Yup. And I should" — Rory waved a hand at the screen — "do all the things I said."

Finn had to ask though. "Are you…are you going to come home with me tonight?"

Rory's eyes watered with fresh tears. "If you want me to."

"Of course, I do." Never had four words felt so inadequate. *Please or I'll die* was more like it.

"Then yes."

"Chinese and *Godstrike*?"

"Chinese and *Godstrike*."

* * * *

Finn and Rory talked about not much of anything on their way home, but once they were in the kitchen hanging up coats and dropping bags, the words fell from Finn's lips. "I called Liz."

Rory whirled to face him. "You did?"

"Yeah. Last night while I…while I was out on my walk. Then we texted a bit more today. The kids are going to come stay here for the weekend in March."

Rory launched their lithe body at Finn and threw their arms around him. "That's great, Finn. I'm so proud of you. And look, last night, when I said —"

Finn cut them off. "It's okay. You were right."

Then they were kissing, quickly moving from soft and tentative to urgent and needy. Finn picked up Rory and their legs closed around his waist. "Oh, that's right," Finn murmured into Rory's ear. "We had plans last night, didn't we?"

"I believe you were going to devour me?" Rory said, holding Finn even tighter.

"Like I haven't eaten in years," Finn said. He carried Rory down the hall to their bedroom and feasted.

That didn't actually solve any of their problems, though.

Chapter Twenty

Cali and Bryson

Finn squinted at his screen and read the email again. "Wow!" he said to Rory, who was flipping quesadillas in a frying pan. "Markos has invited us to the grand opening. Like, everyone. All of Breakpoint and their families."

"No way!"

"It's the weekend Cali and Bryson are coming."

"That's perfect!" Rory hesitated. "That's the weekend of Bailey's party, too. It's Sunday night."

Right. Bailey's party. They hadn't talked about it since their Valentine's Day fight.

"Oh. Okay. That will be so fun for the kids," Finn said, tactfully steering the conversation away from the abyss.

Rory came to read over Finn's shoulder. "I wonder if I can invite my extended family?"

Finn tried not to grimace. Because of course Rory would want to invite the entire family tree. "Park's looking great though," Finn said, changing the subject again, scrolling through the rest of Markos' email. "What's left for you to do before it all goes live?"

"Just have to submit to the app store and get approval, and we'll do some dry runs at the park this week to see how it works real time in the kitchen. You?"

"Not much. I'm supposed to give notes on the new ride but they haven't sent me the files yet. All the ads are live."

"We're in good shape," Rory said lightly, going back to flipping the quesadillas. "It's all going to be great."

Finn's stomach flipped, too.

* * * *

The next morning at work, Finn was walking back from the washroom when Morgan stalked by. He carried a box with a lamp poking out of it, his face bleak. Finn paused, eyebrow raised, waiting for Morgan to offer a quip or explanation of some sort, but he breezed by like Finn wasn't even there. As soon as the petite blond disappeared around the corner, Finn turned on his heel toward Luka's office.

He poked his head in. "Did I just see Morgan carrying a box of his shit?"

"Um. You sure did." Luka exchanged a look with Thomas. "Do you want to grab a drink after work? It's a long fucking story."

* * * *

"Sorry"—Finn placed his hands flat on the table as if attempting to anchor himself to reality—"you were secretly dating *Morgan* last year?" His head was spinning and it had nothing to do with the pint sitting in front of him.

"Oh my God, I know." Luka buried his face in his hands. "I can hardly believe it myself, and I was there."

"I mean...*Morgan*?" Finn said, voice climbing into his upper register.

"He...he could be really charming, okay? And..." Luka blushed.

Finn held up a hand. "So help me God, do not say 'good in bed,' or I'll have to bleach my ears."

Luka covered his face again. "I'm sorry," he mumbled.

"Fuck!" Finn shook his head and took a sip. "How long did it last?"

"Four months. And then one night, the restaurant messed up and they only sent Morgan's food. He just sat there, eating his pad Thai, without even offering to share it with me, and it was like...what the fuck am I doing?"

Finn had to laugh. "So that's what did it for you. You got hungry."

Luka tried to glare at him but a chuckle escaped. "I guess so. I really love Thai."

"I can't believe you didn't tell me!"

"I know, I'm sorry. I wanted to, so many times, but we had to keep it a secret until we told HR, and Morgan didn't want to."

"Wait, so...how did this lead to Morgan getting fired *now*?"

Luka took a sheepish sip of his Bloody Mary. "He blackmailed me."

"He *what*!" Finn looked around for their server. "I'm going to need a stronger drink."

Once Luka laid out the sordid details for him, Finn leaned back in his chair, mind blown. "Okay...I'm getting the reluctance with Thomas now."

"*Thank you*," Luka said, with an emphatic gesture. "I don't need any more relationship drama with coworkers."

"Cheers to that." Finn drained his whiskey.

* * * *

It wasn't officially spring yet, but it felt like it. The snow was gone, and the gray dirt that had piled up along the curbs had been swept away that morning, wet trails still visible on the asphalt. Small green daffodil shoots poked up here and there from damp gardens, and the birds announced the approaching equinox with great joy. Finn had taken the day off, although Rory had gone to work so Cali and Bryson could get comfortable and settled with Finn first. He spent the morning tidying up the yard, and was now freshly showered and pacing, waiting for his family to arrive.

My family.

It felt weird to say.

Then there they were, pulling up in a rusty, nondescript Honda. Before it had even come to a complete stop, a round, redheaded boy tumbled out of the back door and charged up the walkway. Bryson, obviously, even though he looked like an actual child and not the toddler entrenched in Finn's memory. Finn opened the door before the kid could knock, and Bryson streaked right into the house.

"Where's the bathroom?" Bryson squeaked, holding tight to his crotch.

"Uh…" Finn pointed down the hall, and Bryson was off like a shot. Finn stuck his head around the corner to make sure Bryson found the right room, then turned to head out onto the walk.

Liz was hunched over at the door Bryson had emerged from, collecting fast food bags and candy wrappers out of the backseat. Cali had not appeared yet. Finn shuffled forward to greet them.

"Liz. Hi," Finn said.

His sister stood and turned to face him. She looked older than he remembered, hints of gray on the crown of her head visible in the strawberry-blonde waves, laugh lines deeper around her eyes. Of course, Finn supposed he looked older, too.

"Hey Finn. Did Bryson find the bathroom?"

"Yup." He wondered if he should hug her, but the awkward pause stretched on until they had passed the acceptable window of time for initiating such an action, so instead he looked into the backseat. Cali was lost in a book.

"Earth to Cali!" Liz said. "We are actually here, in case you hadn't noticed."

Cali made an irritated noise and snapped her book shut. "I know."

"Hi, Cali," Finn said.

She sighed and unbuckled her seatbelt. "Hi."

"What are you reading?"

She climbed out of the car, squinting at him and shouldering a backpack. "*Number the Stars*, by Lois Lowry."

"Oh, that's a good one."

Her look was pure skepticism. "You've read it?"

"Sure have. It was one of your mom's favorites. I saw it lying around so much that I gave it a go."

Cali's nod was solemn. "Cool."

"Cali has promised not to read the entire weekend, haven't you, Cali?" Liz smoothed Cali's hair. "Engage in conversation, even. I told her she was only allowed to pack two books."

Cali rolled her eyes and ducked out from under her mom's hand, muttering a response that Finn couldn't make out.

"Anyway," Liz said, slightly strained, "give us a hand with the bags, Cal."

"I can help," Finn said, following them to the trunk. "Which one is yours, Cali?"

"It's okay, I got it," she said, reaching for a worn blue duffel.

"Please, let me." Finn hefted it out and nearly pulled a muscle. It felt like it was full of rocks...or books. Cali stared at him, tight-lipped. He winked at her.

Cali and Liz collected Bryson's things and other road trip shrapnel from the backseat, then the three of them headed into the house.

Bryson was rooted to the rug in the front hall, staring up at Finn's painting.

"Oh my God, Bryson, I had to carry your bag," Cali grumbled, shoving his backpack at him.

"What is this?" Bryson asked, attention not wavering from the canvas.

Cali rolled her eyes. "A painting, stupid."

"Cali!" Liz said through clenched teeth. "What did we talk about in the car?"

"It's called *Home*," Finn told him, trying to set Cali's bag down without a thump.

"Who painted it?" Bryson asked.

"I did."

Bryson tilted his head. "What's it supposed to be?"

"That's rude," Cali said.

"No, it's okay." Finn shoved his hands in his pockets. "That's what's so great about art. It doesn't have to be just one thing. When I painted this, I was thinking about the feelings I get when I'm home."

"You can paint feelings?" Bryson said, now tilting his head the other way.

"You sure can," Finn said, smile tickling the corner of his mouth.

"Hmm." Bryson looked up at his mom. "I'm hungry."

Liz shrugged. "You ate all the snacks I packed."

"It's okay. I bought a few extra snacks," Finn said. Rory had, in fact, teased him about all the snacks he had purchased.

Bryson lit up. "You did? What can I have?"

"That's rude," Cali said again, but she fell in behind Finn and her brother on their way to the kitchen.

Finn flung the pantry door wide. Bryson's eyes glowed at the boxes of shiny wrappers laid out in neat stacks on the shelves before him. Even Cali looked impressed, up on tiptoe to check out the higher shelves.

"Oreos!" she squealed, right as Bryson spied the cereal.

"Frosted Flakes! Yes!" he cried

"And there's more stuff in the freezer," Finn said, grinning even bigger than the kids.

"Can I have some cereal?" Bryson asked hopefully.

Liz intervened. "Let's get you settled first, then snacks."

"Perfect. I'll show you where you'll be sleeping," Finn said. The bungalow only had two bedrooms, and one was jammed to the ceiling with canvases and tech gear. So, with Rory's help, Finn had transformed the dining room into a guest room. On each side of the table he had laid out a mattress, then used tablecloths, blankets and chairs to turn each bed into a fort. At Rory's suggestion, the inside was strung with fairy lights, and Finn had made some little shelves out of cardboard where he had left a bottle of water, a bag of crackers, tissue and a small box of Lego as a gift.

"This is awesome!" Bryson exclaimed, then dove headfirst into one side.

"So awesome," Cali agreed, ducking into the other. She put her book on one of the shelves and lay back on the pillow, looking up at the fairy lights.

Liz hung back, smiling. "Thanks, Uncle Finn."

"You're welcome."

There was something about the way Liz was looking at him — like she was…proud of him or some shit. He flushed and looked at his feet.

"I guess I'd better get going," Liz said. "You have Beth's number. She's not too far away — I can be here in twenty minutes if you need me." Liz was staying with a girlfriend in Oakport for the weekend, a nice little getaway for her, too.

"I'm sure it'll be fine," Finn assured her.

"And they can call me before bed if they want."

"You bet."

"Come here and give me a hug," she called to the kids, who were into the Lego boxes. They clambered out of their cubbies to wrap around their mom. "You'd better be good for Uncle Finn," she said, blinking rapidly and kissing the top of their heads.

"We will!" the kids chorused.

Liz pulled back to stare into their eyes. "I mean it."

The three of them waved to Liz's car until it turned the corner. There was no time for awkward silence because Bryson started jumping up and down. "Frosted Flakes! Frosted Flakes!"

"Let's do it," Finn said. If all it took to make kids happy was food, this was going to be a piece of cake.

* * * *

"Can we bake cookies, Uncle Finn?" Cali asked before she had even finished her bowl of cereal.

"Um, sure," Finn said, wondering if it was the best move to start baking cookies only a couple hours before dinner, but he wanted to give them a fun weekend, and if Cali wanted to bake cookies...they were baking cookies. Just like he used to do with his grandma. "What kind?"

"Peanut butter!"

"Excellent choice." Finn looked up a recipe on his tablet and propped it on the counter for her. "Do you bake a lot at home?"

"Sometimes," Cali replied. "Mom doesn't like it when I make messes."

"What's in the freezer?" Bryson swung his legs under the chair like a puppy thumping its tail.

"The freezer?" Finn asked, looking over the cookie ingredients.

"You said there were more snacks in the freezer!"

"Oh, right. You can look," Finn told him while he collected assorted boxes and containers from the pantry. "Can you come grab the baking powder and baking soda, Cali?"

Bryson hopped off the chair and pulled out the freezer drawer. "Freezies!" he exclaimed. "Please, please, please, can I have one?"

Finn dropped his armful of supplies on the counter then dug in a drawer for the measuring cups. Rory had recently rearranged all his drawers and he could never find anything now. "I don't know, maybe after d —"

"Pleeeeease, Uncle Finn! Please! We never get to have freezies! It'll count as my dessert! And I promise I'll eat all my dinner too."

That little pleading face... *Fuck.* "Okay," Finn relented. "If you promise."

"Yes!" Bryson screeched. He tore through the box of freezies and pulled out a grape one.

There was a bang from the pantry.

"Oops," Cali said mildly. "I dropped the baking powder."

Finn scurried to help her collect the rest of the ingredients and sweep up the white powder.

"Can you help me open it?" Bryson said, appearing at Finn's side. He'd found the scissors somehow and held them up for Finn.

"Sure." Finn snipped the end off the freezie and got him a paper towel to wrap around the bottom. "The peanut butter is in the fridge, Cali."

Once they had everything they needed, Cali measured out the wet ingredients while Finn watched and Bryson sat happily slurping in a kitchen chair.

"Can we add chocolate chips, too?" Cali asked, leveling off the flour with a careful hand.

"Sure." Finn retrieved them from the pantry and placed them next to her bowl. "Maybe use the quarter cup?"

"Umm..." Bryson's legs had stopped swinging and he was holding up one purple, sticky hand, staring at it like it belonged to an alien.

Not only were Bryson's fingers purple, so was his shirt, and...the upholstered beige chair he was sitting on. "Oh, no no no..." Finn gasped. He dove for a roll of paper towel and wrapped a few sheets around the leaking freezie, then lifted Bryson off the chair.

"I'm sorry!" Bryson wailed.

"It's okay," Finn said, blotting at the purple stain.

"I might have used too many chocolate chips." Cali frowned at the bowl.

"What? Did you use the quarter cup?"

"Yeah."

Finn grabbed a wet dish cloth and glanced in the bowl on his way by. It was more chocolate chips than dough. "How many did you put in?"

Cali chewed her lip. "Four?"

"You put in four of these quarter cups?"

"It might have been five."

"That's...that's a lot."

Bryson continued to cry while Finn soaked the stain, then worked on blotting up the rest.

"I really like chocolate," Cali said, lower lip pushing out.

"Yeah, but...I meant—" He stopped when her eyes started to water. "It's okay, we'll just add a bit more peanut butter so they stick together."

"Can I have the rest of my freezie?" Bryson said in a trembling voice.

"Yeah, bud. How did this start leaking?" Finn unwrapped the paper towel over the sink. There was a clean slice in the plastic along the bottom. Finn started at it, puzzled. "How did this get cut?"

Bryson sniffled. "I tried to open it myself."

"You—" Finn took a breath. "That's okay. I'll put it in a bowl for you. Maybe you can eat it with a spoon.

Also you'd better change your shirt—oh, Cali, no, hon, that's way too big for one cookie…"

The backdoor opened and Rory came in. They froze when they saw the mess.

"Hey, Rory," Finn said weakly. "Welcome home."

Chapter Twenty-One

Grand Opening

Rory needed only a second to assess the situation. "What can I do?"

Finn got Bryson a change of clothes and left his grape-stained ones in the bathroom sink to soak, while Rory scrubbed the rest of the purple out of the chair and helped Cali get the cookies in the oven. It wasn't until Finn had introduced everyone that he realized— "Cali...did you add the baking soda, baking powder and salt?"

Cali blinked. "No?"

Finn nodded. "Okay. That's okay. There's so much chocolate in them, I'm sure they'll taste just fine."

And they were delicious. Warm and gooey, dense as fudge but soft, and oh, so chocolatey. Finn missed the salt a little, he decided, but overall, not a problem.

They were sitting around the kitchen table with glasses of milk, polishing off the first tray, when Rory asked, "Did Uncle Finn tell you what you get to do tomorrow?"

"No," Cali said, licking a smudge of chocolate on her lip.

Bryson eyed the next tray. "Can I have another cookie?"

"I think maybe ease off, bud," Finn said. The kid had had Frosted Flakes, a freezie —well, most of one—and multiple cookies since he'd been here. "Maybe after dinner."

"I'm too full for dinner," Bryson said, holding his stomach.

"You just asked for another cookie..."

"I'm not full of cookies."

"But..." Finn furrowed his brow, processing.

"What do we get to do tomorrow?" Cali asked.

"Well, Rory and I have been helping redesign an amusement park at work...and we get to go there tomorrow to try it all out!"

"We do?" Cali said. "For real?"

"What's an amusement park?" Bryson asked.

Cali's grin stretched wide. "You know, like rides and cotton candy and stuff."

"Yay!" Bryson threw his fists in the air and thrashed around in his chair in celebration.

Finn laughed. "Sound good?"

"Sounds great!" Cali said. "Can I please have another cookie?"

* * * *

Finn and Rory baked homemade chicken strips for a late dinner, served with veggies and dip, and got the kids to eat some fruit for a bedtime snack, so Finn didn't feel too bad about all the treats. They called Liz to say goodnight, then he supervised the brushing of the teeth and herded them into bed.

Cali curled up with her book, but Bryson didn't stop chattering away to Finn as he clambered under the covers.

Finn waited for him to take a breath. "Your mom said you usually read to her at bedtime. Do you want to read to me?"

"Okay!" Bryson dug in his backpack. "Mom packed these babyish books for me, but I could read you one if you want."

Bryson read a Little Critter story—*Just Me and My Babysitter*—then Finn tucked him in.

"If you need me during the night, you know where my room is, right?" Finn asked them both.

"Yup," Cali said. "Is it okay if I read a bit longer?"

"A little bit longer," Finn said. "We've got a big day tomorrow."

"Okay. Thanks, Uncle Finn." She smiled up at him, the light from the lamp teasing the red out of her auburn hair.

"You're welcome. Have a good sleep."

"Night," Cali said.

"Night," Bryson yawned, eyes already drifting closed.

"Night." Finn flipped off the dining room light, leaving Cali in a pool of lamplight and Bryson clutching his stuffed dinosaur.

* * * *

"They're all settled," Finn whispered, creeping into their bedroom.

"Why are you whispering?" Rory asked from their spot propped up against the pillows.

Finn huffed a laugh. "I don't know." He brushed his teeth, got into his pajamas, and slipped under the covers to cuddle up to Rory. "I can't believe they're here."

Rory snuggled closer. "I know. It was such a fun night. And tomorrow's going to be even more fun. All my little cousins should be there, too." Markos had indeed said Rory could invite their extended family, so invite them they had.

"Who all is going?" Finn attempted to sound casual, although there wasn't much of a point. Rory would know exactly why he was asking.

"Um, I think everyone with kids is coming. And Griffin, of course. He's just a large kid, really."

So Jackson would be there. "Great," Finn said under his breath.

Rory still heard it. "I'm going to talk to Jackson, okay?"

"You are? At Thrill Island?"

"If he won't even call but he'll come for a free day at an amusement park? He can have a conversation with me."

"Okay." Finn kissed Rory's shoulder. "Thanks." It didn't really make him feel any better about the day, but it was something.

Rory patted Finn's hand. "It'll be fine. I promise."

* * * *

"This is amazing!" Cali squealed, bouncing along the boardwalk to the front gate.

Bryson was right behind her. "Look at that guy! Can you take my picture, Uncle Finn?" He dashed to put his face through the cutout for the 'hacker' character. "Cali, come do one!"

Cali chose the 'distraction' in the evening gown. The kids smiled wide for Finn to snap a few pictures, then they ran to use the viewing binoculars to check out the harbor.

Rory took Finn's arm. "Look how excited they are, and they're not even inside the park yet."

"It's pretty great." They hung back, smiling at the kids' antics and waving at the Breakpoint staff they spotted streaming toward the gate.

"Is Luka coming?" Rory asked, scanning the crowd.

"No, he... Well, if you can believe it, he actually asked Thomas out."

"What?" Rory's jaw dropped. "He did?"

"Yup. They're going to Montecalvo today."

"Wow. Good for him."

"Yeah. Hope he doesn't fuck it up." Finn didn't know how much more pining Luka could take. "Ready to head in?" Finn called to the kids. "We're just getting started!"

"Coming!" They ran over and each grabbed onto one of Finn's hands, swinging his arms as they got in line to get their tickets scanned. The place was jumping—besides the employees' family and friends that Markos had invited, the citizens of Oakport had turned out in droves.

The sign above the gate had been totally redone, from the cheesy slasher font to a slick logo in red, silver and black. Goosebumps stippled Finn's forearms when they passed through the gates. Everything was how he'd pictured it, except bigger and better in person. There was sparkling new signage everywhere and fresh paint in the new color scheme. There was already a lineup at the Ziller and the air rang with the joyful shrieking from its occupants.

"This looks incredible!" Rory said when they stopped in the main square to take it all in. A family walked by, each kid carrying a red helium balloon tied with black string—the preteen's balloon read 'I'm the hacker' in white letters, the toddler's said 'I'm the muscle' and an 'I'm the getaway driver' balloon bobbed from a stroller handle.

Finn smiled. The balloons had been his idea. "What ride do you want to do first?" he asked the kids. Bryson was vibrating so hard it rattled Finn's bones.

"Finn!" Rory exclaimed. "You have to use the app!" They held up their phone to show the interface they had so painstakingly designed.

"Oh, shi—shoot, right. Of course."

But Bryson had decided. "That one!" Dancing in place, he pointed at the Thrillcoaster. It was the centerpiece of the park, red tracks twirling and swooping like insect wings unfurled to the sky.

"Does that go *upside down*?" Cali asked, horrified.

"You don't have to go on it if you don't want to," Finn assured her.

"Don't be a wimp, Cali!" Bryson said.

She scowled, but her reply was—fortunately—cut off by a new voice calling to them.

"Rory! Finn!"

Finn turned to see Steffie and Mikala approaching, with Leo and Troy in tow.

Bryson forgot about the roller coaster and studied the two older boys, eyes wide.

They exchanged greetings and Finn introduced his niece and nephew. "We were about to go check out the Thrillcoaster," he said. "Do you want to come with us?"

"Can we, Moms?" Leo asked.

"You bet!" Steffie said. "Looks so fun."

"I am not getting on that," Mikala said firmly.

"Come on, Mom, you can do it!" Troy took her hand and the group made their way across the park, accompanied by happy screams and shouts from the rides they passed.

"What do you think, Cali?" Finn asked when they arrived at the Thrillcoaster.

She tilted her head back and stood staring at the peak of the first drop, lip between her teeth. "I don't know..."

"What if you sit with me and hold my hand? You can squeeze it as hard as you like."

Cali took a breath and nodded. "Okay."

Leo and Troy had similarly talked Mikala into braving the coaster, although she looked much less certain than Cali as they got in line.

The ride was even better than Finn remembered as he listened to the delighted shrieks of his family around him. Cali clutched his hand and howled the whole way, but when they got off, she laughed and exclaimed along with the rest of them, chattering over each other with their gravity-defying tales.

"I screamed so hard that first drop!"

"Oh my God, when it went upside down!"

"Bryson screamed, too!"

"No, I didn't!"

Mikala was white-faced, insisting she was both proud of herself but would never do that again.

Back out in the park, Finn consulted his app. "It looks like now might be a good time to check out The Heist Experience." The VR ride had ended up being ready to go only days before. Rory had said all the tests ran smoothly and Finn hoped it would be a hit.

On their way to the entrance, they passed the exit to the ride. A familiar frame stood with his back to them. Then the voice reached Finn's ears.

Jackson.

" — garbage," he was saying to Amy. Minnie held tight to Amy's hand, brown curls up in adorable pigtails.

"You didn't like it?" Amy asked him. "I thought it was fun!"

"It's the worst ride I've ever been on. Jolting around in a seat while things whizz at my head? I had to close my eyes. Why would anyone line up for that?"

"Are you sure it wasn't just your motion sickness? These types of rides are really popular these days — "

"I think I would know, Amy — "

Minnie saw them approaching and pulled away to jump into Rory's arms. "Ro-ro!"

Jackson's face flashed with annoyance, then a fake smile took over. "Look who it is!"

They exchanged another round of greetings and introductions while Finn's heart thudded. He hated the power Jackson had over him — how he was anxious and angry, one big ball of fight *and* flight.

"Did you like The Heist Experience?" Rory asked Jackson and Amy.

"Loved it!" Amy said. "My favorite part was the car chase at the end."

"I guess I'm not cool enough to get the 3D glasses thing," Jackson said with a fake self-deprecating shrug. "Not really my thing."

An awkward pause hung over the group.

They were rescued by Minnie. "Can we go on the ponies, Mom?"

"Yes, sweetie," Amy replied. "I told her we could do the carousel next because she couldn't go on this one."

"Okay, maybe we can catch up with you guys later," Rory said. "I'm hoping the two of us can talk, Jackson."

"Sure thing," Jackson said, taking Minnie from Rory's arms and hoisting her onto his shoulders. "But this one needs ponies right now."

"Ponies!" Minnie sang, waving goodbye from her perch as the three of them made their way into the crowd.

"All right, who's ready for a heist?" Steffie asked.

The kids cheered as they headed for the back of the line.

When they got to the front, a cheerful employee handed them their 3D glasses and they were loaded into their seats.

Finn loved the ride. It was exactly as he'd imagined it. They were right in the thick of the action, sneaking into a palace in Milan, dodging the security lasers, snagging the jewels then making a break for it through the glamorous party and being chased through the narrow cobblestone streets by the guards.

The kids chattered as they stepped outside again, blinking up at the sharp blue sky in the bright sun.

"That was so fun!" Cali exclaimed. "Did you and Rory really help design that, Uncle Finn?"

"We sure did," Finn said, grinning. "What was your favorite part?"

The story swapping resumed until another ride caught Cali's attention.

"Can we go on that one next?" Cali asked, pointing over to the infamous boat ride, whose sign now read 'Stolen Kisses' on a pair of puckered red lips.

"We don't want to go on the boats!" Leo said. "They're for babies."

"Yeah, we don't want to go on the boats!" Bryson added. "I wanna go on another roller coaster!"

"Let me see what has the shortest lineups right now," Rory said, swiping through the app. "Hmm..."

They frowned. "Nothing's loading. Is it working for you?"

Finn pulled out his phone to check. "Doesn't look like it."

"That's weird…" Rory's thumbs flew over the screen. "The network signal seems to be fine."

Finn tried refreshing the app. "Yeah, I definitely can't get anything to load."

"I'll just check with Markos…"

"Can we go on the Thrillcoaster again?" Bryson asked.

"No, we should do the Diamond Dash! It's a roller coaster in the dark!" Leo said.

Rory slapped a hand to their forehead. "Markos says the park Wi-Fi is down."

Finn bit back a curse. "That's not good."

Rory typed a reply. "They're trying to fix it, but he's hoping people can use their data."

"That'll only work if they have good service here, and right now…" Finn held his phone up searching for a signal. "One bar, off and on."

Rory nodded and continued typing. "I still see the Wi-Fi network, so the access points must be fine. There's got to be some sort of problem in the server room."

"Can we do another ride, Uncle Finn?" Cali asked.

"You bet, we just need a minute… Why don't you guys go check out the fountain?"

"Let's make a wish!" Steffie said, herding the kids over to the burbling water. "I have some coins."

Finn furrowed his brow. "So, if people can't use the app, they can't use the line skipper or order food or anything, right?"

"I knew we should have done a soft open." Rory raked their fingers through their hair.

A beleaguered family rolled up and stopped next to them. The mom had her phone out while children circled her legs, whining about rides and demanding food at full volume. The dad had a toddler on his back and appeared ready to give up on life.

"Hang on," the mom muttered. "This stupid app..."

"I want to go on the fairy wheel!" a small girl cried.

"I'm hungry!" a boy about Bryson's age whined.

"Yeah, I know, I'm trying to order some food, but...urgh! Nothing will load." The mom groaned, tucking her phone into her pocket and picking up the girl. "Guess we'd better go get in line."

The husband sighed as they trudged away.

Finn grimaced and checked his phone again. Now he had no bars. He didn't want to throw the word 'disaster' around, but...

A large shadow loomed in Finn's vision. "There you are!" Markos lumbered up to them. "This is a fucking disaster! I think the load on the cell tower has bogged everything down and now no one can do anything. What the fuck went wrong?"

"I'm not sure... What have you tried for fixes so far?" Rory asked.

"I don't know, I don't know. It's all beyond me now." Markos ran a hand over his head, leaving the few stray hairs on top sticking straight up. "If people can't order lunch, they'll leave. Fuck! An absolute *disaster*."

"It's okay," Rory said. "We can help. Just give us a second."

The kids were lined up along the cement wall of the fountain tossing coins into the spray.

Finn hunched down to talk to Cali and Bryson. "Rory and I need to go help out for a bit. Are you okay staying with Mikala and Steffie?"

"Yup," Bryson said absentmindedly, going right back to Leo and Troy to see who could get a coin to land in the middle of the diamond mosaic on the bottom.

Cali nodded. "You'll be back soon, though, right?"

"As soon as I can." Finn was a little surprised when she hugged him, and even more surprised when his instinct was to kiss the top of her head.

"Okay," Finn said to Markos. "Let's go."

Chapter Twenty-Two

Hot Dog Heist

The three of them strode through the park, Markos' bulk cutting a swath through the crowd. "The customer service line is swamped with people complaining. They can't access the wait times or line skippers, but the biggest problem is they can't order food," Markos explained. "There's a lineup a mile long at the grill because we don't have the capacity for everyone to order in person anymore."

When they arrived at the covered outdoor eating area, they confirmed that the lineup had spilled from the appointed lanes and was twice as long again, winding through tables and nearly out into the park itself. And the people looked…hungry.

As they stood and gaped at the crowd, another family stopped next to them and did the same.

"This is ridiculous. We are not getting in that line!" one of the grown-ups said.

"But I'm starving!" The teenager groaned.

"Let's just go," the other adult said. "We can get food on the way home."

Markos watched them depart like a puppy being left at the pound. "More people are going to start leaving."

Finn and Rory looked at each other.

"Are you going to…" Rory started.

Finn nodded. "I'm gonna try." They gave each other a quick kiss, then Finn turned to Markos. "I have an idea. Can you give me free rein with the grill? I want to give away some food."

"Absolutely."

Markos led them through a staff door into the kitchen and found a tall, lanky woman with a clipboard. "This is my grill manager, Nadya," Markos said. "Nadya, this is Finn. Give him whatever he needs." He nodded once. "Let's go, Rory. I hope you can fucking fix this."

Finn and Rory shared one more look before Rory followed Markos out of the kitchen.

"It's a mess out there," Nadya said. "Things are going fine in here, but we can't get the orders in fast enough."

"I think I can help. Can you get everyone's attention for me?"

Nadya clapped her hands and bellowed, "Listen up, crew!"

The staff paused what they were doing, regarding the large, redheaded interloper warily.

"Hi, everyone. I'm Finn. I'm with Breakpoint, Thrill Island's advertising company. And we need to make a whole bunch of people real happy real quick. I'd like you to cook all the hot dogs you can."

"All?" repeated Nadya.

"All. And I need someone to contact a supplier and get more delivered here as soon as possible. Now, how many can we crank out within the next ten minutes?"

Eleven minutes later, Finn left the kitchen clad in a Thrill Grill apron and carrying a tray of hot dogs, followed by a handful of kitchen staff bearing the same load. The smell of park food — grease and sunshine — made Finn's stomach growl. He would need a hot dog of his own later.

He approached the cranky family at the front of the long line. "We are so sorry about the wait," Finn said. "But maybe you can help me out. I just went on a hot dog heist and I need to get rid of the evidence. Can I interest you all in a complementary hot dog?"

"Really?" the mom replied, eyes lighting up. "Yes, please." She collected a hot dog for each of her family members while the kids cheered. One of the employees behind Finn offered ketchup or mustard from the squirt bottles he carried.

Finn repeated his task with the next family as the other staff spread out with their trays down the line.

"It's the least you can do," a woman muttered at him as she collected a stack of hot dogs. "We've been in this line for forty-five minutes."

"We're so sorry about that, ma'am. We would also like to offer you these coupons for a free slushie after four p.m." Finn handed her a fat stack of glossy coupons.

"Thank you," she said, slightly mollified. "The kids will like that."

Finn continued down the line until he ran out of hot dogs, then he went in to collect the next batch and distributed those, too. A group of teens christened him 'Hot Dog Dude' and tried to get him to stay and eat one with them, but he politely declined. His tray was just about empty a third time when he turned to greet the next family, and came face to face with Jackson, Amy and Minnie.

"Oh, hi." Finn held up his tray. "Um...would you like a complementary hot dog?"

"Are you...working here?" Jackson asked, taking in the apron.

"Just, er, helping. The Wi-Fi went down, so Rory went to deal with that and I was, uh..." He waved at the crowd around him. "Keeping the guests happy while they waited."

That was when he took a moment to look around him. The mood had taken a one-eighty from when they had first arrived. Lots of the guests had taken a seat at the new tables, happy with the free food, while some had stayed in the much more manageable line to add to their meals.

"I love hot dods!" one little boy exclaimed nearby, dancing in his seat while his mom wiped the ketchup sliding down his chin.

"That was nice of you to step in," Amy said. "And yes, thank you, we would love some hot dogs."

"I don't normally eat these." Jackson sniffed. "But since they're free..."

"You're welcome," Finn said. "How about some slushies, too?" He handed Amy a handful of coupons and passed their hot dogs around, then crouched down to talk to Minnie. "Did you have fun on the carousel?" he asked her.

"Yes!" the little girl cried. "My pony was pink!"

"No way! Pink ponies are the best." He smiled at her and Amy. "The gentleman coming up the line behind me has the condiments."

"*Attention, Thrill Island guests.*" A voice cut in over the PA system. "*We are* thrilled *to tell you that the park Wi-Fi is back up and running again as normal. We apologize for the inconvenience and thank you for your patience. Your heist may now proceed as planned.*"

Finn sighed in relief. *They did it.* "Sounds like Rory came to the rescue. I'd better go find them. I hope you three enjoy the rest of your day."

"Thanks, Finn!" Amy and Minnie waved while Jackson nodded, mouth full of hot dog.

Prick. Finn took his tray back inside, thanked Nadya and her staff then leaned against the counter to send Rory a text.

You did it!

Looks like it! they replied right away. *Just finishing up a few things here. Want to come meet me?*

Rory sent directions for how to get to the server room.

When Finn walked in, his heart swelled. Rory was sitting at a console pointing at a few columns of numbers and explaining something while heads bobbed around them.

"Thanks, Rory. I can't believe we missed that," said a bespeckled man in flannel. "So embarrassing."

"Not at all," Rory said. "It was my fault. I have my internal pre-launch checklist to make sure all systems are out of test mode, but I should have shared it with you when Markos nixed the soft open." Rory looked up and caught Finn's eye.

The rest of the room fell away. He walked toward Rory, desperate to have them in his arms. Rory stood and met him halfway.

It was like a jolt of electricity when his fingertips connected with Rory's shoulders. He pulled them in tight for a hug, nose in their hair. Rory sank into him with a sigh of contentment.

Rory let Finn squeeze them for longer than a standard hug, then chuckled and pulled away far enough to look up at Finn. "How did things go at the grill? Did you appease the mob?"

"I think so," Finn said. Rory's lips begged to be kissed. It took all his restraint to not take one of them between his. "They put out their torches, anyway."

"Finn, Rory!" Markos burst into the room. "Christ, what a fucking relief! That almost gave me a heart attack!"

"Glad we could sort it out," Rory said in their typical modest fashion.

"I can't thank you enough. I guess a soft open would have caught that, hey? I'll listen to you next time." Markos let out a booming laugh. "And, Finn! Nadya says you left behind a whole lot of happy customers. The two of you saved the day."

Finn shrugged a shoulder. "Feeding people is never a bad idea."

"We were happy to help," Rory said.

"Thrill Island will be sticking with Breakpoint as long as I'm around, that's for sure. And you two are welcome here free of charge, anytime." Markos shook their hands and they left with promises to follow up next week.

Stepping back out into the sun, Rory texted Steffie to see where their crew was at. It turned out they had just ordered their food, so Rory and Finn headed back to the grill to meet them, balloons bobbing all around them in the crowd. They side-stepped a pack of kids surging off the Thrilloscope, laughing and smoothing their wind-blown hair. The park seethed with joy — smiles, souvenirs and laughter, topped with the scent of sunscreen and popcorn.

Just as they arrived at the grill, Jackson, Amy and Minnie were on their way out.

"Rory! I hear you saved the day!" Jackson said. He shook his head. "I still think you're wasted at an advertising—"

Amy interrupted. "Finn really saved the day, too! I think people in line were about ready to start eating each other."

Rory half-smiled, lip between their teeth. "Before you go, can we talk, Jackson?"

"Ooh, sorry. We've really got to get going. This one's about done," he said, hoisting Minnie up, "and we have to get back to the babysitter. Fiona's getting fussy."

"Sorry, we do have to run," Amy apologized. "But we'll see you tomorrow at Bailey's party?"

"Yup. See you tomorrow." Rory sighed as they watched them leave, then they went to find the others. Griffin had joined the group, and was entertaining the kids by folding paper napkins into bunny ears while Steffie and Mikala went to collect the food.

"Uncle Finn!" Cali cried when she saw him. "We did the Ferris wheel and the Ziller, and it was so fun! It whips you all around like…" She turned in mad circles while Finn laughed and caught her before she could fall over.

"Amazing! I'm sorry we missed it. Maybe we can do it again after lunch."

"Yeah, and the Thrilloscope!"

"And the Thrillcoaster again!" Bryson chimed in.

So they did, and then some. The sun was nudging the horizon when they spilled out of the Diamond Dash for the second time. Cali took Finn's hand while Bryson hopped around with Leo and Troy in some invented game. Griffin laughed at something Rory said and threw his arm around their shoulders. Steffie fed Mikala a piece of cotton candy.

Family.

The word thumped in Finn's chest.

Cali tugged on Finn's arm. "Can we *please* do the boat ride now?"

The boys moaned. "Noooo."

"I'll take these hooligans to the arcade if the rest of you want to go on the boats?" Griffin offered.

It was a short wait in the long willow tree shadows, then Mikala and Steffie loaded Cali into a boat with them. Finn and Rory got the next one to themselves.

Finn stretched his arm around Rory's shoulders once the boat pushed out into the canal. Rory cuddled up against him and laced their fingers together.

The sun was setting, and the cotton-candy-pink light filtered through the hanging branches. The noise from the park was distant and muffled, almost covered by the sound of the water lapping against the boats. The 'Haunted Lagoon' graveyard was gone, replaced by glimmering piles of gems and jewelry, spilling from chests and velvet bags, treasure abandoned, left to wink at them from the long grass.

Finn's chest felt too full. "I'm so proud of you," he said, pressing a kiss to Rory's temple.

"You are?"

"You're—" Finn's voice caught in his throat. "You're so brilliant. Watching you take charge in there and fix everything..."

Rory lifted Finn's hand and kissed his knuckles. "You had half the park eating out of the palm of your hand...literally. *We* fixed it. On top of that, we designed this whole place together, and it's amazing."

Finn's throat tightened until he couldn't speak, so he only nodded and squeezed Rory's hand.

"We make a pretty good team, don't we?" Rory murmured.

Finn nodded and kissed Rory's head again. *Sure do.*

* * * *

"That was the best day," Cali said, tipping her head onto Finn's shoulder and sinking into her seat on the train. She closed her eyes over a sleepy smile.

"Best *ever*," Bryson agreed. He clambered into the seat opposite them and crammed the last of his cotton candy into his mouth.

"Pretty great," Finn added, looking up to meet Rory's gaze.

Rory shook their head, a sweet, slow smile lighting up their face. "Yup. Pretty great."

Finn reached for Rory's hand and pulled them into the seat on the other side of him.

Rory squeezed Finn's knee as they settled. "Should we order some dinner so it's ready for us when we get home?"

"Excellent idea." Finn pulled out his phone. "Are you guys hungry?" he asked the kids.

"Not really," Cali said, eyes still closed. "Just tired."

Suddenly Bryson had a hot dog in his hands. "This is my dinner!"

Finn stifled a laugh. "Where did that come from?"

"Griffin," Bryson said happily. He got to work demolishing it.

Finn made a mental note to make sure Bryson got some extra fruit with his breakfast in the morning. "What do you feel like eating, love?" he asked Rory.

Rory's head tipped into Finn's other shoulder. "Thai, please."

Finn ordered their usuals from their favorite place—lemongrass stir-fry for Rory, panang curry for him. The train slowed at the next station, passengers jostling on their way off, then a few got on. A small blond man bumped Rory's shoulder on his way by.

"Morgan?" Finn said when he recognized the face.

Morgan stopped, expression flat. "Finn. Rory."

He didn't look good—dark circles under his eyes, hair unkempt.

"Are you— How are you?" Finn asked.

A humorless smile pulled at the corner of Morgan's mouth. "So great. Obviously."

Finn couldn't think of a single thing to say.

Thank God Rory was there. "It's nice to see you, Morgan," they said, as graceful as ever.

Morgan's gaze flicked over their held hands. "Sure... You two did it right, you know. I wish that I had..." He looked away, hurt flashing over his face. "Anyway." The humorless half-smile was back. "I'll see you 'round, I guess." He saluted and pushed his way through the crowded train.

Finn wanted to turn and watch him go, but Cali was still snuggled up against him. Instead, he cast his gaze over at Rory. Rory was smiling at him, something extra in their eyes. Something...searching. And all he wanted was to give Rory everything they were looking for.

They drove home from the train station, and by the time they pulled into the driveway, both kids were asleep in the back. Finn carried Bryson in and Rory helped Cali through the door. The kids woke up enough to get into pajamas and brush their teeth, then they both gave Finn and Rory sleepy hugs and were fast asleep again the moment they were tucked into bed.

Finn eased the pocket door to the dining room closed while Rory opened their delivery bag. They pulled out two containers then frowned. "This is only rice and my stir-fry." Rory looked in the bag again and shook some napkins and cutlery onto the counter. "Shoot, they forgot your curry." Before Finn could even reply, Rory pulled a plate out of the cupboard and began scooping out half the rice. "At least the portions are big! Are you good with—"

The words burst from Finn's lips, clear and sure. "Will you marry me?"

Rory froze, staring at Finn, spoon mid-air. "W— What?"

Finn's heartbeat echoed in his ears. He strode across the room, took the spoon from Rory and set it on the plate, then took Rory's hands in his. "Will you marry me, Rory Barrett?"

Rory's eyes filled with tears. "Oh, Finn." They threw their arms around him and held tight. "Yes. Yes, I will."

Finn was crying, but so was Rory, so they just held each other and cried together.

"I'm sorry, I don't have a ring," Finn said with a sniffle. "I wasn't exactly planning to do this, but...today...I know that I want to be with you forever."

"I love you so much," Rory said, fingers creeping into Finn's curls. "*So much.*"

Finn took Rory's chin in his fingers and tilted their mouth up to his. Every thought or feeling he'd ever had about Rory flooded his senses when their lips touched, and it was the most right he'd ever felt.

They kissed and cried and held each other...until Finn's stomach growled.

Rory chuckled, dabbing the corner of their eye. "Let's eat, yeah?"

Finn didn't want to let go, but it rumbled again. "Yeah."

Rory finished distributing half of the stir-fry onto the plate while Finn collected drinks, then they retreated into the living room with their meal.

But instead of turning on a show, they just sat, feet and knees touching, and talked about the day.

"One woman tried to get back in line and get more free hot dogs," Finn told Rory, laughing. "She took off her hat and sweater so she'd look different, and used an English accent the second time."

"No, she didn't!"

"I swear."

Rory laughed and covered their face. "Probably less awkward though than when we first got back to the server room, and Markos suggested people could connect to his phone's hotspot."

They talked and talked until their plates were empty.

Finn set his on the coffee table then regretted it because he had nothing to hold onto. "What will your family say?" he asked, gripping the couch cushions instead.

"About what?"

"About us getting engaged."

"They'll be thrilled," Rory said, with complete confidence.

Finn was much less confident. "Will they?"

"Of course... Maybe we shouldn't tell them tomorrow, though? I don't want to steal Bailey's thunder."

"That's fair." Finn was nervous enough about the party. Putting off the announcement was fine with him. "When do you want to get married?"

"Soon," Rory replied without hesitation. "Very soon."

"Big weddings take time to plan!"

Rory shrugged. "I don't need a huge wedding."

"But...your family."

"I'm not marrying them."

"You're telling me you don't need to have a big ol' Barrett family shindig?"

Rory put their plate down, took Finn's face in their hands and kissed them. "I don't give a fuck about anyone but you right now."

The next kiss got heated, Rory's tongue in his mouth and hands hot under his shirt.

"The kids..." Finn whispered, pulling away with great reluctance.

Rory groaned. "I know... I know."

Finn sighed. "Don't worry...we'll make up for it tomorrow night."

"Promise?"

"I do."

Chapter Twenty-Three

Pink

"Do you like it?" Cali asked, scrunching up her face.

"Hmm." Finn stepped back from the canvas and held up his thumb and forefinger in an L as he examined her painting. "I love it."

"You do?" Her face was shining like a candle glowed from within. She had painted the Ferris wheel with the harbor behind it in broad, bright strokes, the sky a heady mix of blues, and each car packed with boldly-colored people in emerald greens, sunflower yellows and poppy reds.

"Absolutely. Would you let me keep it? I have the perfect spot."

Her eyes widened. "You're going to hang it? On your *wall*?"

"Of course. Bryson's too." Bryson had painted a swirling mass of cotton candy on a red-and-white-striped stick, but had since gone back to his Lego in the dining room.

Cali bounced on her toes. "Where?"

"I'll show you." Finn collected the canvases. "Follow me."

He went into the dining room and took a set of prints off the wall that he'd picked up at the farmers' market when he'd first moved to Oakport. Cali and Bryson's paintings looked much better in that spot.

Bryson crawled out of his fort, Lego spaceship in hand. "What are you guys doing?"

"Uncle Finn is hanging up our paintings!" Cali replied.

"He is?" Bryson stood and gaped at his painting on the wall. "Cotton candy is art, too?"

"Anything you enjoy creating is art," Finn told him.

"That's so cool," Bryson said, voice grave. He held up his creation. "Even Lego?"

"You bet." Finn ruffled his hair as the doorbell rang.

"Mom!" the kids cried in unison and went tearing toward the front door.

Rory had just opened the door, but before they could say anything, Bryson and Cali were hurling themselves into Liz's arms.

"Hello, my babies!" Liz pulled them close and kissed the tops of their heads. "I missed you so much! How are you?"

"Good!" they chorused.

The news came at Liz in a flurry.

"We went to Thrill Island!"

"I rode all the roller coasters!"

"I won a snake at the arcade!"

"And I won a teddy bear!"

She nodded and oohed as appropriate while the kids bounced around her.

"Would you like to come in for a bit?" Finn offered once they ran to grab their prizes and he was able get a word in.

"Sure, thanks. No hurry for us."

"Liz, this is my partner, Rory," Finn said. The word 'partner' echoed in his head. Were they telling people? Should he tell Liz? He shot Rory a questioning look. Rory nodded, so Finn corrected himself. "Actually…Rory and I got engaged last night."

Liz gasped. "You did? Congratulations! That's so exciting. And it's so nice to meet you, Rory." Liz shook Rory's hand. "Hope you didn't mind my crew invading your home for the weekend, especially on the night you got engaged!"

"Not at all," Rory said. "They're great kids. We had tons of fun."

"And the engagement wasn't exactly planned," Finn added.

"Mom!" Bryson came running toward them waving a rubber snake. "Uncle Finn and Rory helped build one of the rides! It was so cool, it crashed you around like—" He made an explosion noise and threw himself on the couch.

"Okay, simmer down, chief," Liz told him. "Are you both all packed and cleaned up?"

"Do we have to go?" Bryson whined. "Can we stay another night? Pleeeease?"

"Nope. I've got work and you've got school. Go make sure you've cleaned everything up. Where do you want them to put their sheets?" she asked Finn.

"Oh, it's fine, I can do it," Finn said.

Liz smiled. "In the washing machine?"

"Sure."

Liz waved the kids back toward the dining room. They groaned and trudged off.

"And make sure you don't leave any socks behind!" she called after them. "Check under the mattresses!"

"Coffee?" Finn asked her.

She nodded. "Wonderful, thanks."

The three adults retreated to the kitchen. Liz and Rory sat at the table while Finn collected mugs from the cupboard. "Cream and sugar?" Finn asked his sister.

"I drink it black now."

"How was your weekend?" Rory said to Liz.

Her eyes sparkled. "It was amazing, actually. I had fuck all to do."

Finn poured their coffees. "That's perfect. You needed a break."

"Agreed. And I can't thank you enough for giving me one."

"It was my pleasure." He set their drinks on the table and sat with them. "So...how are things going at home...with Neil?"

Liz curled her hands around her mug, shoulders tensing. "It's hard. Watching everything you built crumble around you, while the person who was supposed to—" She stopped and pressed her lips together. "Thanks for having them, Finn. They were so excited, and, clearly, they had an amazing time." Her voice caught. "It really means a lot to me."

Finn took a second to collect his words, held back as they were by the squeeze in his throat. "I'm sorry it took me so long."

Liz shook her head. "I get it. You didn't have much reason to stick with me, did you?"

Finn blinked, while twenty years of heartache swirled the surface.

Liz studied his face. "Mom was...well, she was shitty, and I know I took her side a lot. But I...I felt like I had to, you know? She was such a mess. And you...you had it all together. I always admired that about you. Still do."

Finn's eyes were wet. "I didn't feel like I did."

She blinked a tear from her eye, sending it rolling down her cheek. "I'm sorry. I shouldn't have called you selfish. You were just trying to protect yourself."

"I'm sorry too. I wish we hadn't…"

"I know."

Rory sniffled.

Finn and Liz looked at them and chuckled, wiping their eyes.

"You'll have to come visit again soon," Finn said. "Maybe you can join us at Thrill Island next time."

Liz scooted forward in her chair to hug Finn. "That would be great. Thank you."

Finn sank into the hug. He'd forgotten how good it felt to have his big sister's arms around him.

Then Bryson appeared in the doorway. "I want to be an artist when I grow up, Mom!"

Liz smiled at her son. "Do you?"

He skipped over to take her hand. "Yeah! Uncle Finn hanged up my art, come see!"

* * * *

They waved at Liz's car until it rounded the corner, then Finn hooked a finger into Rory's belt with a mischievous eyebrow quirk. "What time is Bailey's party?"

"Oh," Rory replied, eyes darkening. "Not. For. *Hours.*"

"Then," Finn said, tugging Rory close and breathing them in, "I believe I made a promise."

Later, naked and cozy under the covers, the topic of their engagement came up again. Finn kissed Rory's forehead and wiggled right in close so his words rippled over their neck. "So, what should I call you?"

"What do you mean?" Rory asked, lacing their fingers together.

"Do you like 'fiancé'?"

"Hmm…" Rory considered. "You know what? How about 'betrothed'?"

"'Betrothed.' I love it. 'This is Rory, my betrothed.' 'Can't, I'm going for dinner with my betrothed.'"

Rory giggled. "One moment please, my betrothed is calling."

Finn kissed them. "My betrothed is so sexy."

"No, *my* betrothed is sexy."

Finn growled and rolled on top of Rory. "My betrothed is about to get fucked within an inch of their life. Again."

Rory grabbed Finn's ass and pulled him closer. "I always said my betrothed was a generous lover."

Finn earned his title again, this time as Rory's betrothed.

* * * *

Parking in Lainey and Jonathan's driveway was different this time. This time, Rory had chosen him for forever.

He was still nervous to see Jackson, though.

Bailey was at the door to greet them, in a sparkly pink dress and 'Birthday Girl' tiara.

"You look so cute," Rory told her after they exchanged greetings.

"I know," she said with a hair flick.

"Happy birthday, Bailey," Finn said, handing her the gift he and Rory had picked out.

"This is gorgeous!" Bailey exclaimed, holding up the present. "My gosh. Who wrapped it?"

"I did," Finn said, cheeks flushing as they always did when someone gushed over him. He had chosen shimmery pink wrapping paper, multiple pink and silver cloth ribbons, and, instead of a bow, a pink paper flower that was woven with a rose quartz beaded necklace.

"You did? You made this flower?" She marveled over it.

"Yup."

"Isn't my — my partner so talented?" Rory asked.

Finn shared a look with Rory. He could tell how much they wanted to tell her the news. But she would make a big deal about it and it was supposed to be her night.

Bailey didn't notice their meaningful glance, enraptured as she was by the wrapping. "I'll say. This is too beautiful to open. Anyway, come on in. Dad's made a signature cocktail for the party but he hasn't revealed it yet. He's been waiting for everyone to arrive."

"Are we the last ones?" Rory asked. They might have been a little slow getting out of bed.

"Not quite. We're still waiting for Jackson. He's apparently stuck at work."

"Work? It's your birthday!"

Bailey rolled her eyes. "You know him."

They followed Bailey into the living room. It looked like pretty much the full clan was there — aunts, uncles, cousins and a couple faces Finn swore he'd never seen before. Steffie and Mikala waved, but Finn didn't see Dimitri anywhere.

"There you are!" Lainey said when she saw them. "Hello, darling." They swapped air kisses — the Jackson drama apparently swept under the designer rug —

while Jonathan rolled in a bar cart draped in a white cloth.

"All right, everyone!" he called. "Apparently Jackson will be on his way shortly, but I'm not waiting." He paused to make sure he had the room's attention. "First of all, we would like to thank you for joining us for this special girl's birthday."

Bailey smiled and flushed as everyone cheered.

"She is the sweetest, most beautiful person, and we are all so lucky to know her," Jonathan continued.

"Oh, Dad," Bailey said.

"So, in honor of Bailey's twenty-third birthday, I give you..." He paused for dramatic effect before whipping the cloth off the bar cart, revealing a tray of tall pink fizzy cocktails, topped with lime and fresh strawberries. "The Straw-Bailey margarita."

Bailey laughed and clapped her hands over a chorus of oohs and ahhs. "What's in a Straw-Bailey margarita?"

"Magic," Jonathan said. "Just like you. Plus some tequila."

"Aw, Dad." Bailey hugged him, then accepted the first drink. She clinked her glass with his. "Cheers!"

Davis came in carrying another tray of the signature cocktail and circled the room distributing drinks.

Finn and Rory wandered over to Mikala and Steffie to chat as they enjoyed their beverages.

"Did Leo and Troy crash as hard as Cali and Bryson did last night?" Finn asked.

"So hard." Steffie laughed. "I think Troy was sleepwalking by the time we got home. He kept telling me to get off the Ferris wheel."

Finn chuckled. "Bryson just worshiped your boys. It was so nice of them to include him."

"Oh, not at all, they had lots of fun too. They already asked this morning if they could have Bryson over one day."

"Aw, that's so cute. Next time they visit, for sure."

It wasn't long before they were herded to dinner and the adults found their seats in the dining room. The massive table was adorned with white and silver china, pink roses and pink candles.

They had loaded their plates with food—pork ribs, rice pilaf and corn on the cob—when Bailey stood and clinked her glass to get their attention. "I just wanted to say, thanks for being here tonight. It really means a lot to me—"

Jackson dashed into the room in a wrinkled charcoal suit. "Hi, folks," he drawled. "So sorry, Bailey. I couldn't get away." He went to kiss his mom on the cheek.

"Hello, dear," Lainey said.

"We're glad you made it," Bailey said.

Griffin snorted. "Just trying to imagine what you would have said to me if I had rolled in in the middle of dinner."

"You would have been coming from, like, a foosball tournament or something. I was at *work*," Jackson snapped.

"Everything sorted?" Jonathan asked. His cheeks were pink and hair mussed. Finn wondered how many Straw-Bailey margaritas he had sampled before the party.

"For now." Jackson sighed, so put upon. He loosened his tie. "We really need to take another look at our distributor in the south-east—"

"Can I get you a Straw-Bailey margarita?" Bailey interrupted. "Dad made them. They're so good."

"Uh..." He eyed the pink beverages dotting the table. "I'll have a beer, thanks."

Davis slipped from the room with his tray.

"You made it," Amy said dryly when Jackson took his seat next to her.

He muttered something in reply that Finn couldn't make out. Jackson's gaze flicked up and met Finn's.

Neither of them looked away.

Jackson curled his lip and lifted his beer at Finn in a sarcastic salute.

Without breaking eye contact, Finn lifted Rory's knuckles to his lips.

Davis stepped between them as he leaned over to place Jackson's beer on the table and the moment was over.

For now.

Once the meal was completed and the plates cleared, Lainey stood with her drink in hand. "Time for presents and cake!" she announced. "Everyone to the living room."

"Jackson," Rory called, hanging back as the room cleared. "Can we have a second, please?"

Jackson stopped with a sigh. "Whatever you're going to say, can it wait? I've had a long day."

"It can't."

Jackson rolled his eyes and leaned against the sideboard. "So, talk."

"Mom said you were going to call me," Rory said.

Jackson shrugged as he took a swig of beer. "She mentioned I should call you, like once."

"Yeah, and you didn't."

"I've been busy."

"Jackson, I need you to understand something, and I hope I don't ever have to repeat myself, or it's going to be a serious problem. I love Finn. He is the most important person in my life. He's not going anywhere. In fact..." Rory paused to look at Finn and take his hand. "We are engaged."

"You're *engaged*?" Jackson's eyes bugged out.

"That's right. So, you will stop being a fucking snob and you will be respectful to him at all times. And if you pull any more shit again, you won't be invited to the wedding."

Jackson looked back and forth between them a few times, then bobbed his head. "Okay. You're right."

Finn and Rory exchanged a look. "Really?" Rory said.

"Really." He offered a hand to Finn. "I hope you can accept my apology, Finn."

"Er...yeah, of course." They shook.

"And welcome to the family," Jackson added.

"Thanks." Finn's insides itched.

But Rory beamed. "Thanks, Jackson. I really appreciate that. Now come on, we'd better get in there for presents."

Finn filed obediently behind Rory to the living room, unable to tear his eyes away from Jackson's frame.

Bailey was thrilled with every gift, gushing over each item she revealed. She seemed to especially love what Finn and Rory had picked out—a coffee tumbler in trans flag colors, a soft pink scarf and rose quartz beaded earrings that matched the necklace wrapped around the flower on the outside of the present.

The party was winding down, older aunts and uncles saying their goodbyes, when Finn excused himself to use the washroom. His stomach dropped when he heard footsteps following him down the hall. He knew who they belonged to before he turned around. And he was right.

"Jackson." He folded his arms, waiting.

"Finn." The smile on Jackson's face was as slithery and cold as a snake. "I had to ask...was that convincing?"

Finn's stomach bottomed out in his shoes. "Was what convincing?"

"I only apologized to make my mom and Rory happy. But you and I both know you will never belong here. My mom knows it, and, deep down, so does Rory."

Finn nodded, digesting those words as his gaze flicked down the hallway behind Jackson. "And what happens when I tell Rory about this conversation?"

Jackson waved a dismissive hand. "Go ahead. I'll deny everything, and, honestly, it really only matters if I convince the rest of the family. Rory will never go against them, not in the long run." Jackson's eyes glittered. "Get married if you want. You'll lose in the end."

"Jackson. Gene. Barrett." The words sliced through the air like a knife.

Jackson whirled.

Chapter Twenty-Four

Surprise

Lainey stood in the hall, hands on her hips, eyes aflame. Rory was next to her, a twin picture of rage. Amy and Jonathan came up behind, and the rest of the family piled up after them.

A smile tickled at Finn's lips.

The color drained from Jackson's face. "Mom...I— Why are you all down here?"

"Dad thought we should take a look at his new big screen in the basement," Rory said, voice brimming with barely contained fury. "Watch some baby videos of Bailey."

Finn caught Jonathan's gaze. The man gave him the faintest nod.

Jackson went on the offensive. "Look, Rory, I don't know what you think you might have heard, but I—"

"Jackson"—Rory stepped forward to brush an imaginary piece of lint from Jackson's shirt—"and I mean this with every fiber of my being...fuck you." They patted Jackson's shoulder, then took a pointed step to stand beside Finn.

Finn slid his arm around Rory and held on tight.

"Mom," Jackson sputtered, "are you going to let them swear at me like that?"

Lainey sighed and crossed her arms. "I'm afraid...I have to agree with Rory."

"You *what*?" The color returned to Jackson's face, bright spots of pink on his cheeks — the exact color of the Straw-Bailey margarita, Finn noted.

But Lainey wasn't done yet. "You can be a real fucking asshole sometimes," she said to her eldest son.

Finn's jaw dropped.

As did that of everyone else crowded in the hallway.

"Mom!" Jackson said.

Griffin guffawed from the back of the pack. "Amazing."

Rory grinned. "Time for you to go, Jackson."

"Yes," Bailey chimed in. "You are uninvited from my party."

Jackson's gaze darted from person to person and he was met with a wall of ice. "Fine, if you really... Let's go, Amy."

"Nah." Amy raised her wine glass at him. "I'm not done."

Jackon's mouth flapped. "But you... But I... You know what? Fine. Fuck all of you." He turned and stormed through the garage door, slamming it behind him.

"*Such* an asshole." Lainey sniffed. "I can't believe he's mine sometimes." She turned to Finn. "Finn, please accept my apology on behalf of Jackson. We didn't realize... I hope you understand that he does not speak for the rest of us, and we are so happy that Rory has found someone who clearly loves them as much as you do."

"Thank you," Finn said, choking up.

"Thanks, Mom," Rory said. "I—"

"Rory Hayden Barrett!" Lainey rounded on them. "You got *engaged*? And you didn't tell us right away?"

"Er…"

She dove for Finn and Rory and squished them in a tight hug, then pulled away as quickly as she had attacked and held up a finger. "Bailey videos first, and then…then we'll talk. Davis!" she called back down the hallway.

"Ma'am?" came the faint reply.

"Put some more champagne on ice!"

* * * *

"You'll have to get married at the Cerulean," Lainey said on their way up the stairs after the Bailey videos. "We can probably book there for next summer, if we hurry. And I'm sure Alice and Bently will be available for catering with this much notice. I wonder if Simone is still doing wedding flowers? Have you thought about colors yet?"

"Er, no," Rory said.

Finn's eyebrows crept higher and higher on his forehead as she spoke.

"No?" Lainey frowned. "What about a cake? Lemon? Almond?"

"Mom, I don't know if we—"

"You know what would be terrific?" Lainey said. "We'll do a four-piece string for the ceremony, of course, and some sort of band for the reception, but then we should have a jazz ensemble for the midnight champagne toast and refreshments."

"Um…"

Lainey bustled over the sideboard to approve Davis' champagne selection as he set out crystal flutes, while the rest of the group filed into the living room behind them.

"I'm so excited for you!" Bailey said, sliding an arm around Rory then Finn to give them a squeeze. "Congratulations!"

"Thank you. I'm sorry we took over your birthday party though," Rory said.

"Don't be silly." Bailey scoffed. "I'm thrilled."

"Finn!" Griffin wrapped Finn in a bear-hug, lifting him right off his feet. "Fuck yeah!"

Finn's cheeks flushed. "Thanks, Griffin."

"Listen, if either of you need a best man" — Griffin straightened an imaginary bowtie — "I'm available. I have a tux."

Finn laughed. "Good to know."

Davis appeared with a tray of fizzing flutes, Lainey at his elbow.

"Who wants some more cake?" Lainey asked. "We're celebrating!"

* * * *

It was late when they finally left, the streets still and silent as they pulled into their driveway. Finn dropped his keys on the kitchen counter while Rory fell into a chair at the table. "What a weekend, hey?"

Finn poured glasses of water and set one in front of Rory. "It sure was." It was hard to believe it had been only a little over two days since Cali and Bryson had arrived. "So...Jackson? Are things going to be okay?"

Rory lifted one hand in a 'what are you gonna do' gesture. "Jackson is going to be Jackson. But now that everyone has to admit what a dick he is, I imagine he'll shut up about it."

"He's going to hate me forever."

"Hey. You're amazing, and if he doesn't realize that, it's his loss."

Finn leaned over to give Rory a kiss. "I just don't want to make every family gathering...messy."

Rory shrugged. "Families are messy."

Finn reached into the tin on the table and took out an extremely dense peanut-butter chocolate-chip cookie. He took a bite, relishing the flavor melting over his tongue, heavy and delicious. "I'll say."

* * * *

The Monday morning alarm was early and jarring, but once he remembered he was now engaged to the warm lump next to him, Finn couldn't wait to spring out of bed and get the day started—after a kiss and cuddle for Rory first, of course. Finn sang in the shower and whistled while he scrambled eggs.

"Good morning, my beautiful betrothed," he said when Rory joined him in the kitchen.

"Morning, love." But they seemed a little distracted as they sat. Rory ran a hand through their damp hair, frowning at their phone.

"What is it?" Finn asked.

"My mom sent me a list of twenty-five florists."

"Twenty... Are there even that many florists in Oakport?"

"It would seem so." Rory continued to scroll. "Plus, twelve bakeries, eighteen photographers and...and thirty-three bands?"

Finn's heart rate had doubled as Rory continued. "Good God."

Then an idea came to him. An idea so huge, he had to drop the spatula, turn off the stove then sit down before his legs betrayed him.

"Do you..." He took Rory's hands. "What if we got married...today? At City Hall, after work? If you'd like to. No pressure." *My palms are so sweaty*, he thought as his idea hung in the air.

"Today?" Rory repeated, the idea crashing over them.

Finn studied their expression, looking for a sign to backpedal. "Sorry, that's probably crazy. We don't have to—"

But a smile erupted across Rory's face, their eyes sparkling. "We'll need witnesses."

Finn's heart pounded now for an entirely new reason. "So yeah?"

"*Fuck* yeah."

Finn pulled Rory in for a hug. "I love you so much."

"I love you."

They sat entwined in Finn's little kitchen, the room that had seen them from first kiss to *will you marry me* to *let's get married today*. He wondered what other memories they would make there.

Finn sat back in his chair, hands on Rory's knees. "We can go get our marriage license and rings at lunch."

"What about Luka and Thomas as witnesses?" Rory suggested. "And we all have dinner after? Ooh, I can call Dimitri and see if he can get us in at *L'Empereur*."

"Great idea. And you know what would be so fun?" Finn said, as another idea occurred to him. "If we surprised them. Like, let's ask if they're free for dinner after work, then, boom! We're at City Hall."

Rory laughed. "That would be fun." Their gaze met Finn's. "I can't wait to be married to you."

"Oh, my love." Finn kissed them, lips soft and lingering. "Same."

* * * *

"Okay. Be cool," Finn told Rory. They stood outside Luka and Thomas' office, hand in hand.

"You want me to be cool?" Rory snickered. "You be cool! You've got cat that ate the canary going on."

Finn giggled. *Giggled?* "Okay, you're right. You're right." He took a deep breath. "I've got this." They had called City Hall the moment it had opened that morning and confirmed that they could indeed apply for a marriage license during their lunch break. One of the officiants had agreed to stay late and perform a ceremony for them at five-thirty. "Here we go."

They barged in, Finn smiling a normal amount.

Luka and Thomas were hard at work, each engrossed in their screen. Luka looked up and raised an eyebrow at them. "Uh, what's with you two?"

"Are you two free this evening?" Finn asked, sneaking a glance at Rory. "We'd like to take you to dinner."

Luke narrowed his eyes. "I'm free...but what are you up to?"

"Nothing!" Rory insisted, beaming.

Finn tried not to laugh.

Luka and Thomas shared a look.

"Hmm," Thomas grunted. "I am also free and suspicious."

"Great!" Finn chirped. "We'll meet you back here at five."

"Where are we going?" Luka asked.

"We were thinking" — *No big deal, Finn* — "*L'Empereur.*"

Luka whistled. "So you're taking us to the fanciest place in town on a Monday for no reason whatsoever? Sounds normal."

"My cousin works there — remember Dimitri, the one I mentioned at Thanksgiving? — and I told him to call me when they had a cancellation. Can't a happy couple take their friends out to dinner on a whim?" Rory asked, eyes wide.

"Not this couple." Luka gave them a wry look. "I'll be on my toes tonight."

Once the door closed behind them, Finn sagged with relief. "That went well."

Rory high-fived him. "They didn't suspect a thing."

* * * *

"What kind of ring do you want?" Finn asked Rory, standing over a display case of wedding bands. They had snuck out for an early lunch and taken a train downtown, fingers laced tight together, laughing at nothing in particular and blissfully unaware of the world around them.

"Something simple," Rory said, examining a section of white gold bands. "Ooh, look at these." One tray featured bands of varying thicknesses, all with subtle designs engraved upon them.

"Could we see this tray, please?" Rory asked the nearby employee.

"Of course." The man unlocked the cabinet and whisked the tray out.

"Look at this one," Finn said, lifting out a band. It looked like it had been painted in silver, with rich brush strokes wrapping around the band.

"It's beautiful," Rory whispered.

"A Finn ring for you?" Finn asked.

Rory took Finn's hand holding the ring and placed it over their heart. "Perfect."

"Now one for me..." Finn said. His eyes jumped straight to a band with an odd phrase engraved on it — *var love = true;*. He lifted it out. "What does this mean?"

Rory studied the ring, then looked at Finn with wide, watery eyes. "'It's programming code — a declaration. My love is true.'"

Finn's heart skipped a beat. "Does it really say that?"

"Sure does."

Now the two of them were blinking at each other with wet eyes. "Well, we've found our wedding bands."

They got their ring fingers sized and both rings were available in the right size. Finn took hold of the little silver bag and knew that today was meant to be their wedding day.

They picked up falafel wraps from a cart and ate them on the way to City Hall, then took the train back before the lunch hour was up...ish. Finn tried to immerse himself in some of the Thrill Island survey feedback, but the rest of the day crept by at a painfully slow rate.

At five on the dot, Finn and Rory were back at Luka and Thomas' office. Finn was ready to vibrate right out of his skin. "You guys ready?" he asked, barely even bothering to sound casual.

Luka chuckled as he pulled on his coat. "What time is our reservation?"

"Seven," Rory said sheepishly.

"Seven?" Luka scrunched up his face. "It doesn't take two hours to get there."

"Well...we have a stop to make along the way." Rory fluttered their eyelashes, the picture of innocence.

"Aha." Luka smirked. "Not suspicious at all."

"I'm sure we have no idea what you're talking about." Finn took Rory's hand again. "Let's go!"

A light rain was falling when they arrived downtown, but the night was still warm, the promise of spring rich in the air. They scurried under awnings where they could, then Finn and Rory pulled up hard at the steps to City Hall.

Luka looked up at the old brick building. "What are we doing here?"

"We're getting married!" Finn revealed.

Luka gasped, face a mask of pure shock, then happiness. "What?"

Rory nodded, squeezing Finn's arm. "Finn proposed on Saturday."

"He did?" Luka nearly tackled them to the ground with the enthusiasm of his hug. "Congratulations!"

Thomas took his turn hugging them as well. "Congratulations. I'm thrilled for you."

"And you're getting married *now*?" Luka asked.

"We couldn't wait. We came down at lunch to get our license and decided to just do it today." Finn bounced on his toes. "We bought rings and everything."

"With just us here?" Thomas looked sideways at Luka.

"Yes. We'll do some sort of reception later with our families, but we hoped you would stand up with us and be our witnesses." Rory smiled, eyes hopeful.

Luka's lip trembled. "I'd be honored."

"Me too," Thomas rumbled.

Finn thought he might explode from joy. "Then let's get this motherfucking show on the road!" he cried.

They climbed the wet, shining steps of City Hall.

Chapter Twenty-Five

Family

"If you're ready, we'll begin?"

Finn and Rory, flanked by their witnesses, faced Kate, the black-robed officiant.

Finn exhaled with a whoosh. "Been ready since the day I met them."

Rory turned to gaze at Finn. "Me too."

This was it, the moment he declared to the world that he was Rory's and Rory was his. As he stared into their dark eyes, shining like obsidian, the happiness bubbling through Finn was enough for a thousand lifetimes.

Kate began. "This couple has come here today to be joined in marriage, which is the voluntary union of two persons to the exclusion of others. If any person can show just cause why they may not be lawfully wed, let them speak now or forever hold their peace."

Finn, barely able to contain himself, couldn't quell the urge to make the obvious joke. He mock-glared at Luka. "No smart comments from you, Moreno."

Luka obliged, holding up his hands and pressing his lips together, eyes dancing.

Kate turned to Finn. "Repeat after me, please. I, Finn Owens, do solemnly declare that I do not know of any lawful impediment why I may not be joined in matrimony to Rory Barrett."

Finn repeated the words, each one solid and heavy on his tongue, then Rory did the same.

"Marriage is not a single event but rather a progression," Kate continued, "which is not to be undertaken recklessly or irresponsibly, but rather carefully and honestly. Marriage is the faithful union between two persons, the result of which is the formation of a family whose members shall help, support and enjoy each other in good times and in bad. It is the relationship these two persons wish to have declared and celebrated."

Family.

Finn had gone through his entire life thinking he was alone, that maybe a family was not something everyone could have, but standing there, it struck him. Not only did he have his sister and her beautiful children, Rory was his family. And, like it or not, the entire Barrett clan.

Kate continued, "Please face each other as you repeat your vows."

Finn went first. "I call upon those present to witness that I, Finn Owens, do take you, Rory Barrett, to be my lawful wedded spouse." Tears tickled in his eyes. "Rory...I feel so lucky to have found you. I still can't believe that someone as kind and patient and brilliant as you puts up with me and my bullshit. I love you more than I can possibly say, but I will try to show you every single day. I promise to love and cherish you, be there for you no matter what and fall asleep with you in my arms and in my heart for the rest of my life."

Luka sniffled.

Then it was Rory's turn. "I call upon those present to witness that I, Rory Barrett, do take you, Finn Owens, to be my lawful wedded spouse." They took a deep breath. "Finn."

Finn waited, his body held together in that moment only by the need to hear the words Rory was about to say.

"You are my beacon," Rory said. "My bright, shining light of love and enthusiasm and passion for life. You've taught me to look at the world with my eyes wide open, not letting any opportunity for joy and laughter pass me by. Your love gives me strength, sustains me and makes me a better person. I will always love you, and I can't wait to share my life with you."

How was it possible to love someone this much and not explode? Finn dabbed at his eyes with the tissue he had ready in his pocket.

"Do you have the rings?" Kate asked.

They each pulled a wedding band from their pocket. Finn rubbed the brushstrokes with his thumb, itching to slide it onto Rory's finger.

"These rings are a symbol of your marriage, your love and your life together," Kate explained. "Please place the ring on the third finger of the other's left hand and repeat after me. With this ring, I shall love, honor and cherish you, and this ring shall be the symbol of my love."

Finn took Rory's hand in his, their eyes locked. "With this ring, I shall love, honor and cherish you, and this ring shall be the symbol of my love."

Rory slid Finn's ring on and repeated the same words while Finn's heart pounded.

"I, Kate McCurdy, by the powers vested in me by the city of Oakport, do hereby pronounce you to be married. I wish you long life, happiness and prosperity, and may the vows you made to each other today sustain you forever. You may celebrate your marriage with a kiss."

Finn took Rory in his arms. Their lips met in a whispered promise of the love they would always have. Then his tongue touched Rory's, an expression of how much he wanted them in every way. Rory kissed back, heated and urgent, their hearts beating in time with each other. Finn imagined, later, in the quiet of their house, pressing his ear to Rory's chest, listening, until the rhythm of Rory's blood echoed through his entire body. Then...then he would taste them, savor them, soak them into each and every cell of his body.

Luka and Thomas hooted and clapped, an abrupt reminder for Finn that they were in fact still in City Hall, and the wedding was not quite over. The four of them signed the register, then the clerk offered to take some pictures. Finn wrapped his arm around Rory and smiled so hard his face hurt.

"Wait, you know what pose we need to do?" Rory asked. Before Finn could reply, Rory slid one arm under his, then bent down to lift his legs.

"What are you—" Finn said, then he was in the air. "Rory!" he squeaked, slinging both arms around Rory's neck and holding on for dear life.

Rory giggled, staggering under Finn's weight, managing to hold him still enough for a couple photos, then they heaved Finn back to his feet.

"So strong." Finn laughed and kissed Rory on the cheek.

Luka and Thomas were deep in a quiet conversation a few steps away, much too serious for the situation. A sudden surge of affection for the two hit him hard. Because they were his family too, weren't they?

"Hey, you two. Get over here!" Finn called. He put an arm around Rory and held the other one up in invitation. "Family photo."

The four of them lined up, smiling, while the clerk captured the best moment in Finn's life.

They tumbled out onto the sidewalk afterward into one of those perfect early spring nights. The rain had stopped, and the air was warm, moist and scented with beginnings and wet pavement.

Finn held his arms wide and asked the city, "Who's ready to celebrate?" Three voices bounced back, rippling around him like drops in a puddle. They were ready.

Finn had never been to *L'Empeurer* before. Even if he could technically afford it now, for special occasions anyway, it was still drilled into him that a fancy French restaurant like that was 'too expensive.' There were only a handful of tables in the place, each tucked into its own little world in a plush alcove with small bow windows and thick, cream-colored drapery. The maître d' sat them on button-tufted velvet chairs and draped linen napkins on their laps. Quiet violin music played in the background, the lighting low and soothing.

Dimitri appeared as soon as the maître d' left.

"Rory!" He kissed them on both cheeks. "*Toutes nos félicitations!* And Finn." Kisses for Finn too. "*Bienvenu dans la famille.*"

The family.

"Thank you so much, Dimitri. And thanks for getting us in tonight!" Rory said.

Dimitri waved a hand. "*C'est rien*. I am thrilled to be a part of your wedding day!"

"These are our friends, Luka and Thomas."

They exchanged greetings, then Dimitri breezed around the table, collecting the menus the maître d' had just left. "You won't be needing these, *mes amis*! I will take care of you. This evening, for hors d'oeuvres, we are featuring *Palourdes au Gratin*, baked clams with garlic butter and bread crumbs, and Quiche Lorraine. I will bring those out with some fresh bread and a bottle of red for the table to start. *Bon*?" Dimitri was only gone a few minutes before he came back with water, wine, and a basket of warm crusty rolls with herb butter.

"How have you been, Dimitri?" Rory asked, taking a roll.

"*Ça va, ça va*. Max got nipped by a yorkie at the park the other day, *mon pauvre bébé*. He had to get stitches. But he will be okay."

"Oh, yes, Rory mentioned you have four dogs?" Luka asked.

They chatted about Dimitri's dogs—five now, actually—as he poured the wine and they dug into the bread.

"Your parents must be so thrilled for your marriage!" Dimitri said to Rory.

"Er…" Finn and Rory shared a look. "They actually don't know we got married today," Rory admitted.

Dimitri froze with the wine bottle halfway to Rory's glass. "Eh?"

"We weren't even going to tell them we got engaged yesterday, but then Jackson…" Rory trailed off. Dimitri had missed Bailey's party.

"Jackson...?" Dimitri prompted.

Rory told him the whole story, while Dimitri gasped and sighed throughout.

"*Quel connard!*" Dimitri exclaimed when Rory finished. "You need some more wine," he said to Finn, topping up Finn's glass to the brim. "Although I do wonder...perhaps, on some level, Jackson is jealous of Rory's attention being drawn away from him, the big brother Rory always looked up to." He squeezed Rory's shoulder.

"You think so?" Rory asked.

Dimitri shrugged. "*Peut-être.* Or perhaps he's simply a snob! Now...let me see if your hors d'oeuvres are ready." He patted Luka's shoulder and vanished through the drapes.

Finn crunched through the crust of another perfect roll as he thought. *Jackson...jealous? Of me?* Then he banished the idea. He wouldn't waste any energy on that man today.

The appetizers were scrumptious, and Dimitri was an excellent server, warm and friendly, and always appeared before they even thought to look for him. For dinner, they each sampled two main courses — *lemon poussin* and braised lamb shoulder. Finn would normally have eaten until he could barely move, but he was too busy watching Rory enjoy the meal. He might have even fed Rory a few bites of food, like those besotted fools in the movies.

"So, are you moving into Finn's place?" Luka asked Rory as they ate.

Finn hadn't even considered this step. But yes, of course. Of course Rory had to officially, fully move in now. He'd throw out every last painting to make room for the rest of their stuff if he had to.

Rory furrowed their brow. "I'm trying to remember the last time I actually slept in my apartment. I don't even think I've been there in weeks. But yes." They leaned over to press another soft kiss on Finn's lips. "I'll be giving my notice tomorrow."

Finn blinked back a few tears and thought about creating a new space in the house that would be for both of them.

"Will you go on a honeymoon?" Thomas asked, swirling the wine around his glass.

A honeymoon. Another thing he hadn't thought about in the whirlwind of the last few days. And what a thing it was — time away with Rory, just the two of them. "Hmm, we haven't talked about that. What do you think, love?" Finn asked.

"Yes, please." Rory propped their chin on a hand and stared at Finn with a dreamy expression. "Can we find a cabin somewhere without cell service, and hike and sit around a campfire and read and...just be together, only the two of us? For at least a week!"

Cuddled up next to a crackling fire, sparks spiraling up into a sky smeared with the stars hidden by the city... "That sounds perfect." An invisible force drew Finn forward to kiss them again. Then, mesmerized by Rory's beautiful, elegant face, he tucked a piece of hair behind their ear.

Thomas smiled. "I hope you get to go soon."

"Maybe in a couple months when it's a little warmer in the mountains?" Finn said. "Up by Bell Lake?"

"I love it." Rory lifted a bite of lamb to Finn's lips. "Try this."

There was something so sensual about closing his mouth around Rory's fork. Finn's thoughts started to drift to their wedding night.

The meal was winding down, their plates almost empty, when Dimitri arrived to ask about dessert. Finn scooted his chair even closer to Rory's and used the distraction as an opportunity to slide the last bite of his risotto into Rory's mouth, while murmuring into their ear. "Thinking about what I'm going to do to you when we get home."

Rory swallowed the bite, then licked their lips and gave Finn a mischievous grin. "Oh? Do tell."

"Hmm..." Finn took Rory's hand and dragged his nose along their forearm, then planted a kiss on their palm. "No, I think I'll let it be a surprise this time."

Rory's cheeks, already flushed from the wine, turned a darker shade of pink. "Oh my..."

"Oh, your *something*, that's for sure." Finn nibbled at the soft skin of Rory's inner wrist.

"Finn..." Rory said with a hitch in their breath.

Finn grinned and shifted in his chair, wondering how fast they could eat their dessert.

Not that fast, it turned out. Dimitri had them sample everything—crème brûlée, chocolate mousse, raspberry tart—plus the specialty coffees. It was approaching midnight when Dimitri cleared the last of their dishes.

"*Mes amis*, the first bottle of wine was a wedding gift from me, and, as I have said, the desserts were on the house. And the rest of your bill has been taken care of."

Finn blinked, confused. "What?"

"By whom?" Rory wondered, looking around the table.

Thomas avoided their gaze.

"Thomas! You didn't!" Rory cried.

He squirmed a little. "As a wedding gift."

"No, that's too much!" Finn insisted. "We wanted to take you out."

"It is already done," Dimitri interjected. "He snuck his card to me earlier."

"Thank you so much, Thomas," Rory said. "That's so kind of you."

"So kind," Luka repeated. "Thanks for me, too."

"You're welcome," Thomas said, gaze locked on Luka's.

Finn had, admittedly, been rather focused on Rory that evening, but it was all he could do not stand up and scream *'you obviously like each other!'* at the two morons. Instead, he settled for rolling his eyes at Rory as they made their way to the door.

"Remember not to say anything to my parents yet!" Rory said as they hugged Dimitri goodbye.

"*Bien sûr!* My lips are closed!"

"Thank you, Dimitri," Finn said with his hug. "We'll see you soon, yeah?"

"Indeed. The next family celebration looms." Dimitri winked.

Now, in the middle of the night, a chill had settled over the sleepy city. Finn and Rory clung to each other as they made their way down the sidewalk, a little tipsy. Finn looked back. Luka and Thomas were behind them in a similar pose, locked together arm in arm, heads practically touching. Finn turned back, chuckling.

"What is it?" Rory asked.

"Those two lovebirds behind us. I don't know who they think they're fooling anymore. They're perfect for each other and clearly in love."

Rory's laugh danced around them, high and musical. "We've gone over this. Sometimes when you're in it, you can't tell."

"Well…" Finn pulled Rory closer and kissed the top of their head. "I don't want them missing out on this feeling."

Rory squeezed his arm. "Me neither."

When they got to the station, there were more congratulations and thank yous all around.

"Thank you for being here, Luka," Finn said, hugging Luka tight.

"I wouldn't miss it, my friend," Luka replied. His blue eyes pierced Finn's. "Thank you for including me."

"I apologize for the hangover you're going to have tomorrow." Finn chuckled. "At least I got a spouse out of it."

Luka laughed, eyes flicking unconsciously over to Thomas. "Worth it."

Finn grinned and clapped him on the shoulder. "Get him on his train safe, hey, Thomas?"

Thomas took Luka's arm. "I've got him."

"Yeah, you do."

* * * *

A blurry train ride, then back in the kitchen. Their kitchen.

Finn pressed Rory against the counter, in the exact spot of their first kiss.

"I love you," Finn said. He kissed Rory's cheek.

"I love you, too," Rory whispered.

"I love you," Finn repeated. He kissed the other cheek. "I love you." A soft brush of lips across Rory's forehead. "I love you." Along their jaw. "I love you." Neck.

"I love you. I love you. I love you," and again, until there was nowhere left to kiss, until Finn's heart was so full there was no room left inside him for words, until all he could do was hold Rory and recognize how their bodies slotted together like they were made to love each other.

A perfect fit.

Epilogue

Sunset

Two months later

"It's fine if you hate it," Finn said, white-knuckling the sheet. "Honestly, totally fine. You can tell me. I won't be offended. That's the thing about art, it's really a subj—"

"Finn," Luka interrupted.

"Yeah?"

"Show me the fucking painting."

Finn almost laughed despite the nerves clawing at his belly. He'd never done this before—set out to paint a portrait of someone important to him, with a whole big *reveal* like this. But when he had seen Luka on stage for the first time, so fucking talented and gorgeous up there with the voice of an angel, strumming his guitar like a goddamn rock star, he'd known he needed to paint it.

"Come on, love," Rory said, running a soothing hand over Finn's back. "It's brilliant. Let's see it."

"Okay. But—"

"Finn!" Rory and Luka cried in unison.

Thomas chuckled from where he was leaning against Rory's desk, hands in his pockets.

Finn took a deep breath and pulled the sheet off. He couldn't look at Luka's face, so he stared at Thomas instead.

But that didn't work, because Thomas' face didn't give much away. He was just watching Luka with soft, schmoopy eyes.

It was too quiet in the studio. Finn forced himself to look at the subject of his painting.

The subject had a hand pressed to his mouth, eyes big and watery.

"Uh…" Finn scrunched his face. "Do you…"

"I love it," Luka said through a sob. "Is that really me?"

The four of them studied the canvas together. The shapes and colors suggested the outline of a man holding a guitar, eyes closed and singing his heart out, but all around him was magic—light and stars, shimmering golds and silvers and blue the same color as Luka's eyes. The piece was titled *Joy*, because that was the only word for Luka up there.

Finn rubbed his beard. "Yeah, I—"

Luka threw himself at Finn and crushed him in a bear-hug. "Thank you." His words were muffled in Finn's shoulder.

Finn hugged him back. "You're welcome."

"It's gorgeous, Finn," Thomas said. "Really."

Rory beamed at all of them.

Sniffling, Luka let go, then slid himself under Thomas' arm.

Thomas pulled him close and kissed his cheek. "That's exactly what you look like up there, you know."

Luka gazed up at him with a smile that outshone the sun. "Do I?"

"Absolutely."

They kissed properly, sweet and lingering.

"You two!" Finn grinned. "So fucking cute."

Luka and Thomas blushed in unison.

"Nah," Luka demurred with a hand wave.

"Please," Finn said. "So cute I could puke."

Luka and Thomas had finally — finally, *finally* — admitted their feelings for each other a few weeks earlier. It had gone right down to the wire in dramatic fashion — of course, since Luka was involved — mere minutes before Thomas was supposed to leave town for his next Breakpoint VP gig. They had kissed in the rain and everything, the whole fucking romantic movie finale.

And they had been inseparable and achingly adorable since.

"Hey, you know what?" Luka said, pulling out his phone. "Can I send a picture of this to the manager of the coffee shop? They have all kinds of work by local artists up on the wall. I bet you he'd love to display it."

"Um…" Finn bit his lip. "I don't know…"

"You don't know?" Rory said. "You don't *know*? Finn! Love. I think it's an amazing idea."

"Really?"

Rory barked a laugh. "Yes, really. I'm going to keep telling you how gorgeous your work is and how everyone should see it, over and over, as many times as it takes to convince you."

"You have to say that," Finn grumbled. "You're married to me."

"There was nothing in our vows about that," Rory said, eyes twinkling. "So you can trust me."

Finn nodded and sucked in a deep breath. "Okay. Sure. You can send it to him. But tell him no pressure—"

"Done!" Luka said, thumbs already dispatching the message. "I'll let you know what he says."

"The food's almost done," Thomas reminded them with a look at this watch. "Is everyone ready to eat?"

The two couples had made dinner together—rigatoni with pan-roasted cauliflower and capers—except really Thomas had done most of the work. Finn's mouth watered as they gathered around the dining room table, although his gaze was momentarily drawn from the feast to the wall behind their guests.

Cali and Bryson's paintings were in the center, next to framed photos of the kids at Thrill Island. Finn and Rory's wedding photos were beside those, including one with Luka and Thomas. There was an old picture of him and Liz that she had sent him, two kids smiling on the front step of the house they grew up in, the pair of them with matching scraped knees and lopsided smiles. A picture of the Barrett clan, rows of shining faces, and one of Finn and Rory from Halloween, so happy in their costumes.

The family wall. There was lots of space for it to keep growing.

The four of them dug into their dinner, cutlery clattering in the quiet that descends at the start of a good meal.

Luka broke the silence first. "I make the most amazing pasta," he said wistfully. "Really, I'm so talented."

Thomas raised an eyebrow. "Oh, are you?"

Luka booped him on the nose. "I sure am. You're lucky to have me."

Thomas shook his head, completely smitten. "That I am."

Luka beamed at Thomas, cheeks flushed, eyes glittering. The man was drunk on love. "Oh, that reminds me," he said, tearing his attention away from his boyfriend and back to his hosts, "do you two want to go to Montecalvo with us Saturday? Thought we'd have dinner at the pork pastry place."

Finn was about to say 'Sounds great!' but Rory placed a gentle hand on his arm.

"Oh, we can't. That would be lovely, but it's Griffin's birthday."

Finn sighed. "Right."

"How are family things going?" Luka asked Rory as he helped himself to a piece of garlic bread. "Has your mom settled down yet?"

Rory and Finn shared a look. Lainey had not taken the City Hall wedding news well.

"She's still not…thrilled?" Rory said. "We've agreed to have a reception at the Cerulean next summer, but we're holding strong on not doing another ceremony."

Finn snorted. "'Not thrilled' is putting it mildly. There was a bit of a scene at Easter."

Luka raised an eyebrow. "Oh?"

"Let's just say that this time, it was Griffin talking my mom out of the bathroom."

Thomas tapped his chin. "I wonder whose mom was more pissed—Rory's, when you told her you secretly got married, or Luka's, when she found out Luka had lied about when we got together?"

Rory gaped at Luka. "You lied to your mom about that?"

"I merely...*assumed* that we were going to—" Luka gestured with his wine glass. "That is, I knew that we'd end up..." He took a sip and nodded. "Yeah, I lied."

Thomas snickered. "We fake-dated for his parents at Easter."

"You did not!" Finn cackled. "That's amazing. How did she find out it was a sham?"

"Well, once it was official"—Luka smiled at Thomas—"I didn't want to have to lie to my family about how or when we got together for the rest of our lives."

Finn could practically hear Thomas' heart skip a beat in the silence that followed.

"Luka..." Thomas said, emotion thick in his voice.

Luka looked at him shyly. "Sorry if that's too much. But that's how I feel."

Thomas leaned over to kiss him. "I feel the same."

Finn's heart swelled with happiness for his friends. Seeing two people exactly right for each other end up together... He squeezed Rory's knee under the table.

Luka cleared his throat and went back to his pasta, cheeks pink. "And are things getting any better with Jackson?"

Finn shrugged. "He didn't say a word to me at Easter but...I guess that's better than him being an outright asshole."

"Speaking of assholes!" Luka cried, nearly choking on his food. "We forgot to tell you! We watched the final episode of season three!"

Rory smacked the table. "Can you believe it?"

"I swear to God..." Luka pressed a hand to his chest. "The whole time I thought the snake was acting up because of Ophy's evil twin, but then..." He shook his head, lips pursed.

Finn chuckled. They had managed to get Luka and Thomas hooked on *Godstrike*. "Come on, the snake was just—"

"Do not defend that creature!" Luka howled. "He—" His phone buzzed. "Ooh!" Luka held it up, beaming. "Nam loves the painting! He says he'll definitely display it, and he asked if you have a couple others, too."

After the initial shock, the feeling in Finn's chest was a strange one, like the fear that had been sitting there for so long was cracking, falling away piece by piece. "Yeah, I could do that." He swallowed hard. "I've got a few in the garage…"

* * * *

One month later

"Here we are." Finn's truck rolled to a stop at the top of the long, winding dirt drive.

They stared out through the windshield for a beat, then another.

"It's perfect," Rory said, a little choked up.

The cabin was small and simple, but exactly what Finn had imagined when they'd planned their honeymoon. The weathered front porch faced a small mountain lake, where a rowboat waited at a rough dock.

They carried their bags inside and stood together in the doorway, taking in their home for the next eight days. The back half of the cabin contained a bedroom and bathroom, and the front didn't hold much besides a wood-burning stove, a simple kitchen, a faded plaid couch and a tall shelf crammed with books as weathered as the building itself. They had electricity and plumbing, barely, but cell service had given out at the bottom of the drive.

"It's perfect," Rory repeated, floorboards creaking under their feet as they went to examine the bookshelf.

"Hmm, I don't know..." Finn said, hands on hips. "We'd better check out the bedroom to be sure."

Fortunately, the bed was sturdy. A little squeaky when Rory clutched the headboard, but there were no neighbors within shouting distance, so a little—or a lot—of noise wasn't a problem.

"What do you want to do tomorrow?" Rory asked later, when they were naked and wound together like two sleepy puppies in a basket. "Hike? Paint?"

"Sure." Finn kissed the paintbrush tattooed over Rory's heart.

"Aren't you excited to paint?" Rory asked, sliding their fingers through Finn's hair. "The mountains, the trees... You'll be so inspired. Plus, you have fans waiting for new work now."

"'Fans,'" Finn scoffed. "Hardly."

"Yes, fans," Rory insisted. "Especially Jackson."

A smile twitched at the corner of Finn's mouth. Okay, that was a little true, and it felt really good. Rory had talked Finn into giving Griffin a painting for his birthday...and Jackson had gone nuts for it.

"You painted that?" Jackson had asked as the family stood around admiring Finn's work. The gears turning in Jackson's head were practically visible.

"Yeah," Finn had said. The painting was titled *Brother*. Finn had tried to imbue the bold, shining lines with a sense of vulnerability and uncertainty.

"Isn't it beautiful?" Rory had asked.

"Yeah, listen..." Jackson had scratched his chin. "We're redecorating the office at the plant and I'd love to have a piece or two like this."

Finn had managed to keep his jaw from hitting the floor. "Um..."

"Sorry," Rory had cut in. "Finn's showing his work right now, so inventory is a little low. But we could maybe sell you something down the road."

Jackson had pouted the rest of the night. Finn smiled at the memory.

"Or..." Rory continued in their bed, wrapping a curl around their finger. "We could stay right here all day?"

"Yes." Finn kissed the letter 'F' Rory had added to the tattooed vines on their arm. "Anything you want, my love." They had a whole week of days ahead and Finn didn't care how those days were filled, as long as Rory was with him.

So, they did all those things and more—hiked, painted, sat by the campfire, read, stayed in bed for hours, took the boat out—together. On their last night, they climbed into the rowboat for one last turn around the lake, just as the sun was setting.

Finn pushed off the dock, then settled across from Rory on the bench, oars in hand. The water lapped against the boat as it slid through the water, the only sound besides frogs chirping at them from the reeds.

"So romantic," Rory said dreamily, reaching down to trail their fingers through the water. The curve of their long white neck, the shining ripples in the water... A firefly flickered near the shore. Finn filed the image away for a future painting.

"It reminds me of..." Rory looked up and froze. "Finn, look at the sunset."

Finn turned to look over his shoulder. The sky above the mountains was lit up in fiery pinks and oranges, so bright it looked like brushstrokes on a canvas. "Stunning," Finn said. "You were so right about this trip being inspiring for paint—"

He trailed off because Rory was staring at him, eyes wide with wonder.

"What?" Finn asked self-consciously.

"Your hair…" Rory breathed, reaching to touch Finn's curls like they were on display at a museum. "It's catching the light from the sunset and…you're on fire."

Finn took Rory's other hand and threaded their fingers together. "I burn for you, Rory."

They kissed, one silhouette dark against the orange glow.

Acknowledgements

Publishing is a ride, and I need to thank the people who have been in the car with me, keeping me on track and feeding me snacks.

First, my dad, who is the proudest anyone could ever be of their child. Thank you, Dad. I love you.

My husband and children, who know how much I love to write and are supportive of the time I carve out for it and cheer me on the whole way.

Hanna Kubicka, John and Andrew, who continue to be the best, most helpful and supportive trio of beta readers and friends. They encourage me when things are rough and celebrate with me when things are more 'HOLY F***, IS THIS ACTUALLY HAPPENING?' I am so lucky that this crazy universe allowed our paths to cross.

Rebekah Rodriguez-Lynn, one of the loveliest people I've ever met, who makes my books so much better with her insights and suggestions. Thank you to early reader Gwen for being so excited to keep reading this trilogy.

Thank you to my agent Jordy Albert and my editor Anna Olson for their work, and Kelly Martin for another beautiful cover—it's always such a thrill seeing the characters come to life!—as well as the rest of the TEG team.

This book was both a thrill and a challenge to write and I'm so grateful that you're here. Thank you for reading *A Hard Fit*. I hope it made you smile.

Sign up for our newsletter and find out about all our romance book releases, eBook sales and promotions, sneak peeks and FREE romance books!

Want to see more from this author? Here's a taster for you to enjoy!

Falling Hard: A Hard Note
Jennifer Moffatt

Coming Summer 2025

Excerpt

It was all the Thai restaurant's fault.

If they hadn't forgotten Luka's order that night, Morgan wouldn't have gotten fired.

But there he was, standing on the sidewalk outside Breakpoint Advertising, holding a box full of his office shit, like a total asshole.

There was only one place to go.

He thumped the box of shit on the bar at the Bitter Exchange and slumped onto his favorite stool. Luckily, the pub had just opened for the day.

Kazio, the owner, came over and eyed the remains of Morgan's office life with distaste, as he did most things. "Morgan. What can I get you?"

Morgan scrubbed his face. "Twelve shots of tequila."

"Let's start with one," Kazio said, raising an eyebrow, "and go from there."

Morgan's brain spun as Kazio poured.

The text from Luka last night — *"I'm sorry I hurt you, Morgan. I was a jerk when I broke up with you."*

The words Morgan had blurted this morning at the meeting — *"It's true, what Luka says. I blackmailed him."*

His boss—*ex*-boss—frowning at him across her desk—*"I'm afraid we have to let you go, Morgan."*

"Taking an early lunch?" Kazio placed the tidy glass of amber liquid in front of Morgan, gaze drifting over the lamp poking out of the box.

Morgan laughed, dry and humorless. "Guess you could say that." He raised the shot. "Cheers." It vanished down his throat. "I'll take the other eleven now."

Kazio leaned on the bar. Morgan noticed his toned arms, not for the first time. Kazio's long white-blond hair was half tied back, but a few pieces had slipped out to frame his sharp nose and discerning eyes. "Were you let go?"

Morgan shifted, eyeing the only other patron at the bar, but they were oblivious. "Not so much 'let go' as fired. Thanks to Luka."

"Ah," Kazio said, as if that made sense.

"What do you mean, 'Ah'?"

Kazio wiped the bar with a rag like every bartender in the world had before him. "Luka was in here last night."

Morgan blinked. "And?"

"And...he asked why I don't like him." A smile hinted at the corner of Kazio's mouth. "Aside from his labor-intensive drink order, I might have told him about the time I saw you heartbroken over him."

"What? You told him about that?" The day after Luka had broken up with him—actually, *dumped* was a better word—about seven months ago, Morgan spent a long night at the bar with Kazio, exact same stool even, and he wasn't sure what drunken confessions he had made. He and Kazio had never talked about it again. But now the sudden text from Luka last night made so much more sense.

"I'm sorry I hurt you, Morgan. I didn't mean to. I didn't even realize I had. I was a jerk when I broke up with you. And I'm really sorry."

That fucking text had sat in Morgan's head all night, festered there, seeped into his conscience, put down roots and blossomed into a confession for his boss that morning. *"It's true. What Luka says. I blackmailed him."* The relief at telling the truth had almost outweighed the humiliation of getting fired. Almost.

"What happened to the bartender code?" Morgan sniffed. "Aren't you supposed to be like a priest? Keep all confessions to yourself?"

Kazio shrugged and poured Morgan another shot. "I thought Luka should know he was an ass. That guy is too smug for his own good."

"Thank you!" Tears nearly sprang to Morgan's eyes. "*So* fucking smug! And everyone just adores him. Everyone but you, I guess," he corrected at Kazio's raised eyebrow.

"How did he get you fired?"

Morgan shook his head. "If he had... When Thomas..." He downed the second shot. "I don't really want to talk about it." Thomas was no doubt partly to blame too, the smoking hot VP Luka had been drooling all over since the moment he had arrived.

Another customer came and sat a few stools over, waving at Kazio. Kazio bobbed his chin at the man and collected two bar menus. He placed one in front of Morgan. "You need food. I'll come back for your order in a minute."

"I don't want any food," Morgan grumbled, but the wings were really good, and he was a bit hungry.

The man down the bar was hot, a toned silver fox type, in a nice suit. Reminded him a bit of Thomas, actually. Normally Morgan would have chatted him up. He had certainly made a go at Thomas, that was for sure—a desperate attempt to regain a sliver of confidence that had only led to further humiliation. The memory of Thomas shutting him down was enough to keep him glued to his stool. Besides…how could a man hit on someone with the sad contents of his desk sitting right there in a box?

Kazio served the man a pint, then was back.

"Can I have another drink?" Morgan asked, pretty sure he managed not to slur.

"After you eat something."

Morgan rolled his eyes. "Are you kidding me? What are you, my dad?"

"Are *you* kidding *me*? You're looking to get smashed and I could lose my license for feeding you twelve tequilas in a row."

Morgan sulked and pushed the menu back across the bar. "I'll have the chicken wings. Honey garlic."

Kazio left the menu where it was. "Be right up."

A plate of wings and another tequila shot later, Morgan's face was hot and his blazer was off. "You know the wors' part about Luka?" he asked Kazio, undoing the top button of his dress shirt.

Kazio tapped his tablet and appeared to be only half listening. "Hmm?"

"Luka…" Morgan waited for the right words to settle on his tongue. "Luka…actually liked me. They hardly ever really *like* me, you know?"

"What do you mean?" Kazio collected a signed bill, filed it into his till then went back to wiping down the bar.

"I mean… I had a chance—a real chance—and it all got fucked up."

Kazio poured a glass of water and placed it in front of Morgan. "Drink this. And how about some fries?"

* * * *

Kazio spread out his next three shots, then cut him off. "You'll thank me in the morning." He slid Morgan the bill. "Fries are on the house."

Morgan fumbled for his credit card. "Guess I'll take my business elsewhere."

"Go home, Morgan." Kazio tilted his head and studied him in a way Morgan didn't like. "Have some more water, take an aspirin and go to bed. Things will seem better tomorrow."

"Easy for you to say." Morgan shrugged his blazer back on. "You're not an unemployed loser."

"You'll be okay," Kazio said.

Morgan wished he could believe him.

* * * *

Since it wasn't quite rush hour yet, the train wasn't as busy going home as it normally was, so he used the seat next to him for his stupid box. He glared at his lamp, page-a-day calendar, sticky note dispenser and Freddie Mercury bobblehead while the train swayed around him.

He picked up the sticky note dispenser and turned it in his hand. An office job had never been his dream anyway. The approximately college-aged person sitting across from him looked like he used lots of sticky notes. Morgan held it up. "You want this?" he asked when the guy looked at him.

"Huh?" The guy pulled out his earbud.

"I said, do you want this thing? I don't need it anymore. I got fired."

The guy gave him a look like he was diseased. "I'm good, man." He put his earbud back in and shifted away from Morgan.

Morgan wasn't sure why that made his eyes water, but it did. He chucked the dispenser back into the box. It bounced off the lamp with a clang. Everyone on the train turned to stare at him.

An ugly smile stretched across his face as he blinked up at the destination display.

* * * *

Morgan kicked open the door to his apartment and dropped his box on the floor. The lightbulb broke when it hit the sticky note dispenser, shards of glass tinkling as they fell.

He laughed so he wouldn't cry.

More tequila.

He poured himself a healthy shot, tossed it back then stumbled down the hall to his bedroom, dragging one hand along the wall for balance. His work clothes landed in a corner and were replaced with his comfiest sweats. Back to the kitchen for more tequila. Then he cracked open a lime-flavored hard seltzer and flopped onto the couch to order a pizza.

"Fuck Luka. Fuck Breakpoint," he muttered, scrolling through his contacts. In a moment of strength, or maybe it was more like a tantrum, he deleted Luka and the other Breakpoint employees. He didn't need any of them. His screen was getting blurry, so it took him a few tries, but he sent a message to his band's group chat.

Anyone up for an extra rehearsal this week before the gig on Saturday? I'm free whenever.

"Really fuckin' free," he mumbled. It was their first gig, at The Sphinx, a shitty bar downtown, opening for a band Morgan had never heard of, but it was a start.

A message from Todd, the bassist, popped up right away.

Maybe Friday? If my wife says it's okay.

I can probably do Friday, Andre, the other guitar player replied.

Can you do Friday, Felix? Morgan asked the drummer.

Some bad news actually, Felix chimed in. *We can't use my cousin's garage anymore for rehearsal. They got too many complaints.*

Fuck. Morgan took a long pull from his seltzer. *Of course.* If he was being honest, it wasn't like another rehearsal mattered anyway. The band was nothing special, and one more session wouldn't make a difference. Andre was so blah—he never took sides or did anything interesting musically. Todd could never remember his part, plus he was like a bump on a log onstage. Then there was Felix. It had taken Morgan months to put the group together, rejecting one drummer after another until he found him. Felix was decent...and pansexual, really hot—Morgan was sure he hadn't imagined the sexual tension between them— and most importantly, came with a rehearsal space.

Had come. *Fuuuuck.* Morgan didn't know what to reply that wasn't a long string of expletives. He threw his phone toward the cushion at his feet, covered himself in a fuzzy blanket and turned on some stupid show featuring gorgeous actors in loincloths. He fell asleep before the end of the first episode.

* * * *

A high-pitched noise shrieked its way through Morgan's tequila-fogged brain. He groaned. His alarm. Time for work. He sat up, fumbling for his phone in the cushions, desperate for the snooze button.

He found it, then cradled his head in the ensuing silence, stomach heaving. *Oh God. What did I do?* His mouth tasted like concrete and his head pounded like it was being jackhammered. *I cannot go to w...*

Work. The events of the day before hit him like a dump truck. *I don't have to go to work.*

The shame washed over him again.

He curled up under his blanket and went back to sleep.

* * * *

What the fuck do I do all day? Morgan wondered when he woke up three hours later.

For starters, he scrolled his phone. Four messages from the pizza delivery person—shit. They had apparently decided to leave the pizza on the planter out front of his building when he didn't answer. No messages from anyone else except for a few in the band group chat... Oh right, they had lost their rehearsal space, too. *Terrific.*

I guess no rehearsal before the show then, he added to the chat. *But try to run through the set a few times on your own.*

He didn't feel like cleaning up his place and he sure as hell wasn't doing laundry. Probably looking for a new job should be high on his list. But who the fuck was going to hire him? He couldn't use Breakpoint as a reference and now had a year's gap in his already scant resume.

So no job hunting today. He should be allowed a day to wallow in his patheticness, at the very least. And to shop. Shopping always made him feel better.

He had a shower, then put on white cuffed chinos and a blue button down. His face looked a little tired and puffy, and he wasn't the hottest guy in the world to begin with, but the power of confidence and his light gray eyes were usually enough to reel in hotter guys — like Luka.

Morgan took the train downtown to his favorite shopping area, but as he was eying a really sweet pair of pricey Reggie Hill loafers, he realized there was a slight problem — he was no longer getting paid. Now was not the time for retail therapy. He was about to sulk his way back to the train station when the Shoe Shack caught his eye.

Felix was the manager of the Shoe Shack. Felix was hot. And a fuck sounded better than shopping. And cheaper. Morgan smoothed his blond hair and pushed through the doors. Felix was at the back, eyeing the clearance shelves with a clipboard in hand, looking yummy in tight jeans and sexy professor glasses. Morgan made his way over.

"Oh, hey," Felix said when he saw him.

"Hey." Morgan gave a casual head toss.

"What are you doing here?" Felix said.

"I...need some shoes." Morgan chuckled. "Obviously."

"Cool. Let me know if you need help finding anything." Felix went back to his clipboard.

"Okay." Morgan smiled weakly and wandered over to the men's section, pretending like he was on the hunt for some off-brand running shoes. He snuck a glance over at Felix who was chatting with another employee, but whipped his gaze away when Felix's head started to turn. *You know what, fuck it.* He grabbed the cheapest shoes he could find—a pair of flip-flops that were on sale.

He sidled back over to Felix with the sandals tucked under his arm. "So that sucks about the garage."

"Yeah." Felix puffed his cheeks up, then blew the breath out as he counted boxes.

"What if we put up some more soundproofing, or stuck to certain hours—"

"Nah, don't think so." Felix scribbled on his clipboard. "My cousin was iffy about letting us in there in the first place."

"Oh." Morgan bobbed his head, then pouted to make sure his lips were full and tilted his hips toward Felix. "So, listen, what are you up to—"

"Hang on." Felix frowned and pressed his ear piece for a second before turning his attention toward the till. "Sorry, the new guy needs me to do a return. I gotta go."

"Sure."

"I'll see you at the gig Saturday."

"Yeah…" But Felix was already gone.

Cheeks burning in humiliation, Morgan jammed the flip-flops back onto the nearest shelf and got the fuck out of there.

* * * *

Nothing much happened the rest of the week. There was some more tequila and falling asleep on the couch. The box of office shit still sat by his front door. No laundry or job hunting yet, but he did run through their set until Mrs. Bagshaw-Smythe, his upstairs neighbor, pounded on her floor.

"Fine," Morgan muttered, putting his baby back in its case. It wasn't like he actually had the guitar plugged in, and he had very thoughtfully not gone all-out on the high notes.

Saturday was even less eventful. Morgan got to the shitty bar three hours early instead of the agreed-upon two. Sure, he was bored, but their first gig was a big deal. An hour early was better than two minutes late. He had just put his gear down in the itty-bitty opening act "dressing room" slash storage closet when a message from Felix popped up on his phone.

I'm really sorry, guys, but I can't make it.

Morgan's brain took a second to process. *No, surely not.* He stared at the message in the group chat, mere hours before showtime.

I have to work, Felix continued. *Everyone called in sick and the store is slammed.*

What the fuck, was all Morgan could say in reply. *I'm already here! I'm literally in the dressing room and we go on in less than three hours.*

Don't know what to tell you. I can't leave.

Panic coursed through Morgan's veins as his dream — everything he had imagined for his band — crumbled around him.

It's our first gig, Felix! Come on! What are we supposed to do without you?

See if the headliner's drummer can sit in.

"Sit in? That selfish piece of..." Morgan's fingers flew, faster than his pounding heart.

Fuck you. You're out. Your drumming sucks anyway.

Fine. And fuck you too, you arrogant prick.

Felix left the group chat. Morgan seethed.

Todd piped up. *If Felix is out, I can't make it tonight either. My wife is sick and she's pissed I was planning to leave.*

Morgan wanted to throw his phone.

What am I supposed to tell the bar manager?

No one bothered to reply. *Fuck all of them.*

The manager was furious. "I'll tell you what, you guys are blackballed. You'll never play here again, and I'll make sure to tell all the other clubs, too."

"Seeing as how I don't even have a band anymore, I couldn't fucking care less." Morgan flipped him off over his shoulder as he stormed out, guitar on his back.

He got on the train, an equal mix of hurt and angry, and pushed through the jostling crowd, looking for a seat. He bumped the shoulder of someone seated who, out of the corner of his eye, looked awfully familiar.

"Morgan?" a voice said.

Morgan stopped and looked at the two people sitting there. "Finn. Rory." A couple from Breakpoint. Close friends with Luka. They had no doubt had a good laugh about him getting fired.

Finn's gaze roamed over him, judging. "Are you — how are you?" Finn's ginger curls were ridiculously shiny and pissed Morgan off to no end.

His gut curdled. "So great. Obviously."

There was an awkward pause while Finn stared at him.

"It's nice to see you, Morgan." Rory stepped in, as sickeningly sweet as ever.

Morgan studied their fingers woven together. "Sure… You two did it right, you know. I wish that I had…" He looked away. "Anyway. I'll see you 'round, I guess." He saluted and pushed his way through the crowded train to get as far away from Finn and Rory as he could.

About the Author

Jennifer firmly believes that there are so many more stories to tell than the ones that have traditionally been lined up on bookstore shelves, and she wants to write as many of them as she can. She lives with her spouse and two children in beautiful British Columbia, Canada.

Jennifer loves to hear from readers. You can find her contact information, website details and author profile page at https://www.firstforromance.com

ENTWINED PUBLISHING